Rapid Eye Movement

GW00383462

Amanda Sheridan

First published in e-book format by self-publishing via Amazon (Kindle Direct Publishing) in 2020.

Copyright © Amanda Sheridan.

Amanda Sheridan asserts the moral right to be identified as the author of this novel. Therefore, no part of this book may be reproduced, or stored in a retrieval system, or transmitted in any form or by any means, electronic, mechanical, photocopying, recording or otherwise without express written permission by the author, Amanda Sheridan.

This book is a work of fiction. Names, characters, organisations, places and events are either the products of the author's imagination or used fictitiously. Any resemblance to any to actual persons, living or dead, is purely coincidental.

Rapid Eye Movement.

A unique phase of mammalian sleep characterised by random movement of the eyes, low muscle tone throughout the body, and the propensity of the sleeper to dream...vividly.

Wikipedia.

Chapter 1 – Cyprus

Nine days ago.

The pale blue Lexus sped along the road through the darkness and the relative, albeit temporary, safety that the moonless night offered.

Ilan Ben-Levi's dark eyes flitted back and forth from the road in front of him to the rear-view mirror. He was searching for the tell-tale glow of a pair of headlights travelling behind him. Following him, gaining on him, and maybe catching him. What the occupants of the car would do to him, if they caught him, was something he preferred not to think about.

He reckoned he had put at least half a mile between himself and his pursuers, possibly more, since he knew these roads like the back of his hand and they didn't. He was also trained in evasive tactics, so it was second nature to him. Better trained than they were, he hoped.

Less than two hours ago he had been compromised. A casual face in the crowd and a spark of recognition was all it had taken to set events in motion that led him to this moment. It had always been his worst nightmare and now, because of that recognition, they were fleeing for their lives. He slammed his palm against the steering wheel in anger and frustration.

Ilan glanced at Jennifer beside him in the passenger seat. From the dim glow of the instrument lights, he could see his wife's pale features. Worry and shock etched lines that hardened her face and he could tell from her posture that she was terrified. He hated himself for having brought all of this to their home and into their lives.

She had asked what was wrong when he rushed in through the front door and quietly, but firmly, told her they had to leave immediately.

'Someone recognised me at the airport. We need to go right now,' he said. The icy calmness of his voice emphasised the seriousness of their situation.

Jennifer followed him as he hurried into the spare bedroom and opened the wardrobe door. From behind rarely used winter coats and spare blankets, Ilan retrieved a dark blue backpack. He carried it into their bedroom and set it down on the floor. She watched him as he opened the wall safe and emptied it of its contents.

Two false passports first. One for each of them. The knowledge that there was another passport with her photograph but a different name hidden in her home was something she always found disturbing. It was a reminder of an unspoken possibility that one day they could be forced to become other people entirely. That day had arrived.

As well as the passports, the safe contained cash in US dollars, UK Sterling and Euros – about fifteen thousand pounds in total. Ilan took the bundles of cash along with the passports and put them inside the backpack.

Jennifer stepped back with a small shudder of revulsion when Ilan took his gun, pancake holster and two ammunition clips from the safe. He loaded the weapon with one of the clips, attached the holster to his belt and placed the gun in the holster. The spare clip went into the front zip pocket of the backpack.

He removed two unused mobile phones, batteries and pre-paid sim cards from the drawer beside the bed. He quickly installed the batteries and sim cards into the phones but did not switch them on.

'Keep this with you at all times,' Ilan said as he handed her one of the phones. He dumped the chargers into the backpack and placed the other phone in the pocket of his jacket.

'Ilan, what's happened?' Jennifer asked as she turned the phone over and over in her hand.

'We have to leave here,' he said and his eyes met hers briefly, almost ashamed to make contact. 'I am so sorry. Can you gather up some clothes for us? Just a few things?'

Jennifer nodded and pulled a second small backpack out of the wardrobe. From the chest of drawers, she quickly gathered up jeans and tops, underwear and socks – enough for both of them for a couple of days. In the bathroom she collected basic toiletries – toothbrushes and a tube of toothpaste, a packet of wet wipes, some deodorant, and her make up.

She placed these items into her backpack, mirroring Ilan filling his with the cash, passports and phone chargers.

Jennifer barely had time to take one last look around the house but, her eyes brimming with tears, she silently said one last heart-breaking goodbye.

Goodbye to her large open-plan kitchen with the pretty, old-fashioned curtains. There had been times she was tempted to modernise them but had never been able to find a pattern that suited the room so well. Goodbye to the spacious living room with the comfortable leather sofa.

Although she spent a lot of time on her own in this house when Ilan was away, it was still home because her life had never required his constant presence. Her own career kept her busy and she learned to adapt and be happy, whether he was with her or not. And she tried her best not to worry about him.

When he came home it was a different story. The longer he was away, the longer it took them to get back to normal and for a few days they were strangers – hesitant and wary of one another. Ilan would be remote, tired and uncommunicative when he came back from wherever, and whoever, he had been.

'Until I can get into my own skin again,' was his way of describing it to her when she complained about his remoteness.

In time, he would relax and once more become the man Jennifer had fallen in love with. They would be like newly-weds all over again and they couldn't get enough of one another. Unable to stop reaching for one another. Needing the physical contact equally as much as they needed the emotional reconnection.

Now, with her eyes full of tears, Jennifer said goodbye. She closed their bedroom door for the last time and remembered the countless nights and days they had shared the big, comfortable bed. Their desire for one another never waned over the years. It never became some routine ritual they performed as part of their marriage contract. Maybe because he was away from her so often that their love life remained fresh and exciting, or maybe it was good sexual chemistry between them. But, whatever the reason, their lovemaking had always been perfect. And it remained that way to this day. The love they felt for one another had never lessened or diminished. Tears welled in her eyes again as she silently said goodbye to the ghosts of the couple who had shared this bed for so many years.

A quick glance out of the window and she could see the terrace where the jasmine was in flower. This was her favourite part of the house. It was where they would sit in the evenings, watching the setting sun, sharing a bottle of wine as they chatted and relaxed together. This was frequently the place where their reconnection would begin.

I love this house. I don't want to leave it. Abandon it. I want to sit here drinking wine with Ilan and surrounded by the scent of the jasmine.

Almost all her life with Ilan had been lived in this house and it was her haven when he was away on 'business' as he insisted on calling it. And it was their home in the truest sense of the word when he returned. Jennifer knew she was standing in her home for the last time. Tears rolled down her face and her heart ripped into pieces at the thought of leaving it.

What about everything in the house? The furniture? All our belongings?

Jennifer desperately wanted to grab a few treasured possessions to take with her.

But which ones? What do I treasure the most?

'Someone will pack up everything for us.' Ilan seemed to read her mind. 'You don't have to worry. Everything will be kept safe for us.'

'The cats! Ilan, what about the cats?'

'They will be taken to a foster home.'

'They won't be... put to sleep, will they?'

'Of course not,' he rolled his eyes that she would think such a thing of him. 'I promise. We'll get them back when we are... settled again.'

He squeezed her hand in comfort as they hurried out the door, closing it behind them for the last time.

It doesn't matter. There'll be another house somewhere else. As long as we're together, it doesn't matter.

Ilan checked the rear-view mirror again. Was that a car headlight? He couldn't be sure, and he couldn't take the chance that it wasn't. He pressed his foot against the accelerator pedal, appreciating, now more than ever, the power in the big V8 engine. He was thankful he had bought this car instead of the little Fiat that Jennifer had wanted because it was 'so bloody cute.'

'What the hell happened?' Jennifer finally managed to speak. The tension in her voice was obvious.

'Someone recognised me and now he wants to kill me,' he told her.

'Why? Who?'

'It was someone I once had occasion to interrogate. A Russian operative. I believed he'd been killed years ago. But now it appears he's very much alive. Do you need me to go into the specifics?'

'No. But are you sure?'

'Yes. Unfortunately, I am sure,' he said.

Ilan spotted the unmarked side road to their right up ahead. Unlit and wooded, it was the perfect escape route. Without hesitating he made the turn. The tyres squealed in protest as he sharply cornered onto the smaller road and accelerated quickly into the darkness.

Maybe they would survive this, he thought as he allowed a little of the tension to leak out of his back and shoulders.

'I am so sorry, neshama,' he told her.

'Sorry for what?'

'This! Fucking all of this!'

'No Ilan, don't say you're sorry.'

'This is my fault, is it not?'

'No,' she told him firmly, shaking her head to emphasise the fact.

Well, okay. It is your fault in a way but there was nothing you could do about it.

'I got you into this,' he said.

'That's ridiculous. You told me what you are, Ilan. What you do. I walked into your life knowing there'd be risks and that this could happen. It doesn't... it will never change how I feel about you.'

In the soft green light of the dashboard, Jennifer couldn't make out the expression on her husband's face, but she knew exactly what was going on in his head. She reached for his arm and gave it a reassuring squeeze.

'I'm frightened. Of course, I'm frightened. But I have faith in you to get us to safety.'

In the darkness, Ilan smiled. He was confident in his training and ability. Confident in himself. All he had to do was put a good deal of distance between themselves and the Russians and get to a safe house. They had two in the area for exactly these circumstances. One nearby that was quite luxurious and another less comfortable one in Larnaca – a good three-hour drive from their present location. Its proximity to the airport rendered the second house the better option.

Once there, he would call Tel Aviv, explain what happened and ask for assistance. Assistance he knew would be available immediately. Then they would lie low, with armed guards discretely protecting them, until they could be extracted to Israel. The thought of returning home, even under these circumstances, felt good. He had been away far too long and he knew that Jennifer would love living in Israel. Despite the threat and the danger, everything felt positive. Even the sharp pang of homesickness suddenly felt good.

Impatient now, Ilan floored the accelerator and the car surged forward. He checked the mirror.

'Shit,' he exhaled. 'I think I see headlights.'

Jennifer twisted around in her seat and peered out of the rear window.

'I don't see anything,' she told him.

Ilan ran a hand down his face and replied. 'Probably just me being paranoid. It's unlikely they could have followed us down this side road.'

Could they have taken this side road? It was unlikely, but not impossible.

It'll be okay. Ilan's a pro at this. He knows what he's doing. We'll get away and lay low for a while in one of those safe houses or whatever they call them, and then we... well, we'll probably just go somewhere else.

'We can do this,' Jennifer told him.

'I know. I just wish we didn't have to. Once again, I apologise for –'

'Shit happens, Ilan,' she told him gently but firmly. 'We deal with it and we move on. Now, stop apologising and drive. Get us away from here!'

Ilan checked the mirror once more. Nothing. No lights. No cars. He began to relax again and lifted his foot off the accelerator pedal a fraction to allow the car to slow down slightly. He took the bend carefully on his own side of the narrow road.

Then he saw it. A massive truck lumbering along towards them in the middle of the narrow road.

Jennifer screamed.

Ilan slammed on the brakes and yanked the steering wheel as hard as he could to the left, praying he could avoid colliding with the truck.

They hit it almost head-on. The front right side of the Lexus smashed into the solid block of the truck. The airbags activated and did their best to absorb the energy of the impact. But they couldn't absorb all of it.

The impact bounced the car off the truck. Metal folded in on itself, destroying the front of the car. The force of the impact spun the car around. Once. Twice.

Then it slid off the road and rolled over before it came to rest in a small ditch.

The ear-splitting noise of metal on metal and of breaking glass as it fell all around him. His entire body aflame in agony, but, worst of all, Jennifer's terrified scream had been silenced. These were the last things Ilan remembered before the darkness enveloped him.

Jennifer groaned in pain and managed to open her eyes. In the darkness, she could just about see her husband lying beside her. He was sleeping and his head seemed to be resting on the flattened pillow the airbags provided. He looked so comfortable and peaceful that she was almost reluctant to waken him. She tried to call his name but she was so tired herself all she wanted to do was fall into a deep, deep sleep. She closed her eyes and allowed the darkness to take her.

Chapter 2 - Yorkshire

Nine days ago.

There was an alarm, faint and far away in the distance. It grew louder the closer it came, and she slowly opened her eyes. Lying beside her, he groaned.

From a narrow gap in the curtains, a sliver of early morning sunlight streamed onto her face and she dipped her head under the duvet, away from the brightness.

'Reset it for seven-thirty before you go please, love,' Charlie mumbled, still half buried under the duvet. His arm snaked out, blindly groped for the source of the noise, found it and switched off the alarm clock.

Wide awake now, Lucy stole a few minutes beside Charlie before reaching across him to reset the clock. She kissed him lightly on the cheek, grinning as he yawned and snuggled deeper under the bedclothes. For a moment, she was tempted to do the same. It would be nice to stay in bed a while longer, but she had work to do and the weather forecast promised plenty of sunshine with not a single drop of rain. It was exactly the kind of weather she needed.

Lucy sighed as she climbed out of bed and made her way to the en-suite bathroom. She washed her face and applied moisturiser, carefully appraising her features in the mirror as she did so, searching for the wrinkles she dreaded to find but knew were inevitable. Her hazel eyes smiled back at her and told her she still looked pretty good considering she was a mother of two and she would be thirty-three in less than four months. She brushed her teeth, ran a hairbrush carefully through her long, brown hair and tied it up in a ponytail.

Back in the dressing room she stepped into her old jeans and pulled on a T-shirt. As an afterthought, she got her hoodie from the wardrobe. It might be the height of summer but this was Yorkshire and it would be chilly up on the moors, especially this early in the morning. 'Stupid o'clock' as Charlie, who loved a lie in on a Saturday, insisted on calling it.

Lucy tiptoed down the stairs, being careful to avoid the boards that creaked, and into the kitchen. She filled the kettle and switched it on. While she waited for it to boil, she made roast beef and tomato sandwiches, wrapped them tightly in tin foil and placed them inside her small dark blue backpack, adding a couple of pre-packed chocolate biscuit bars.

With her picnic lunch packed, Lucy shook a generous amount of muesli into a bowl, added milk and ate it standing at the kitchen window while she enjoyed the view of her back garden.

Her breakfast finished; Lucy checked the backpack one final time and got a spare fully-charged camera battery from the charger on the kitchen counter. She slipped it into a side pocket of the bag, along with her mobile phone.

She filled the thermos flask and placed it upright in the backpack, adding a small jar of instant coffee, a spoon, and a half-full carton of milk from the fridge. She gathered up her car keys and sunglasses off the kitchen table and was almost ready to leave the house when she sensed a pair of eyes watching her.

A tail thumped, more in hope than in anticipation. It was Ross, their Border collie. He was sitting upright in his dog bed in the corner of the kitchen, begging Lucy to take him with her. 'Even if it's only to the corner shop to get a carton of milk, I don't care,' the eyes and the thumping tail pleaded with her. 'I wanna go!'

Lucy grinned at the quivering dog. 'Do you wanna go for a ride in the car with me?'

Ross replied with an excited high-pitched bark, indicating he would be delighted to go.

Lucy stepped into her comfortable, well-worn hiking boots and laced them up. She picked up her bags, then patted her thigh in a 'come here, boy' gesture. Ross leapt out of his bed with a click of claws, as he scrabbled across the tiled floor. He knew all too well what was coming next as he halted at the door, sat down and stared up at the handle, willing it to open. Lucy barely got the door opened before he barged outside and ran down the driveway, pausing only to lift his leg and pee on one of Lucy's shrubs before he raced on. He was already waiting beside the Land Rover by the time she closed the door behind her.

She unlocked the tailgate. Ross climbed in and settled down on top of the old duvet they kept there for him.

With a smile, Lucy climbed into the driver's seat, started the engine and set off down the bumpy lane towards the main road. She turned left towards the higher Dales and drove for about four miles until she came to the small carpark that served the hiking trails in the area. This early in the morning, the carpark was empty. *Good. No annoying tourists.*

She set off up the hill, her camera slung over her shoulder, stopping to take a few photographs while Ross raced on ahead.

When she came to the tumble-down remains of a dry-stone wall, Lucy stopped and looked around. This was her first chosen spot and it was ideal for the scenic views she wanted. She immediately got to work, firing off a couple of dozen shots in quick succession, stopping only to briefly check them on the small screen.

Satisfied, she walked on, every now and then repeating the process – stop, take some shots, check, and repeat. The light was perfect and the colours were sharp and well-defined as the rays of the early morning sun shone through the scattered clouds on the horizon.

Lucy was in her element. She worked steadily as she walked up the hill, enjoying the workout her thighs and legs were receiving and eyeing up potential shots, debating whether or not they were what she wanted. She took photos of those she deemed ideal and rejected the ones she considered not worthy of her beloved camera.

Finally, she stopped, lowered the camera and worked the stiffness out of her shoulders and back. She had taken over five hundred high-resolution photographs in the space of three hours and it was time for a lunch break before moving on to a different location. She had a couple of places in mind and hoped to cover both before calling it a day and heading back home.

She whistled loudly. Ross stopped and raised his head. He looked in her direction and weighed up the possibility of a treat against the fun he was having zig-zagging back and forth as he followed the exciting smells. The smells won and, with barely a glance in her direction, he put his head down again and continued his back-and-forth pattern across the ground as his nose picked up another scent. Grouse, or possibly a rabbit.

Lucy laughed as she watched the antics of the dog that, from the day they brought him home as an eleven-week-old puppy, had been 'highly trained to ignore our every command.' These were the words Charlie lovingly, and frequently, used to describe Ross's often wilful behaviour.

He could never replace their first dog. She had died so young and so tragically but, within a day or two of coming home, Ross became a much-loved and important member of their family.

Still watching him, Lucy found a nearby rock to set the camera on, safely away from the damp grass. She took the thermos flask and mug out of the backpack and made coffee, sniffing the milk before pouring to check it hadn't spoiled during her long hike. *Must remember to buy a cool bag next time I'm in town.*

She reminded herself to do this every time she sniffed a carton of milk. It smelled okay and she added a small amount to the coffee.

She nibbled slowly on the sandwiches and drank her coffee, at the same time drinking in the spectacular views. Views that were so familiar, yet never ceased to captivate her and fill her heart with pure joy. To put it simply, there was nowhere on earth she would rather be than up here on this beautifully bleak and rugged land or a few miles down the road in the old farmhouse where her family would now be up and about. They had called it their home for the last ten years. She sipped her coffee as she thought about her life with Charlie and their two beautiful daughters.

Amy was approaching the age where she was becoming a handful – testing both of her parent's boundaries. She seemed to need to push them almost, but not quite, to the limit of their tolerance and discover how best to work both her and Charlie off one another to get what she wanted. Chloe, two years younger than Amy's seven, was watching and taking note and no doubt in a couple of years would be playing the same game.

Lucy glanced at her watch. Lunchtime was well and truly over. One more mouthful of coffee then she rinsed out the mug with a splash of hot water from the flask and returned it to her backpack. Ross suddenly appeared by her side, barking and wagging his tail. She gave him the crust from her last sandwich as she gathered up the bag and camera, and set off towards the higher hills. The dog had grown tired, or maybe just bored, with his frenzied zig-zagging, and was content to follow at her heels.

It was a long hike and Lucy took time to enjoy the fresh air and the summer sun. This was the best part of her job. Or career, or hobby, or whatever it was called. She was never completely sure how to define it. She enjoyed it far too much to consider it merely a job. A job implied hard work and boredom and what she was doing could, by no means, be defined as hard work. Nor was it boring. Yet calling it a career seemed a little too pretentious and it was, without doubt, so much more than a hobby.

She crouched down on one knee to photograph the small waterfall.

Whatever it is, it's interesting, it's fun, and it earns us more than enough to afford all the extra luxuries in life.

By the time Lucy decided to call it a day it was much later than she realised, and she had travelled further than intended. It was now roughly a two-hour walk back to the Land Rover. Although there was no mobile phone signal, she fired off a quick text to Charlie, telling him she was running late but would be home soon. The message would go as soon as she managed to pick up some semblance of a signal.

Ross was also keen to go home, the thought of food and his comfortable bed instinctively leading him back in the direction they had come that morning. Lucy let him go on ahead of her, content to follow in the knowledge that his natural sense of direction was all he needed to direct her back to the car.

She walked along a natural path formed by both sheep and hill walkers. It was worn smooth in some places but rugged and uneven in others, which made it easy to stumble and trip if one wasn't careful enough. She was so engrossed in the scenery she didn't see the rabbit hole.

Down she went. Her ankle twisted painfully as she tumbled forwards. She fell about eight feet down the slope and her head struck a small rock as she tried to protect her camera bag.

Muttering a string of swear words, Lucy rolled into a sitting position and grimaced as the wet ground soaked into her jeans. Her right ankle screamed in agony and she cursed some more until the pain eased slightly.

The first thing Lucy did was check the camera. She switched it on, took a couple of photographs and checked them on the screen. It was intact. The lenses, encased in bubble wrap, were also undamaged but her coffee flask had a dent that matched the one it already had. Her sunglasses were smashed beyond repair but she had another pair in the glove compartment of the Land Rover.

Having ascertained her camera and all its related accessories hadn't suffered any damage, Lucy took stock of her own injuries. She briefly rubbed the side of her head where she had struck the rock. It was painful and there would probably be a lump tomorrow but it wasn't bleeding. Her next, and much more serious, concern was her ankle. It hurt like hell and she was tempted to take off her boot to have a look at it. She was about to do so when she remembered reading something, somewhere – or she could have seen it on TV – that it was all about the importance of keeping footwear on to strengthen and protect an ankle injury. Her hiking boots would do just that so she decided to keep the boot on until she got home.

Lucy looked around her. It was only a short distance to the carpark and she could probably get there slowly on a sprained ankle. Since it wasn't her left ankle, she would still be able to operate the clutch pedal and therefore drive home using her right foot, cautiously, on the accelerator. Provided it was only a sprain.

There was one sure way to find out. She rolled over onto her hands and knees and got to her feet, keeping her weight off her wounded ankle, afraid for a moment or two to even attempt it. Ross watched her with a puzzled expression on his face.

She took a deep breath and gingerly placed her foot on the ground, keeping most of her weight on her left leg as she tested her tolerance limit. 'Oh, bugger!' She yelped in pain, eliciting an echoing yelp of concern from Ross. It hurt more than she thought it would, but she had no choice.

She hitched her backpack over her shoulder as she took a careful step forward on her right foot. It was not as painful as she expected it to be – the sturdy boots helped. Yes, it was sore, there was no doubt about that but, favouring her left leg, Lucy was able to take a second careful step, then another, and then another. She limped slowly down the steep slope.

Although it was only a short distance to the car park, it took Lucy much longer than she had anticipated. Charlie would be wondering where she was. She checked her mobile again and this time there was a signal. Her earlier text had been sent an hour and forty-five minutes ago, according to the time read-out. She quickly typed in a second message – **Home soon. Have the wine well chilled. It's been a long day! Luv u heaps!**

Two x's for kisses and a smiley face like she usually did and she hit send. It went immediately. There was no reason to mention her fall and worry him unnecessarily.

Lucy slipped her phone back into her pocket and carried on, still limping, to the car park. Ross had walked alongside her the whole way but he increased his speed once the end was in sight and raced towards the car. He waited for her to open the tailgate, then jumped in and collapsed onto his comfortable bed where he promptly fell asleep. He did not waken until they had pulled up at home where he leapt out and rushed in through the open back door, no doubt looking for his dinner.

'Where are the girls?' Lucy asked, as she hobbled into the kitchen and set her bag down on the floor. She eagerly accepted the glass of white wine Charlie poured for her.

'You're limping. What happened?'

'I tripped and fell,' she told him. 'I think I've sprained my ankle. You know how clumsy I can be.'

'Are you okay?'

'Yeah. Nowt that a bit of rest and a bag of frozen peas won't cure. I hit my head too, but it's okay. It's the thickest part of me, or so you keep telling me!'

'Lemme see it,' Charlie frowned as he placed his bottle of beer down on the table.

Lucy took another swig of wine and tilted her head towards the light so Charlie could inspect it.

'I'm okay. It's just a bump, and it doesn't hurt half as bad as my ankle does. That's the part that needs sympathy right now,' she told him as he checked her head with a frown on his face. 'Seriously, Charlie, where are the girls? You haven't gone and sold them again, have you? We talked about this, remember? It's illegal to sell them.'

'Your head looks okay but it'll probably be sore for a day or two. I haven't sold them. Claire phoned to invite them to a sleepover and I had them bound and gagged – I mean, washed and dressed,' he grinned, 'and into the car in fifteen minutes flat. I think that's a world record. Of course, we have to return the favour next weekend but hey, that's next weekend. Now, I have two steaks marinating in garlic, a salad prepared, and more wine chilling in the fridge. If you're up for it, that is?'

'It sounds perfect. You bet I'm up for it,' she said, planting a kiss on his cheek. 'I'll feed the dog and load these photos onto the laptop, have a quick shower, and then I'm all yours.'

'Are you going to work on the photos tonight?' he asked.

'God no! I'll just upload them and leave them until Monday morning.'

'Perfect. I'll light the charcoal while you're doing your thing with the camera. I'm guessing it wasn't damaged when you fell?' he asked and Lucy shook her head. 'Okay, good. As soon as you're ready, sit yourself down and I'll get you some ice for that ankle.'

The salad was prepared the way Lucy liked it, plain and simple, and the steaks were cooked to perfection. Charlie was one of the best barbeque cooks she had ever known. The wine was delicious and plentiful. The pain in her ankle had eased considerably thanks to the ice, and she had forgotten all about the bump on her head. As a result, she was feeling a contented, happy buzz as the two of them sat together out on the patio, watching the sunset.

Ross lay fast asleep near Charlie's feet. Every few minutes, his paws twitched and he woofed quietly as he chased rabbits or grouse in his dreams.

The sunset, like the evening, was perfect and the remainder of the night promised much more.

Despite the ache in her heart caused by the absence of the girls, it was good to spend at least one evening without them. She relaxed in the knowledge that the girls were safe and sound in the company of Claire – and Gavin, her crazy Scottish husband. They had three children of their own, all of a similar age to her two girls.

I'll phone Claire tomorrow and thank her. Invite them over for a barbeque, while the weather's still good.

She glanced at Charlie, now drinking red wine and she hoped he wouldn't drink too much and fall asleep the moment his head hit the pillow. She had plans for him tonight that did not involve sleep. He returned her gaze and his eyes, in the light of the setting sun, told her that sleep was the last thing on his mind.

Much later Lucy lay sated from their lovemaking and lingered halfway between sleep and wakefulness. She thought about her life. Charlie, two years older than she, was not only her husband, but her perfect lover and best friend all rolled into one. Amy and Chloe – her two beautiful, funny, loving daughters that she cherished beyond all reason. And this beautiful home they had made together was full of happiness and laughter and so much love. It was all she needed and wanted. She whispered a silent prayer that it would be like this forever. She could feel a slight headache coming on and blamed it on the wine. Her eyelids grew heavy as sleep caught up with her.

Chapter 3

The next morning.

Charlie was already up and about when Lucy came downstairs. He had a gleam in his eye and he was whistling out of tune. She joined him at the kitchen sink and was admiring the morning light when a wave of dizziness washed over her. It was powerful enough that she had to grip the edges of the worktop to keep from falling to the floor.

'How's the ankle this morning?' Charlie asked as he slipped his arms around her waist and kissed her cheek. She leaned against him for support while she waited for the dizziness to pass.

'It's okay, but I...' she hesitated.

'What?'

'I'm fine. What do you want for breakfast?'

'Coffee and a slice of toast would be great.'

Lucy filled the kettle, switched it on. They skilfully danced around each other as they got mugs, cutlery and plates from the cupboard and drawers. As the water came to the boil, Charlie spooned instant coffee into the mugs and got butter and marmalade from the fridge while Lucy caught the toast as it popped up out of the toaster. It was a dance they had perfected over the years.

Her backpack was on the floor by the back door, where she'd left it last evening, the flask and mug she had taken on her hike yesterday still inside. The milk would probably be sour now.

She lifted the backpack and removed the flask and the mug. As she did so she felt dizzy again and a powerful memory coursed through her mind that made her stop what she was doing.

An image of another backpack appeared before her eyes. It was dark blue in colour and it was similar in idea if not in style. But this one contained two passports and a considerable number of banknotes in various currencies.

The image reminded her of the dream she had awakened from. Something about a fast-moving car and a sense of panic and terror to see a truck parked in the middle of the road? She could only remember fragments but not enough to piece together the narrative. The details seemed to be hovering around the edges of her memory, like a name on the tip of the tongue. But try as she might, and much to her annoyance, she couldn't recall any more of it.

'What do you want to do today?' Charlie asked as he buttered the toast. He switched on the radio to listen to the news and any chance Lucy had of remembering the dream – if it was a dream, it seemed more like a memory – drifted away like early morning mist.

Shrugging her shoulders and putting any further thoughts about the images in her mind onto the back burner for now, she turned to look at him.

The pain in her head was fierce. A knife had been driven into her skull. It twisted and turned as it pierced her brain. The agony mixed with the dizziness sent the world around her into a spiral of pain and fear. Then out of nowhere came the nausea and she vomited up last night's dinner. The remains of the meal and the wine she had drunk appeared in front of her on the kitchen floor. Frightened, Lucy stepped forward towards her husband, reached out to him, and collapsed into his arms.

From far, far away she could hear Charlie calling out her name over and over again. Then he was talking to someone else. His voice sounded frightened.

Has something happened to one of the girls?

The blackness faded in and out as she lay there wondering what was wrong. She felt her head being gently lifted and something – a cushion, maybe – was placed underneath it. She could hear the noise of a siren in the distance and she tried to ask Charlie what was happening but she couldn't speak. Try as she might, she couldn't form the words.

Everything went completely black and Lucy's world became silent.

Chapter 4

Eight days ago.

The excruciating pain in her head took her breath away and turned her soul to ice. It was a sharp knife that penetrated her skull, twisting and turning in her brain. Destroying tissue and brain cells and all that made her who she was.

Moments later it disappeared, leaving only numbness in its place and an inky blackness that engulfed her. Her senses had abandoned her and she could neither touch nor taste nor smell. Nor could she see or hear anything. The blackness surrounded her and she was drowning in it. She screamed, but she could not even hear herself screaming.

Am I dead? Is this all there is?

Then she saw it. A light in the distance in front of her. A bright warm light. A feeling of relief flooded through her veins and she eagerly took a step towards it when she glimpsed something to her left. Another light that beckoned her towards it.

Confused, she stopped.

Which one?

She had to make a choice but which one?

Did it matter?

Without even coming to a decision, she walked towards the light on the left.

Through this light, she could see colours and objects. But they were hazy and unclear as though she was watching an old television set that was losing the quality of its picture, or perhaps a window covered with the dust and grime of many years.

But in the distance beyond the light, she could hear the welcoming sounds of voices and laughter and a feeling of warmth and love and happiness washed over her. All the things that made up her world.

With a sense of relief, she stepped back into that world.

And screamed.

Because this was not her world. She was not meant to be here.

She tried to step back. Tried to retrace her steps back into the darkness where she could choose again. This time she would make the correct choice. She would walk towards the right-hand light and go back to her own world, where she belonged.

But before she could do so, some unknown force blocked her way and pushed her forward.

Into a life, and a past, that did not belong to her.

Chapter 5 - Cyprus

Ten years ago. Lucy's dream.

'You are here on holiday from the United Kingdom? Yes?' The tall man with the dark hair asked as he leaned his elbow on the edge of the bar.

'Um, no. I live here now. I moved to Cyprus eight weeks ago,' Jennifer replied.

He smiled and nodded thoughtfully, his dark eyes studying her face as he took another sip of whiskey then pointed to her empty glass, indicating if she would like a refill. Jennifer nodded in agreement. Another drink had been the reason she had walked up to the bar in the first place, having failed to get the attention of the waiters. All of them were pretending to be too busy to take an order for a mere *one* drink.

Well, another drink had been *one* of the reasons. A closer look at the tall, very sexy, man propping up the bar was the *main* reason. Now, seeing him up close and personal, he looked even better.

He was wearing faded designer blue jeans that fit him like a second skin and a khaki-coloured T-shirt. He was tanned and had a full head of black hair with the merest hint of grey at the temples. This, coupled with his muscular build, dark eyes and the fashionable beard stubble he sported had Jennifer almost licking her lips. He was definitely very sexy and more than a little mysterious. She liked what she was seeing.

'Yes, please, I'll have another vodka and tonic,' she answered his unspoken question.

A couple of drinks can't hurt, can they?

Jennifer had not planned to spend the evening in the bar but a strange dream the night before had left her with a lingering melancholy she could not shake off. In the dream she was someone else, living another life entirely and she had wakened disturbed by it. She had been out of sorts all day and considered having an early night but the thought of going to sleep and maybe dreaming again had lured her out to the bar. Now here she was, in the company of this handsome stranger. They had spotted an empty table in a secluded corner of the terrace and nabbed it before anyone else could. It was a perfect place to sit, well away from the noise in the bar and the rowdiness of the tourists out in the street below.

Less than ten minutes later Jennifer found herself telling her life story, such as it was. He seemed easy to chat with – open and friendly, and a good listener. Easy in a way that made her realise she was beginning to fancy him like crazy.

'Why did you move to Cyprus?' he asked.

'I love it,' she said and took a sip from her vodka and tonic. 'My family always came here for holidays when I was a kid. My dad was in the army and he was based here for a few years. He fell in love with Cyprus and always found an excuse to come back on holiday. When they got married, mum and him spent their honeymoon here and when my brother and I were old enough, we would come here for a family holiday a couple of weeks every year.'

'You were a barrack brat? Yes?' he asked.

'A what?' Jennifer asked and raised her eyebrows at the unfamiliar expression.

'Please, it is not meant to be derogatory. It is merely the name given to the offspring of serving soldiers who spend their childhood on military bases. Does the term describe you?'

'No. My dad left the army before he and mum got married. He only served for a few years, in Cyprus and in Northern Ireland, then he got out and spent the rest of his working life as a car mechanic. I think he only joined up to see a bit of the world and learn a trade he could use in civilian life. And that's exactly what he did. He spent almost forty years in the motor trade then he officially retired last year, but he still likes to tinker with old cars and motorbikes. These days he's busy restoring an old classic car, when he isn't away at local car rallies or motorcycle races, that is.'

He nodded but didn't comment.

By the time the second round of drinks were ordered and placed in front of them they had exchanged first names.

'Jennifer,' he repeated it softly in a way that made it sensuous coming from his lips. He nodded as though in approval then raised his glass to her.

'I am delighted to make your acquaintance, Jennifer. My name is Ilan and I hope with all my heart that we become the very best of friends.'

From his formal use of English, it was obvious it was a second language to him. His accent wasn't local and Jennifer wondered what his native tongue could be.

They touched glasses and each took a sip of their drinks. Jennifer was enjoying the smiling laughter in his eyes as they toasted their new-found friendship. There was something decidedly suggestive in the way he looked at her and the slight hint of emphasis he put on the words – the very best of friends. She found herself hoping it would go farther than friendship.

But not wanting to take this too far on a first date, if it was a date, Jennifer raised her eyebrows at him and told him Ilan wasn't a Cypriot sounding name.

'You are quite correct, Jennifer. It is not a Cypriot name,' he replied, flashing his most charming smile in agreement. Despite her questioning frown, he declined to elaborate any further on his nationality. Nor, she couldn't fail to notice, did he say much of anything about himself.

'So, where are you from then? I've tried but I can't place your accent?' she asked, refusing to give up.

Ilan quickly deflected the question by ordering another round of drinks from a waiter who appeared at his side. He took their order, placed refilled bowls of salted peanuts and popcorn on the table in front of them and spirited away the empty ones.

Before Jennifer got a chance to repeat her question about his nationality, Ilan skilfully manoeuvred the topic of conversation back to her again.

'Are you also in the military, like your father was, and based here in Cyprus?' he asked.

'Me? Oh, no. I'm... well, I'm an interior designer.' Jennifer cringed inwardly at her hesitation. Her lack of conviction annoyed her. She glanced down at the glass of vodka in her hand, unable to meet his eyes and the mocking laughter she was certain she would see there. She concentrated on the contents of the glass, swirling the ice cubes around, as she tried her best to ignore what she thought would be his reaction.

'It sounds interesting, but I must confess I know very little about interior designing, other than – if I find a room comfortable and appealing then I like it, without ever thinking too much about how it came to be. You must tell me about it, please. What does interior design entail?'

Jennifer glanced up at him, surprised at his interest. She shrugged her shoulders. 'There really isn't that much to tell you.'

'What made you decide to become an interior designer?' Ilan asked.

'I'm not sure I ever actually wanted to be one,' she told him, fiddling with a piece of popcorn that had fallen out of the bowl. 'At least not at first. But I've always had a flair for colour and I loved to be able to create a mood or a theme using colour and fabrics and light. It's a bit hard to explain, but I seemed to be able to imagine what worked and what didn't and so the natural thing to do was study it at university. That's what I did and well, here I am. And now I love it.'

'And the reason you chose Cyprus?' Ilan asked.

'You mean aside from the fact that I love this place?' Ilan nodded.

'Well, it was my brother's idea to begin with. He's an architect and one of his mates recently started up a business here in property development. Since Cyprus joined the EU, the increase in tourism has been a thousand-fold. That, and all the EU funding being pumped into the country, means there is a fortune to be made in new ventures in hotels and apartments, and in private homes.'

Jennifer paused and took another sip of her drink. She was beginning to relax in his company and her words – like the alcohol – flowed freely.

'So, David – that's my brother – convinced me to meet this guy, find out what he was looking for and pitch a few of my ideas to him. Let me tell you, I was so nervous going into the meeting that I nearly turned and ran. But I forced myself to go through with it. I must have made a good impression because the next thing I knew, he was offering me megabucks to turn my ideas into reality. Well, not quite megabucks but eyewatering enough for me. Anyway, we shook hands and I was booked on the next flight to Larnaca. Although I suspect my brother had played a part by pushing him a little bit into hiring me.'

'Why?'

'Ahh, David believes he has to look out for me and thinks I need to settle down and do something with my life. I've been jumping from one job to another. Travelling, then coming home, then getting itchy feet again. David reckons I should be married and have kids and a steady job like he has.'

There was also a more personal reason for leaving – a man who told her he was madly in love with her but omitted to tell her he was married. She kept this part to herself. There was no reason for him to know her past in that much detail. Especially a part of her past that had caused her so much hurt and embarrassment.

'And you do not agree with his line of thinking?' Ilan asked.

'I haven't met the right man to do all that with. Well, not yet. And I'm not sure about the whole 'having children' bit.' Jennifer made air commas as she explained it to him. 'I love being an auntie to his kids – he has three – but I think that's as far as it's ever gonna go with me. I don't think I have the motherhood gene, or something.'

She took a mouthful of her drink, very much aware that he was studying her intently.

'But I'm happy where I'm at,' she continued. 'This job, living here, it's good. I'm finding the work interesting and I have nearly full control over how I turn my ideas into something tangible.'

'What sort of ideas? I am intrigued.'

Jennifer ran her fingers through her spiked, short blonde hair and puffed out her cheeks while she formulated her answer. 'You know, initially they were nothing very special. Nothing out of the ordinary that would change the face of interior design for years to come and launch me onto the world stage and I'd win the Nobel Prize for interior design. If there is a Nobel Prize for interior design. Is there one?'

'Somehow, I very much doubt it,' Ilan laughed. 'What won him over then?'

'You mean, aside from my good looks and sparkling wit?'

'Yes, aside from your beauty and sparkling wit.' His eyes met hers. 'Although I must confess, that would be more than enough to win me over.'

She blushed at the obvious compliment and took another sip of her drink, hoping he didn't notice the slight tremble in her hand. 'Okay, this is the idea I pitched to him. He's building a holiday complex – hotels, apartments, swimming pools and bars, and the like. Now, most tourists and holidaymakers come from Europe, mainly Northern Europe – the Scandinavian countries, plus Germany, Austria and the likes of Holland and such.'

'They also come from the UK,' Ilan said.

'Yes, that's true but a lot of them are from the Scandi countries. My idea is to have themed rooms and apartments which reflect Northern Europe. Now, before you stare open-mouthed at me in horror, when I say themed, I don't mean in a glaringly obvious way. I mean it in a very, very subtle way using only the right colours and fabrics and lighting and such. I want it to be so delicately subtle you would hardly notice it. But I want it to be enough so the family arriving from Denmark, or the honeymoon couple who have just flown in from Norway, arrive at their apartment or check into their hotel room and, without even realising it, they instantly feel at home. Not in a 'we-might-as-well-have-stayed-at-home' kind of way, but I want them to have a warm, fuzzy 'we've-chosen-the-best-place-to-stay' feeling. It's simple but brilliant, even if I do say so myself.'

He nodded thoughtfully and chewed his bottom lip, his eyes watching her.

'Say something, Ilan. Say it is brilliant. Or crap. Just say something.'

'I have been to Norway on several occasions and Finland once. I found both countries beautiful, but the cold did not appeal to me. I can, however, visualise what you are implying when you bring a little of those countries here to offset the heat. It does make sense and I would very much like to see some of your work.'

Inwardly Jennifer was thrilled. He had described her work and her ambitions perfectly and she was delighted that he understood her.

Ilan ordered another whiskey for himself but Jennifer declined.

'So, you've heard my story Ilan, now it's your turn. What is it that you do?'

'Mmmm, let me say that I am in the... import and export business,' he replied, somewhat evasively.

Jennifer frowned, suddenly not liking the tone she was hearing. A seed of doubt crept in and she began to wonder who he was and what he did. *Something illegal, I bet. He's an arms dealer or a drugs dealer, or involved in people trafficking. Maybe it's time to call a halt before this gets out of hand.*

'Well, it's getting late,' Jennifer said as she glanced at her watch and stood up. 'This has been lovely, Ilan. I've had a great evening but I really think it's time I was going –'

'Please do not go,' he deftly caught her wrist. 'I can assure you that my employment is quite legitimate if that is your concern.'

'Oh yeah, right,' she said loudly. 'Let go of my wrist or I'll –'

Her voice caught the attention of a few people nearby who frowned and glanced in their direction. One man started to get up.

'Jennifer, please. You have taken a little too much to drink,' Ilan's voice was quiet but firm. 'Please let me call you a taxi to take you home.'

Jennifer sat down again. She was a lot more intoxicated than she realised.

He leaned forward towards her. His voice was low as he whispered in her ear. 'I am Israeli, Jennifer, and we tend to be naturally reticent. What I do is very important, but it is not something I am able to speak freely about. However, if you want me to, in time, I will tell you anything you wish to know. But not tonight.'

She caught the look in his eyes. The sincerity in them was obvious. 'I'm sorry,' she told him, praying she hadn't frightened him off.

'Apology accepted,' he smiled and nodded. 'Now, I will take you home and I will return early tomorrow morning to see if you require something to cure your hangover. I suspect that you will.'

Ilan held her hand lightly, but firmly, in his as they walked along the footpath in the general direction of the line of waiting taxis. Yet they were not in any hurry. The cool breeze was beginning to clear Jennifer's head and she relaxed in his company and her hand inside his felt good.

He was enough of a gentleman to walk her up to the front door of her apartment and he took her key from her and unlocked the door. It was on the tip of her tongue to invite him in for a coffee. Before she could do so, he

kissed her briefly on the lips, a gentle touch, then he
turned and walked swiftly away towards the waiting taxi.

Chapter 6 - Yorkshire

Ten years ago. Jennifer's dream.

The single-track road was narrow and winding and barely wide enough for two cars to meet and pass by without scraping wing mirrors. Then one more corner and there was a lane with the dry-stone walls on either side. A 'For Sale' sign, faded and battered by the elements, was planted in the hedge near a large oak tree.

'What have you found?' Lucy smiled as she glanced at her husband in the driving seat.

'Wait and see,' Charlie replied as the car bumped along the lane. The suspension clunked and rattled in protest at every pothole. He braked to a gentle stop near a grove of large fir trees then inched the car forward until the farmhouse came into view.

'Oh my God! I love it, Charlie! I bloody well love it!' Lucy screamed in delight. 'It looks perfect. It is perfect! This is exactly what I imagined the house of my dreams would look like!'

Memories of the dream she had awakened from began to disappear as they parked the car and got out to investigate the lovely old farmhouse. But it was one of the strangest dreams Lucy had ever experienced. Almost as if she had been watching through someone else's eyes while she sat and chatted to the tall, good-looking man with the black hair and dark eyes. And the disturbing memory of his kiss still lingered in the back of her mind, and on her lips.

'To be honest pet, perfect is the one thing this house isn't. It hasn't been finished and it'll need a lot of fixing up. There'll be a lot of work and we'll need to get it for a good price and if we –'

'Who cares? You're a builder you can easily sort it. Look at it, Charlie, it's so beautiful.'

'Well, let's take off the rose-tinted glasses and go have a proper look, shall we?'

Charlie switched off the engine. From the glove compartment, he produced a bunch of keys that the estate agent had given him. He jangled them, teasingly, in front of Lucy before putting them in his pocket as he opened the car door.

'Come on!' Lucy shoved open her own door and was out of the car in seconds.

Laughing at her enthusiasm, Charlie slowly got out and locked the car. She was almost hopping from one foot to the other with impatience as he deliberately took his time.

'Come on Charlie! I want to see inside! I want to see what the rooms are like. I want to see what sort of kitchen it has. A big old-fashioned farmhouse kitchen probably. Maybe there'll be an Aga stove. I hope all the rooms have fireplaces and the floors will be tiled and there'll be beams on the ceilings!'

'Steady on girl. Savour the moment. Look around you. Look at these views, Lucy. Aren't they something else?'

'Yeah, yeah, they're lovely. Really spectacular. But I can look at them later. Right now, I'm more interested in the inside of the house.'

Lucy was like a little kid standing at the entrance to a fairground, wanting to have a go on all the rides but unable to make up her mind which one to jump on first. Charlie took her hand and together they walked up to the front door. They marvelled at the spectacular views the countryside offered them, and the old, beautiful trees that surrounded and sheltered the property as they approached it. But at the same time, they took note of the negatives.

The overgrown garden, the tumbled-down walls, piles of builder's debris and what looked like old farm machinery – several ploughs, or possibly one plough that had been broken into several pieces. There was also an old hay bailer and even an old vintage tractor that had almost disappeared in the tangled mess of long grass and weeds.

Lucy quickly glanced over all the various instruments with the keen eye of someone who would carefully restore some of them, especially one piece that looked like an old horse-drawn plough. She could either to sell it or possibly utilise it as a rustic bespoke garden feature. It would look great cleaned up and maybe painted pillar-box red, sitting where it was now, but surrounded by a tidy, well-manicured lawn.

Charlie, on the other hand, frowned at them with the critical eye of someone weighing up the cost of either having to haul them all away for disposal or their potential value as scrap metal.

'What's the asking price?' Lucy asked, suddenly coming back down to earth.

'Shhhh, let's go and have a proper look at it first.'

Charlie kept hold of her hand as they walked up to the front door, only releasing it to retrieve the bunch of keys from his jacket pocket. The lock was stiff from the elements, and he worked it back and forth a few times until the mechanism loosened enough to unlock it. The wood in the old door was swollen, as was the frame, and he had to push hard to force it open. They peered inside, wrinkling their noses at the musty, unlived in smell. Thankfully it wasn't as strong as they had anticipated.

'It'd better not be haunted,' Lucy commented as she stepped over the threshold.

To her left a window, about three feet by three feet, let in what little light there was on this dull November afternoon and softened the dark granite walls of the small porch. An oak door beckoned them further into the house. Charlie, after several attempts at finding the correct key, finally unlocked it and they walked inside.

'Oh shit,' Lucy said, her eyes wide with amazement. This was not what she expected.

They had stepped into a large entrance hall that was the centre of the house. The floor was natural wood, light in colour, with several doors leading off it to various rooms. But it was the magnificent staircase that caught their attention.

'Not your typical farmhouse,' she remarked. The staircase, in the same wood as the floor and the doors, was so beautiful she wanted to weep. A large skylight in the ceiling above bathed the area in pale light and begged her to climb the steps to see what was up there.

'Nah. Most of the old house was torn down, apart from the outer and inner structural walls and then it was rebuilt, restored and modernised by the current owner,' Charlie informed her, as he took the estate agent's brochure out of his other pocket and read through it. 'He ran out of money before he'd finished so he gave up and put it on the market. I'm not sure what kind of restoration he's done or how good it is though.'

'Well, knowing you, it won't be good enough. What is this room?' Lucy opened the door and peered inside.

He checked the brochure. 'This'll be the living room.'

'Okay. My god, would you get a look at that fireplace!'

The room was large with exposed original stone walls and the beams, Lucy had been longing, for across the ceiling. It was bigger than what would be commonly called family-sized and the stone and wood fireplace took up most of one wall. The slate hearth stretched out well in proportion to the size of the fireplace. A wooden beam mantelpiece, probably pitched pine, was naturally distressed and gave it an ancient, yet still functional, appearance. The small grate looked completely dwarfed in this vast space and Lucy shook her head in disgust at how inappropriate it was and imagined how much nicer a wood-burning stove in the centre of the fireplace, glowing warmly on a cold winter's evening would look. A basket full of seasoned pine-scented logs sat nearby for when the fire got low. She could see Charlie and herself curled up on a big leather sofa, each drinking a hot whiskey, or maybe an Irish coffee, and happily planning their first Christmas in their new home.

Two large windows and double patio doors threw natural light into the room, albeit not much on this dark, rainy day but come the summer and the longer days, this room would be filled with sunshine. Lucy's keen sense of direction had already told her the compass points and where the sun would be at various times of the day and season.

'Oh, Charlie this is perfect. I love how the old stone walls have been exposed, and this floor is genuine wood, not that laminated shit you find everywhere nowadays. Imagine a big furry rug in front of the stove and lovely chestnut coloured leather sofas – a three-seater here and a two-seater over there, an antique coffee table or two, and heavy curtains to keep out any draughts. We could have dimmed lights. Or candles and –'

'Fire hazard,' Charlie said.

'Eh?'

'Candles are a fire hazard. In fact, they cause about three per cent of all home fires.'

'Three whole per cent. Wow, that is a lot.' Lucy rolled her eyes.

'I'm just saying.'

'Well, we'll use tea lights then. They're less dangerous. Anyway, back to the wood-stove –'

'A wood-stove? Are you sure? I was thinking a large open fire in here would look the part.'

'Nah, we need a wood-burning stove. You can burn any type of wood in it – all those pallets you get at work that end up burned on site can be used in a wood-stove and you don't have to worry about, first the rug, then the whole house catching fire from any sparks. I can imagine a big basket full of perfectly shaped, pine-scented logs but they are just for show.'

'What else are you imagining?'

'Oh well, I can see a dog dozing contentedly on the rug. And there's a tabby cat strategically positioned on one of the window sills so he, or she, can get warmth from the radiator and look out of the window at the same time. She's female, an old mother cat, and she's relaxed and content and very thankful to be indoors where it's warm and snug. I can see dark-coloured, heavy, full-length curtains – possibly a deep maroon shade, but any colour so long as they are dark – on the windows and on the doors, to keep out the draughts, and the window sills are handmade and wooden and stained in a lovely dark mahogany. I've put cinnamon scented tea lights burning in their holders on the hearth and larger ones on top of the mantelpiece, in case the electricity goes off, which is likely because outside the wind is really howling and there's going to be a blizzard before morning. If you peek outside, you can already see flakes swirling around and falling on the ground so we'll probably be snowed in for a few days.'

Lucy rambled happily, completely lost in her imagination. 'And I'm not at all concerned about the blizzard because the larder is well-stocked, we have plenty of wine, and you've been working so hard all afternoon chopping wood for the fire that we won't get cold.'

Charlie grinned at her. 'How come it's always me that ends up outside in the bitter cold chopping firewood?'

'Oh, you won't be even a little bit cold because all that chopping is gonna keep you nice and warm.'

'So, while I'm outside in this blizzard this weird imagination of yours has conjured up, freezing my arse off, you'll be indoors parked in front of the fire, all warm and comfortable and cosy, and knowing you, there'll be a big glass of wine in your hand.'

'Yep, that sounds about right,' she nodded in mock seriousness.

'Okay you win,' he said as he pulled her gently out of the room. 'Let's go see the rest of it.'

The next room they investigated was the kitchen. This had also been restored by the owner while he still had funds and it was obvious a considerable amount of money had been spent on it. The exposed stone walls, recessed lighting on the ceiling and underneath the eye level cupboards, the polished granite worktops and the tiled floor, gave it a modern feel that successfully managed to compliment the age of the building itself. Whoever had designed this kitchen had certainly pulled off the complicated blending of old and new and had done so in a way that worked extremely well.

Charlie nodded in approval as, with a builder's eye, he studied the workmanship of the units, the tiling and the electrical sockets.

Lucy watched him as he peered into every nook and cranny, trying to read his face, but he was giving nothing away and it made her nervous. All she could imagine as she gazed around the large kitchen was food cooking on the stove. A table set for two with subtle lighting and a glass of wine within arm's reach while she stirred the stew – for some reason, in her mind, it was a heart-warming winter stew. She blew gently on a spoonful of it before tasting it. In her imagination, it was delicious.

Charlie winked at her. 'Well, so far as I can tell everything looks okay.'

Relieved, Lucy let out a slow breath as they continued in this vein, checking out the remainder of the house. It was all wood and stone, and even in its present state, stripped bare and unlived in, it looked beautiful.

Upstairs was every bit as enchanting as downstairs and Lucy was almost in tears when she walked into the master bedroom. She gazed in wonder at the open fireplace with its amazing pitched pine mantelpiece, similar to the one in the living room, although more compact in size, to allow for the smaller area.

The windows on either side of the chimney breast looked out over the part of the garden where the old ploughs and other assorted junk hid in the overgrown grass and weeds. From another, much larger window, Lucy could see the narrow road and the lane they had travelled along to approach the property and beyond that, the dales. This window would allow the early morning sunlight to shine in, brightening and warming the room.

Another door led off the bedroom and Lucy assumed it was an en-suite bathroom. When she opened it, she was delighted to find a spacious dressing room, big enough for a large wardrobe and a good-sized dressing table. She squealed in delight when another door in this room led her into a comfortable sized en-suite with a bath, wash hand basin, toilet and an unfinished shower. Only the tray had been fitted.

Charlie stood behind her and rested his chin on her shoulder. 'That shower tray looks dodgy so I'd rip it out, and the bath, because it's cracked. Then I'd tile the floor and walls, and it needs a proper extractor fan which I could incorporate in a central light. I'd put in a new shower, one of those large walk-in ones because we have the space. And one of those nice stand-alone baths and a more modern wash hand basin and toilet. What do you think?'

'It sounds perfect. Is it a lot of work?'

'Ripping the old stuff out is the hardest part. Don't worry about it.'

There was nothing about the house Lucy didn't love already. From the three other bedrooms, another main bathroom, a second living room downstairs – this might be the one she would put the wood stove into and keep the open fire for the larger room. There was also an integrated double garage and a small shower room downstairs. It was perfect. This was her dream home and the several houses they looked at previously with a view to buying, paled in comparison to this stunningly beautiful old farmhouse.

But would Charlie, a builder who knew when something was dodgy enough to walk away from, think this beautiful house would make a home for them? She knew he would look at it coldly and clinically, concentrating on what needed to be done rather than see the finished product. Still, if he was as good a builder as his reputation said he was, he could easily see the finished article. Couldn't he?

They spent the better part of another two hours exploring every nook and cranny in the house until they had seen all they needed to see. Lucy pictured only the good and imagined it all furnished and lived in. Charlie frowned and scratched his head. He even sucked in air through his lips in a way that Lucy knew meant if they bought it, they would be laying out a considerable amount of money and time on it.

He was making her very nervous. She was worried he would carefully add up all the faults he had found and decide that it wasn't a good deal. If he did, she would be heartbroken. She prayed he would want it as much as she did, and all the faults and the subsequent repairs and renovations would not cause him to walk away.

'Well, what do you think?' Charlie locked the front door and turned to his wife. He laced his fingers through hers as they walked around the exterior of the house.

Lucy hesitated as she looked around her, taking in the wonderful views, the large garden and finally her eyes were drawn back to the old farmhouse itself. 'Oh, I love it, Charlie. I really love it, but...'

'But what?' he asked.

'But can we afford it? How much is it? Is it worth buying? Is it going to be worth finishing the renovations? How much work is there? I dunno Charlie, it's a big undertaking.'

'There's a fair bit of work but there's nowt that can't be done with a bit of hard graft. Most of the important renovations are done and they all seem okay. I'm concerned about the bathrooms as they might have to be pulled out and redone with waterproof plasterboard, but that's not an issue if I'm going to modernise them anyway. I'd also plaster over maybe a quarter of that exposed stonework. It's nice but there's far too much of it. It's a bit like living in a mediaeval castle.'

'But can we afford to do all of that? What if we run into a major problem that could cost us a fortune?'

'Well, I know a bloke who works for the estate agents. In fact, it was him who told me about it because I did some renovations for his mum and dad a couple of years ago. He told me we could probably get it for a fair bit under the asking price, especially if I pointed out all the things that need sorting out. You know, get a proper survey and a detailed list of what's what. If I take it to them, they should accept our lower offer. It's the kind of stuff that your average person wouldn't want to take on when they're buying a house. That, plus the fact that it's been on the market for over sixteen months and there's been little or no interest in it.'

She couldn't speak. She looked at him with hope shining in her eyes.

'Lucy, if we play our cards right,' Charlie told her. 'We could steal this place.'

She could tell by the gleam in his eye that he wanted it as much as she did. He was itching to get his builder's hands on it.

'So, how much are they selling it for?'

He told her and she let out a long, slow whistle. Charlie could see her mentally making the calculations and a light of determination, and realisation, shone in her eyes.

'We could manage that if we —'

'Come in with a lower offer and use Auntie Ethel's money,' he finished. His aunt, his mother's only sibling, had died eight months ago. Since Charlie was her favourite nephew as well as being her only one, she had left him a very tidy sum of money.

'Are you sure? I thought you wanted to keep that money for a rainy day?'

Charlie looked at her, standing in front of him on this cold, wet November day. The drizzle made her long, brown hair go limp, and she looked cold and wet and miserable, but there was a look in her eyes that filled him with happiness and made him want to buy her the world.

'Sweetheart, if this isn't a rainy day, I don't know what is.'

Chapter 7 - Lucy's Dream

The annoying sound of the doorbell awakened Jennifer from a dream-filled sleep.

Walking around a musty old farmhouse and then outside in the cold with the winter rain plastering my hair to my scalp, soaking into my bones. What was that all about? And why does it seem more a memory than a dream?

She opened her eyes and the dream disappeared like a leaf on the breeze. The doorbell chimed again and she groaned. All she wanted was for it to go away and bloody well leave her alone. Her head ached and her mouth tasted like sandpaper. If only she could close her eyes and sleep for a couple more hours.

It's Sunday morning for Christ's sake. Whoever you are, go away!

Then she remembered. Last night in the bar – the one on the corner she had never ventured into before. And the lovely evening she had spent there with the tall, dark-eyed, mysterious, and very, very sexy Israeli guy.

'Oh my God! He's here!'

Jennifer threw back the sheets and quickly pulled on a light cotton dressing gown. It was then she remembered he said he would pick her up early. At the time, it seemed like such a good idea. But now, and with a nasty hangover, it didn't seem quite so wonderful.

Jennifer checked her appearance in the mirror. She needed a shower, but there wasn't time. She rushed to the door and opened it. Ilan was standing there with a wry smile on his face.

'Ilan. Hi there. Look, I'm not quite ready but come on in. Can you give me a few minutes?' She held the door wide open and swept her arm to usher him in.

'Good morning,' Ilan said. He flashed her the brightest of smiles and walked in as if he owned the place.

Maybe he does.

Jennifer had no idea who owned the apartment she was living in, as it was leased through the company she worked for. Not that she cared all that much who owned it. It had been paid for in advance for twelve months with a further lease option at her own expense if she wished to continue living there. She hadn't made up her mind yet whether to stay or look for a property. Part of her baulked at the thought of owning a house and being tied down. But another part of her, the part that realised her brother was correct when he said it was time she settled down, knew it was something she should be considering.

Well, buying a house is certainly the definition of settling down.

'Is it a good morning?' she replied and took a moment to admire his body encased in tight jeans and a black T-shirt. He carried a brown leather jacket which he threw casually over the back of a chair. His face was clean shaven and he looked like a million dollars.

'I thought it was still the middle of the night,' she said grumpily, and wondered how he could possibly look so good this early in the morning.

'It is a beautiful morning and we should make the most of it before the tourists awaken and come out of their lairs on the prowl for breakfast and suntan cream. Yes?'

Jennifer nodded and yawned. 'I'm sorry, I'm still a little bit sleepy. You kept me up quite late last night.'

'Are you badly hungover?' Ilan asked.

'Nothing that two paracetamol tablets and a full English wouldn't cure,' she replied.

'A what?' he asked with a frown.

'A full English breakfast – fried eggs, fried bacon, fried sausages, toast, mushrooms and baked beans. Maybe some black pudding thrown in. It's the best cure for a hangover known to man. That, or a double cheeseburger, or maybe a chicken curry. Mmmm, nothing beats a chicken curry. Okay, that's probably not a breakfast dish but still...'

'Would you like me to make you some coffee while you shower?' Ilan asked, looking slightly queasy at the thought of her breakfast menu suggestions.

'Yes, please. The kitchen is that way. There's coffee in the cupboard above the toaster, and you'll find mugs in the same cupboard and milk in the fridge. I'll be twenty minutes, no more,' she smiled at him. 'I'm really glad you're here.'

'Go and shower. Quickly. Or the coffee will be ready before you are.'

Jennifer nodded and fled back into the bathroom. She stared at her reflection in the mirror.

Well, if this doesn't frighten him off...

Her hair looked okay on one side of her head but the other, the side she slept on, was flattened against her scalp. She showered and dried herself in record time. Then some styling wax smeared onto her palms and in no time her hair was spiked into the style she preferred. A thorough brush of her teeth and some moisturiser on her face and she felt almost able to face him.

Jennifer took a deep breath and feeling somewhat more awake, emerged from the bathroom. Dressed now in denim shorts, a loose white T-shirt and tan leather sandals, she felt a hundred times better.

Ilan was seated on a stool at the breakfast bar and swivelled around towards her. He looked her up and down appraisingly and nodded his approval as he drank a mouthful of coffee, then poured one for her.

She sat on the barstool beside him and added a splash of milk, noting that he preferred his coffee black. She took a sip.

'This is delicious, thank you.'

'My pleasure,' he replied. 'What would you like to do today? I have an idea I think you will enjoy but if you have something specific already planned that is okay.'

'I don't know. I'll admit I have a bit of a hangover and I had this crazy dream. It was about a house strangely enough, but not like anything here. More like an old English farmhouse. Is that weird or what?'

Ilan shrugged as he sipped his coffee. 'Dreams tend to be whatever they want to be. Are you homesick? Was it a house you know?'

'No. It was old and a bit decrepit, like so many old farmhouses I've seen dotted around the countryside, but it wasn't somewhere I recognised. And I'm definitely not homesick.'

'I am disappointed in you Jennifer. I had hoped you would have been dreaming of me.'

'Yeah, I was disappointed myself. It's your fault, you know,' she told him with a smile.

He looked at her with feigned shock, but then he grinned and his grin was full of mischief. 'My fault? Why do you say that?'

Her heart began to thump in her chest. 'You need to give me something to dream about. To keep me from having strange dreams of old, tumbled down English farmhouses.'

'Do you mean something like this?' Ilan said and carefully set his coffee mug down on the worktop. He pulled her towards him. His lips met her own, gently at first, a mere taste of coffee and mint toothpaste. Then he kissed her more forcefully. His arm went around her waist and rested lightly on the small of her back. His other hand cupped the back of her head.

Jennifer could feel the heat from his body emanating through the light clothes they both were wearing and her lips parted in response to his touch. She moaned softly as he pulled her closer to him, holding her tightly in his arms. She returned his embrace, kissing him deeply with a passion and a hunger that surprised her. Yet it felt like the most natural thing in the world.

Then he stopped and stood up, extricating himself from her arms. He looked at her with a question in his eyes and what seemed to be regret.

Did he regret kissing me, or regret stopping?

Jennifer hoped it was the latter.

'Is that enough material for your dreams, neshama?' Ilan asked.

'It's a beginning,' she told him. 'Probably good enough for a dream or two. But I'll need more than that. A whole lot more.'

'You are very greedy,' he grinned. 'But if it is what you wish, then who am I to say no to you?'

Why do you call me neshama?' she asked. 'What does it mean?'

'It is a Hebrew word,' he explained, taking both of her hands in his. 'Literally translated it means 'my soul' but it is commonly used as a term of endearment. The closest translation in English would probably be... sweetheart, or maybe darling.'

'My soul. That is so beautiful,' she told him.

'It is a beautiful language. As for material for your dreams, well, I think I will have to work on that. But now we should go. Do you have a swimsuit and a pair of trainers or deck shoes?'

'Yeah, I've got both.'

'Good. Bring the swimsuit with you and wear the trainers.'

The black BMW convertible was exactly the sort of car Jennifer expected him to be driving. The fact that it was old, somewhat battered, and extremely dusty, came as a bit of a surprise. The engine sounded a bit suspect, too. But Ilan seemed confident that it would get them from A to B so she got in and settled back into the passenger seat.

He drove quickly but carefully through the small resort then out onto the main road heading southwards. Jennifer didn't know where they were going. They were driving away from the more well-known tourist areas, but she was content to sit back, relax and admire his skill behind the wheel.

After about fifteen minutes they pulled off the highway onto a dusty gravel road that took them back down towards the coast again. She looked out at the crystal-clear water and smiled. This had all the makings of being a perfect day.

Ilan pulled into a small parking area that had been finished in the same loose gravel surface as the road. Although calling it 'finished' was stretching the definition of the word somewhat. He circled around and parked in the shade under a sprawling fig tree.

'We are here,' he told her as he got out of the car.

Jennifer opened her door and stepped out. She reached into the back of the car and gathered up her beach bag. Ilan took her hand in his as they carefully made their way down rough-cut stone steps that took them to a small cove with a beach and a marina. Several boats were moored there. The largest being a medium sized, expensive looking yacht and the smallest – a simple rowing boat with an outboard motor attached at the rear. Six jet skis were tied up at the wooden jetty and there was a patio area to the left which housed several tables and chairs underneath large umbrellas. Behind the patio area, she could see a small café.

'Where are we going?' Jennifer asked.

'Breakfast first,' he told her and ushered her through the indoor seating area and out onto a balcony that overlooked the cove. The wooden floor beneath their feet gave a boardwalk feel to it and the sprawling fig tree the balcony was structured around seemed to grow up out of the floor. Still holding Jennifer's hand, Ilan led her to a table that overlooked the beach. The fig tree gave them shade from the morning sun. At this early hour they were the only customers.

Jennifer gazed out over the bay from behind her sunglasses. 'This is beautiful.'

'It is,' Ilan replied. 'But I expect in a couple of years they will have developed it with hotels and apartments and it will be full of tourists. For now, I like to come here and enjoy the tranquillity and the unspoiled naturalness of it.'

'Is development such a bad thing?'

'No. It will bring income to an area that desperately needs it. I regret my selfishness, but I dislike watching an area becoming commercialised. But of course, you want commercialisation – so many more hotels and apartments for your designs.'

'I can see both sides, Ilan. There are areas where development can be a good thing. It brings economic security where it is needed, but I'm on your side too as it's important to keep some places... unspoiled.'

'I know. I am not disagreeing with you,' he smiled. 'How is your hangover?'

'I'm okay. Maybe a little bit tired and very, very hungry but I'm not really hungover.' She was, but she was not going to admit it to him.

Almost on cue, a middle-aged, smiling waiter approached their table and greeted Ilan like a long-lost brother. Ilan stood up and the pair of them shook hands, then they hugged and finally they slapped one another on the backs.

Jennifer was unable to keep up with their conversation. Her Greek consisted of what little she had learned from a tourist phrase book and the rapid-fire exchange between Ilan and the waiter, or possibly the owner of the café, went over her head completely. From their expressions and their delight in being in each other's company she managed to deduce he was an old friend pleased to see Ilan once again, even while he chided him for not dropping by more often.

Then it became apparent they were talking about her. Favourably she hoped. The waiter asked a question and Ilan shook his head. He immediately switched to heavily accented English, informed her that his name was Dinos and he welcomed her to his humble restaurant.

'Thank you,' she responded as he wiped the table with a damp cloth. He placed two menus in front of them then walked away, leaving them to decide what they wanted.

'Is he a good friend of yours?' Jennifer asked as she studied the menu, not that she could understand much of it.

'Yes. He is a very good friend,' Ilan replied. 'He is also a wonderful cook and the food here is excellent. You should order something light. Croissants and coffee. But if you must have something more substantial for your hangover then I recommend the Eggs Benedict.'

'Why something light?'

'Because we are going swimming and it is not a good idea to swim after a large meal.'

'Okay, if you insist. But I have to warn you, I'm not much of a swimmer.'

'You will be fine,' he smiled.

Jennifer wondered what he had in store for her as she ordered scrambled eggs and croissants, and a large, black coffee. Ilan placed the same order.

They lingered over the meal, making only small talk while they ate. Despite her reservations about who he was and what he did, Jennifer found that she was happy and content to be in his company. She began to relax and enjoy herself. Thanks to his presence, and the two paracetamol tablets she had taken with her coffee, her headache had all but disappeared.

They laughed and talked as they finished their breakfast. Jennifer chased a crumb around her plate with her fingertip and tried to entice Ilan to talk about himself. But he very carefully deflected all of her probing questions. With a mental shrug of her shoulders, she gave up and played along with him and his light-hearted conversation.

Eventually he went back inside the café to pay the bill, once again chatting in Greek to Dinos. When he returned a short time later, he was carrying two life jackets over his shoulder, a blue and white cool box and a set of keys.

'Let's go.'

Jennifer slung her bag over her shoulder and followed him down to the jetty where they walked out to a small speedboat.

'Is this yours?' she asked.

'No, it belongs to Dinos, although he has been trying to sell it to me. I take it out on test runs and each time I come back, I tell him that I have not decided yet,' he said with a shrug and a grin. 'Dinos knows I have no intention of buying it, but he lets me take it out every now and then. It is a little game we enjoy playing.'

'Somehow Ilan, I suspect you play many little games,' Jennifer told him as she took one of the life jackets from him and climbed into the small craft. 'Are you going to tell me what's in the cool box? Body parts? Drugs?'

'Lunch,' he told her with a mocking glare as he set the box down inside the small open cabin and put the keys in the ignition. He pulled off his T-shirt and, much to Jennifer's surprise and delight, unzipped his jeans and stepped out of them. To her disappointment, he was wearing swimming shorts underneath the jeans. She watched him as he neatly folded the jeans and T-shirt, placing them on top of the cool box. Part of the seating area held a small storage compartment underneath and Ilan tidied away the cool box, his clothes and Jennifer's bag.

'Change into your swimsuit and store your clothes in here,' Ilan told her as he handed her a large beach towel. 'They will remain dry inside.'

Jennifer wrapped the towel around her as she changed into her swimsuit and then folded her clothes on top of his in the compartment.

As Ilan helped Jennifer put on her life jacket, she noticed the scars. One on the front of his chest high up near his right shoulder and a second one on his right thigh. They were circular and compact and when he turned around, she noticed another one on the back of his thigh, this one larger and more ragged. She had never seen a scar from a bullet before except on TV, but it was obvious, even to her, that at some time in his life he had been shot. Twice.

Ilan noticed her staring. 'I was in the military.'

'Yeah, but most people don't get shot twice.'

'I am not most people. In Israel it is different.'

'Did it hurt?' Jennifer asked as her fingertip gently traced the outline of the perfect circle on his chest.

'At the time yes, it hurt like hell because the round clipped my collarbone. Even now it aches when I am tired. The one in my leg went straight through. The exit scar makes it appear more serious but it was by far the lesser of two evils. Do they disturb you?'

Her blue eyes looked into his. 'It disturbs me to think you could have been killed and I would never have met you. And it disturbs me that, because of these, you were in pain.'

She leaned forward and gently kissed the scar on his chest as if to make it better. It was just a light touch of her lips but enough to make him gasp, though not in pain.

Ilan pulled her roughly into his arms and kissed her, pulling her tightly against him as his tongue probed her mouth. She felt the heat of him despite the cool sea breeze and she pressed her body against his. There was no doubt in her mind, he wanted her as much as she wanted him.

Jennifer pulled back and looked at him. There was so much she wanted to say. So much she wanted to ask him – she was not sure she trusted him completely – and she needed to trust him before she could give herself to him. She needed to resolve this conflict. But how?

'Slow down,' she said and regretted her words almost instantly.

'What?' he asked. He released her and he took a step back.

'Not yet, Ilan. Let's take our time, please.'

He held her chin in his hand and tilted her head upwards and smiled into her eyes. 'I understand, neshama. We are merely going sailing and swimming today. I want you to relax and enjoy yourself, nothing more. I want to take you to a beautiful cove not far from here where we can swim and I will teach you to snorkel and maybe scuba dive. Do not worry if you are not a strong swimmer, I will look after you. Okay?'

'Okay,' she agreed.

'Please do not think that I will expect more from you,' he continued. 'Do you believe me?'

Jennifer looked at him for a long while. She could see the sincerity in his eyes. 'Yes. I believe you.'

'Good. We will spend some time getting to know one another. For now, we sail and we swim and this afternoon we will enjoy a pleasant day in each other's company. Yes?'

'Okay. I guess I'm up for that,' Jennifer told him with a smile.

Ilan started up the engine. With a flourish, he spun the boat around and out to sea. She sat back and admired the scenery – not just the coastline but also the handsome man steering the boat – and she allowed him to take her wherever he wanted to go.

Chapter 8 - Jennifer's Dream

'Ahh cheers. You're a darling,' Lucy smiled as she took the mug of industrial strength tea from Jimmy. He was the youngest of Charlie's labourers and a good worker but, more importantly, he made the best cup of tea. She gently blew on the hot liquid to cool it and glanced at her watch. It was only a quarter past ten. She had been working all morning and, by her reckoning, it should have been nearly lunchtime. Her stomach rumbled at the thought of lunch and she realised she was starving. Two chocolate digestive biscuits and a mug of tea were not going to cut it.

Charlie sat down on the floor beside her. He took a drink of tea from his own mug then placed it on the floor beside him.

'Tired?' he asked.

'I'm bloody knackered,' Lucy told him.

'It'll be worth it though,' he nudged her shoulder with his. 'Won't it?'

'Oh, don't get me wrong, I absolutely love it,' she said. 'I love every room. Every wall that needs painting and skirting board that has to be cleaned then oiled. I just didn't realise how unfit I was until now. It's this whole – coming home from my day job, then up here working until late evening, back for a quick shower before crashing in front of the telly with a glass of wine. Only to fall asleep after one mouthful. Oh yeah, it's the best fun I've had in years. And the best part of all, I get to do it all over again the very next morning. It's class!' She gave him a tired, rueful grin. 'Here I am, on my day off, and guess what I'm doing?'

'I know. But we'll be finished one of these days and all this hard work will be behind us. On the plus side, you're so tired you're sleeping deeply and you've stopped having those crazy dreams every night. You have stopped, haven't you?'

'Yeah, sure,' she told him. 'I haven't had one in ages. I'm probably too tired to dream, and if I did dream, it would most likely be about woodworking or something.'

She hadn't the heart to tell him she was still dreaming every night and that they were increasing in intensity and becoming more and more vivid in their details. It was almost as though she was living another life every night when she closed her eyes. More and more often she found herself, in that second or two after she awakened, wondering who and where she was and sometimes, she didn't even know which reality was her reality. That was not a good feeling.

'Hey? Earth to Lucy. Come in Lucy,' Charlie nudged her shoulder with his, almost spilling her tea in the process.

She looked at him blankly for a moment. 'I'm sorry, I was miles away. Did you say something?'

'What were you thinking about?' Charlie asked.

'Nothing in particular.'

'No, seriously Lucy. You were completely gone there for a few seconds. Like someone pressed your 'pause' button. You didn't hear a thing I said or even react in any way. It was weird, and a little bit frightening. Is something wrong?' Charlie frowned at her. She could see the concern on his face.

'Ah no, pet. I'm just tired and I was dreaming about getting finished up and having a long, hot soak in the bath this evening. I was imagining the warmth and the steam, and sinking slowly into the hot water. And the wonderful smell of the bubble bath. Mmmm. For a second, I believed I was in the bath! The power of suggestion is wonderful, eh?'

She tried to laugh it off, convincing neither of them as the look of worry on Charlie's face only increased.

This morning she had awakened from another dream about this other life she was living. And in this life was this tall, dark-haired man with well-tanned skin and eyes that were full of laughter. This man had taught her to sail and snorkel. And even though it was a dream, she remembered how nervous she had been the first time she put her head under the clear blue sea. It was strange because, despite being a good and confident swimmer in real life, Lucy had experienced a moment or two suffocating panic as the water closed in around her. The snorkel mask seemed too tight and she was afraid to breathe in case she inhaled the water. Then this man had taken her hand in his and she had been reassured simply because he was beside her.

Who is he? Why am I dreaming about him every night? I feel like I'm falling in love with him? How could I tell Charlie all of this?

She couldn't. That was the answer to her question.

Draining the contents of her mug, Lucy got to her feet. Wincing at the stiffness in her legs and back, she held out her hand to Charlie. He reached for it, threatening to pull her back down beside him before allowing her to help him to his feet.

'Are you sure you're okay?' he asked.

Lucy nodded and smiled. 'I'm fine, Charlie. Honestly.'

Chapter 9 - Lucy's Dream

'Well, if this isn't a surprise? A stray dog showing up on the doorstep at midnight!' Jennifer flung open the front door in response to the insistent ringing of the bell.

'Hi,' Ilan said giving her a sideways grin.

'Do I know you?' she asked sarcastically.

Is he drunk?

She couldn't smell alcohol on his breath but he was swaying a little.

'It is entirely possible you do,' he replied.

'Well, you're either the stray cat I've been feeding or a homeless dog that needs a sofa to sleep on.'

'What about a stray, hungry Israeli who has missed you very much?' he asked.

'I think I might know one of those,' she replied.

Ilan stepped inside and planted a kiss on the side of her cheek. Off came the light jacket he was wearing, then the shoes. He hung the jacket on one of the hooks near the door and parked the shoes on the floor.

There was a glass of red wine sitting on the coffee table, alongside an open bottle and a paperback novel. Ilan lifted the glass and drank the wine then refilled it from the bottle. He took another mouthful.

'Are you drinking alone, neshama?' He raised an eyebrow at her then lifted the book and glanced at the title. It was a crime thriller. He read the blurb on the back cover, but set it down again without comment.

'I haven't had much choice. Good company has been scarce lately,' she replied.

Jennifer didn't want to tell him she had dozed off, the book face down on her lap and the wine hardly touched. She hated to admit it, but escaping from another evening spent on her own was her life now. Although escape was hardly the correct word. After only a couple of pages and a sip or two of wine, she had slowly drifted into another dream about the old farmhouse in England.

By now, she had discovered it was in Yorkshire. While it was a good, solid building it had only been partially restored and it still needed a lot of work. But in this dream, she was artfully trying to avoid discussing her dreams with someone. It was confusing as hell.

What is that woman's problem with discussing her dreams with that Charlie guy? He seems to care about her so why is she being so secretive? And why am I dreaming about another woman's dreams?

'I thought you preferred white wine?' Ilan said.

'Oh, I felt like a change,' Jennifer replied as she tucked away her thoughts about last night's confusing dream.

'You mean you have run out of white wine.'

'Yeah, okay,' Jennifer laughed and put her hands up.

Ilan refilled the glass and took another sip. Jennifer lifted her book, folded the page at the corner to mark her place and put it on the nearby shelf where it joined a dozen or so other paperbacks. Mostly crime novels and thrillers. She went into the kitchen and got another glass from the cupboard.

When she returned, Ilan had settled on the sofa and was drinking her wine. She poured another for herself.

'So, where have you been? And what have you been up to?' Jennifer asked, keeping her voice casual. Pretending it didn't matter that she hadn't seen or heard from him in over three weeks. She tried to tell herself she hadn't missed him. But, looking at him sitting on her sofa in her small living room, barefoot and drinking her wine, made her realise that every day he had been gone had been so terribly lonely without him.

A surge of annoyance coursed through her.

How dare he? How dare he show up on my doorstep, half-drunk, expecting me to be delighted to see him after three weeks of waiting and hoping he would get in touch? He ducked out of giving me his phone number or where he lived, so I couldn't contact him. Does he expect me to wait until he decides he wants to see me?

She was about to tell him exactly what she thought of him and ask him to leave when she noticed the dark circles underneath his eyes.

Ah, not drunk. Merely tired.

Ilan's eyes had a haunted look, as though he had witnessed something no one should ever have to witness.

His eyes, and the tired slump of his shoulders, made her anger disappear as quickly as it had manifested, to be replaced by affection and concern for him.

'Are you okay?' she asked.

Ilan looked at her and blinked in a moment of confusion. He appeared surprised by her question and seemed unsure how to answer her. Then, as though he had flicked a switch, his weariness was replaced by his usual cheeky grin. His eyes sparkled with laughter, despite the dark circles surrounding them.

'Yes, I am okay,' he replied, 'but I am extremely hungry. I think I mentioned that when I came in.'

'Of course. Yes. Sorry,' Jennifer exclaimed. 'I've some leftover homemade lasagne in the fridge. I'll heat it up for you.'

'It sounds delicious and I would very much appreciate it, Jennifer. Thank you.'

'Okay, sit there and relax. It'll take about thirty minutes.'

Ilan listened contentedly to the comforting sounds of her moving around in the kitchen. Turning on the oven, opening the cupboard to get a plate. The clatter of her removing a knife and fork from the kitchen drawer and finally the noise of the oven door opening and shutting. In a few moments, he would be able to smell the enticing aroma of food and his stomach growled at the prospect.

Jennifer appeared before him, faintly embarrassed. She pursed her lips, squinted and said, 'I'm sorry but I'm not sure if this is... well... kosher. Is that the correct word?'

'Do not worry about it. I am hungry enough to eat almost anything. Except, perhaps, a full English breakfast,' he patted the seat beside him on the sofa. 'Sit with me while we are waiting.'

The gravity of her longing to feel Ilan's touch drew her down beside him. Her knee bumped the table and jiggled the nearly empty bottle of wine.

'Careful, neshama,' he said as he reached to steady both her and the bottle.

She settled in next to him and basked in the simple pleasure of her thigh against his. His warmth made her want to touch him but mild resentment held her back. Ilan reached over and tenderly caressed the contour of her hand with his thumb. She caved like a house of cards as she leaned her head on his shoulder. Ilan closed his eyes and rested his head atop hers.

Please stay this time. Please don't make a fool out of me.

'I've missed you,' she whispered.

Ilan gently squeezed her hand and pressed his head on hers in agreement.

'Those few days we spent swimming, sailing and enjoying ourselves were so wonderful. I had such a good time,' she told him. She sipped her wine at an awkward tilt for a few drops of liquid courage. 'You left without a word. I thought it was something I had done or said to annoy you.'

He shifted his head and softly rubbed his cheek against her hair. A deep breath as he took in the scent of her scalp. They sat in silence for a moment. Ilan seemed to be contemplating his answer as he remained silent and unmoving except for his slow breathing. Then he resettled his head back on hers.

Jennifer held her breath a moment as she waited for him to respond.

It had better be a bloody good excuse!

'It was nothing you said or did,' he said. 'I had to go immediately and I did not have an opportunity to tell you I was leaving. I am back now, though.'

Yeah. Like the proverbial bad penny, you've turned up again. Are you a bad penny, Ilan?

'While I was away from you, I found myself thinking about you,' he continued. 'All the time I was not concentrating on my work you invaded my thoughts. Late at night I would awaken and wish you were lying beside me. I could almost imagine you were beside me. That is the measure of how much I wanted to be with you.'

'Is that a good thing or a bad thing?' she asked.

Ilan laughed quietly. 'That would depend entirely on you, my beautiful Jennifer.'

She was about to ask him what he meant when the oven pinged, reminding her she was cooking his supper. She left her words unsaid and hurried into the kitchen.

A glass in each hand and the wine bottle under his arm, Ilan followed her into the kitchen. He took a seat at the small breakfast bar and watched her while she served the food onto a plate and placed a bowl of tossed salad beside it.

As he tucked in to the food, Jennifer got her own fork and sat down beside him. Every now and then she would take a small forkful from his plate and nibble at it, more for the ceremony of sharing a meal with him than hunger on her part. She ate mostly the cheese he scraped off the lasagne, which he pushed to the side of his plate.

He either doesn't like cheese or – haven't I read somewhere about not mixing meat and dairy in Jewish cuisine? I'd better read up on it before I cook for him again.

'That was delicious,' he said as he pushed back his empty plate and smiled at her.

Jennifer gave herself a pat on the back. She wasn't the best cook in the world but lasagne was one of a couple of dishes she had mastered. It could be split it into portions and either frozen or, as in this instance, keep her fed over the weekend. Now Ilan had devoured it.

'So, where have you been?' she asked. They had resumed their seats on the sofa, a second bottle of wine now opened and their glasses filled once again. She wondered if he would tell her the truth. *But what is the truth?*

Ilan took a mouthful of wine then set the glass down on the table. He was silent for a moment, lost in thought. 'I was in Turkey. Then I was in Berlin, but I was sent back to Turkey for a few days.'

'Doing what?' she asked. *Sent? Who sent him?*

'It was business.'

'That doesn't tell me much. What kind of business?'

Ilan shrugged his shoulders. 'It is not easy for me to explain.'

She remembered a report she had seen on the news the day before yesterday. 'There was a bombing in Turkey earlier this week. Were you –'

'Involved?' he finished. 'No.'

'I was going to ask if you had been caught up in it.'

'I was not.'

'Why would I ask if you had been involved?'
Jennifer frowned. *Good question. Why would I think that?*

'Because you hardly know me,' he replied.

'That's not my fault. You know practically all there is to know about me but I know nothing about you. I wish you would tell me.'

'There is not much to tell.'

'Please.'

'Do you have any more wine?'

'Yes.'

'Get it and I will tell you all you wish to know over another glass or two.'

Jennifer found two bottles of red wine in the larder. Despite a quick rummage in the back there wasn't a forgotten bottle of Chardonnay and she kicked herself for not nipping out to the supermarket when she had a chance. It was red wine or nothing tonight.

She shook a bag of potato chips into a bowl and set it on the coffee table, refilled both their glasses and joined Ilan on the sofa again. They both reached for the wine. Jennifer delicately lifted a chip and nibbled at it. Ilan didn't appear interested in them.

Jennifer raised a silent toast to Ilan. 'I'm looking forward to this.'

'You enjoy a good tale?' he asked.

'I do indeed. But while I normally love a good thriller, in this instance I think I would prefer non-fiction.'

'What do you wish to know?'

'Everything.'

Ilan took a moment and a mouthful of wine. He settled deeper into the comfortable sofa and reached for Jennifer's hand.

'Well, my name is Ilan Ben-Levi and I –'

'What age are you?' she asked.

'I will be thirty-eight on my next birthday which is on the seventeenth of October.'

That makes him nine years older than me. Is that too big an age gap?

'What do you work at?'

'I have two sisters and three brothers, or rather I had three brothers. Like me, Dovi stayed in the army but he was killed whilst on manoeuvres with his unit.'

'I am so sorry. When did he die?'

Ilan paused for a moment and stared at the floor, remembering. 'Three years ago. And I miss him even to this day. I am the youngest son and I have one sister who is older than me and one a year younger than me. My father was a lawyer, but he is now retired. My mother is a doctor. She is semi-retired and works three days a week in a nearby walk-in clinic. They live in a nice, quiet suburb of Tel Aviv. At the last count, I have eleven nieces and nephews.'

'What do you work at?'

'When I went to university, I began studying law. My plan was to become a lawyer and join my father's practice. But before that I did my national service – this is mandatory for all citizens over eighteen. I joined the army and I found that I enjoyed it so much I decided to remain in the army where I worked my way up the ranks to major. Also, I was married with a child on the way, so the military pay, such as it was, was a better option than university fees.'

'You're married?' Jennifer's shoulders slumped as the sadness and disappointment washed over her.

That's why he didn't contact me. He was at home with the wife and kids. Just my bloody luck. Again.

He took a deep breath. 'I was. And I have a daughter. She is seventeen and about to join the IDF.'

'What's that?'

'The Israeli Defence Force. She is looking forward to training and I suspect she will probably stay and make a career of it.'

'I wish you had told me you're married with kids,' she gave him a look and moved to the end of the sofa. She kicked off her sandals and swung her legs up and tucked her feet underneath her, needing to put some distance between herself and this married man who was sitting on her sofa.

'I am no longer married,' he told her. 'And I have only one kid.'

'You're divorced then?'

'No.'

'I don't understand.'

'My wife died of ovarian cancer when Nurit – that is the name of my daughter – was three. She was raised by my sister and her husband. But, despite that, we are very close.'

Oh, shit. Now he's gonna tell me he isn't over her but I look a lot like her.

'I am so sorry about your wife.'

He took another drink of wine and settled lower into the sofa. 'It was a long time ago.'

'You've never met anyone else?' Jennifer untucked her legs and stretched out, relieving a cramp that was beginning to develop in her left thigh. She shifted around and threw her legs up onto his, her bare heels resting near his knees.

He laughed. 'I have met plenty. But I never wanted to marry any of them, despite my mother!'

'What do you work at?' Jennifer persisted.

'Would you like to learn Hebrew?'

'Later,' she waved his offer away. 'What do you work at?'

'Todah.'

'Excuse me?' Jennifer asked, with a frown on her face.

'Todah is Hebrew for thank you. So, todah for the delicious lasagne, the wine and the company.'

'You're welcome.' Jennifer smiled.

'In Hebrew, the response is bevakasha. It translates as – you are welcome.'

'Well, that's good to know. What do you work at?'

'Were you perhaps a police interrogator in a past life?' Ilan raised his eyebrow.

'I'm serious, Ilan. What do you work at?'

He reached for the bottle on the coffee table. 'Would you like another glass of wine?'

'I would, but after you tell me what you work at?'

'Red or white? Oh wait, you have no white. Red will have to do,' he smirked.

'Ilan…' Jennifer's face grew stern. She was determined to get an answer out of him even if it killed her.

'Okay,' he sighed. 'If I tell you that I am a boring civil servant will that satisfy you?'

Jennifer's eyes widened in surprise, then narrowed again in suspicion. 'That's it? I don't believe you.'

'I am a civil servant. I do not know why you keep insisting that I tell you when there is nothing to tell. Are you disappointed?'

'If you are a civil servant then why are you here in Cyprus? Are you on an extended holiday or something?'

'No. I live, or I should say I am based, here at present. I work anywhere I am sent.'

Sent? There's that word again. Who sends him? And why?

'Are you a diplomat?' she cocked her head to the side.

He's either a diplomat, a spy or a criminal. Or his job is so boring he's being mysterious to make him seem more interesting than he is. Typical man.

He laughed. 'Well, some aspects of my work require a degree of diplomacy so in a way perhaps I am.'

Interested now, Jennifer leaned forward. 'Please tell me more.'

He glanced at his watch. 'No. That is enough for now. It is getting very late. I am tired and I do have to go.'

'Oh, come on! You can't tell me half and leave me dangling. That's not fair,' Jennifer frowned. 'I want to hear the rest.'

Ilan laughed, making light of her questions. But she detected a hesitation in him. A wariness. Some sort of ingrained reluctance that only made her want to know more,

'Please tell me.'

Ilan took a deep breath. 'Jennifer... I... I am sorry. I cannot go into detail.'

'Why not?' She wanted to know but, at the same time, she didn't want to push him too far.

He set the wineglass down on the table and turned towards her. His face was drawn and serious. 'All I can tell you is that my work is important. It is not possible for me to tell you anything at this stage. All I can do is ask you to trust me. Please. And believe in me when I tell you this.'

Jennifer looked at him thoughtfully. *Is he sincere? Is he telling me the truth? What on earth is his big secret? I wish he would trust me enough. Will this secret of his always be between us? Okay, if that's what he wants, I'll go along with it. For now.*

Ilan touched her cheek gently, pressing his palm against her skin. She leaned her face into the cup of his hand. 'I will tell you. In time. But for now, I must go.'

'Stay,' she said. The words were out of her mouth before she had time to think of the implications. She wanted him so badly.

Ilan chewed his bottom lip thoughtfully, considering her offer and what it could mean. 'I will sleep here then,' he said and patted the sofa.

'I would like you to sleep with me,' she told him, removing her hand from his face to emphasise her good intentions. 'I mean actually sleep in my bed. It's much more comfortable than the sofa and I can see how tired you are. You'll get a better night's sleep in my bed. I'll behave.'

'Somehow, I doubt that,' he grinned.

'I'm serious. I promise you faithfully I will behave myself. I just want you here with me. I've missed you.'

'Okay. I would like that very much.'

The matter decided, Jennifer got up and went into the kitchen to rinse the plates in the sink. She couldn't be bothered washing up, but hated the thought of them sitting there with food drying on them. By the time she returned, Ilan was stretched out along the length of the sofa, snoring quietly and contentedly.

She stood there watching him for a moment or two, taking the time to admire and appreciate his good looks. His black hair held only a hint of grey at the temples and the stubble on his face had only the tiniest dusting of grey. His rugged features were softened by the fullness of his lips. The bottom lip slightly fuller than the top one and this, in her opinion, gave him a very sexy pout. She loved to kiss those lips and could barely resist the temptation. But he looked so peaceful, asleep on her sofa, she didn't have the heart to wake him. There would be plenty of other opportunities and not for the first time did she give silent thanks that she had met him.

But who, and what, are you?

She tiptoed into the spare bedroom and retrieved a fleece blanket which she carefully placed over him.

'So much for my plans to have my wicked way with you,' she whispered ruefully. Hopefully I'll dream of you tonight and not that musty old farmhouse.' She blew him a kiss, turned off the light and went to bed.

Chapter 10 - Jennifer's Dream

'The internet is on the blink again,' Lucy said as she considered buttering a second slice of toast. *How many calories in a slice of toast? Bugger. Can't be that many.* 'I've stuff to do, so I phoned Claire and we're going to spend the day in town. Shopping, a bite of lunch wherever we can find good food, wine and free wi-fi. I'll take the bus in and probably get a taxi home. Or is there anything you really, really need me here for?' Lucy nibbled at her toast and waited while Charlie swallowed a mouthful of scrambled eggs, scratched his head and thought about it for a moment.

I know exactly what you're thinking, pet. You're thinking I need a break from the house. You're thinking a break with Claire, even if only for a day, will do me the world of good. Claire and me will have a good old natter, take in some retail therapy, and I'll come home all perky and a little bit tipsy and what's on my mind will have resolved itself. Close, Charlie. There's definitely something on my mind but it's not what you think. And I really wish I could tell you but you wouldn't understand.

Lucy knew he was thinking there was something not quite right about her. He repeatedly asked her if she was still dreaming. She repeatedly told him she wasn't. She was lying. And she knew he knew she was lying.

Days that became weeks that dragged into months waiting for the house purchase to be finalised had been stressful and the work had been as hard as they thought it would be. Still, Lucy insisted on getting stuck into it every evening, and on weekends from early morning until late at night. She had done this until he made her slow down before she killed herself with exhaustion.

They had settled into a routine. They worked from a steadily diminishing list of things still to be done, or finished, or in some cases started, and Charlie made her knock off at a decent time. Weekend evenings were strictly for relaxing and recharging their batteries.

But that didn't stop him from watching her carefully and commenting on the faraway look she often got in her eyes. At first, she tried to tell him it was exhaustion. But she was sleeping well, from the moment her head hit the pillow until the alarm clock told them it was time to get up. No matter what she said to reassure him, something in his eyes made Lucy realise he was worried about her.

Lucy fondly remembered the day she met him. She had a summer job pulling pints in a dingy pub. It was easy work but it was boring. Lucy stuck with it because it supplemented her student grant. It must have been Charlie's local, because he would drop in a couple of evenings a week. From the moment she spotted him walking towards the bar, catching her eye and smiling in a way that stopped her in her tracks, Lucy fancied him. It seemed to be mutual because he began to show up every night, rain or shine. He would nurse a pint all evening, taking only small sips to try and make it last as long as possible. Lucy reckoned it was because he couldn't afford to drink more than one or two.

Then there came three weeks of nervous, cringe-worthy comments about the weather or the football results, which neither interested nor impressed her. He did manage to compliment her a few times on her hair or her clothes. Playing it cool, she had responded with a thank you and a welcoming smile. She didn't like to say but she was more than a little relieved he quit trying to talk about football with her.

One evening, Charlie finally managed to pluck up some courage and said, 'I'm Charlie. Would you like to, uh, go out on a date with me? Or something?' He immediately gulped down half his pint of bitter, as if extreme dehydration had suddenly struck him.

Lucy remembered how nervous he had been. *And I was so tempted to play him a for a bit but I couldn't. Besides, I wanted to go out with him. That's why I said yes immediately. And I didn't need a drink for the courage!*

He took her to the movies that night and, while she couldn't recall much of the movie other than it had too many car chases – Lucy remembered how happy she had been in his company. Their second date was two days later; dinner at the new Italian restaurant everyone was raving about. Over dessert – tiramisu, she remembered – Lucy told him she was beginning to think he didn't fancy her and she assumed he was some sort of low-grade alcoholic with a two-pint limit.

'So why didn't you ask me out then?' he had asked.

'I dunno. I could tell you I was too shy, but the truth is you make the evenings a bit more bearable. I stand behind that stupid bar, pulling pints and listening to drunks telling me their life stories. If we started dating you wouldn't have been there every evening looking all handsome and sexy with your long hair tied back, and those icy, but very sexy, blue eyes that follow me everywhere. Of course, it did cross my mind that you might be a pervy stalker or something, so maybe that's why I hesitated.'

'You thought I was either a part-time alcoholic or a perverted stalker? You had a really poor opinion of me, hadn't you?'

'First impressions are usually way off, so don't worry yourself about it. However, I have to confess I did like your builder's, er, build.'

'So, in the space of three weeks, I went from being an alcoholic stalker to eye candy in your eyes? I'm doing really well here, aren't I?'

She shrugged her shoulders and tried to keep a straight face. 'Probably. But don't worry, I have a sweet tooth.'

Lucy knew she was in love with him. This was the only man she wanted and she hoped and prayed he was in love with her. He seemed to be, because after about six or seven sessions of amazing, but uncomfortable, sex in the back of his old van – never enough privacy at her place with three other students sharing the flat, and him still at home with his mum and dad – he mumbled something about how they could have a proper shag in a proper bed if they moved in together. Not the most romantic way of putting it, but Lucy didn't care. It was what she wanted anyway.

A few months of scrimping and saving, a small loan from both sets of parents and they had enough for a rental property. Within a few weeks they found what they were looking for – a small semi-detached house convenient enough for his work and within a stone's throw of the university for her.

Not long after that, he bought an engagement ring and plucked up the courage to propose to her. She said yes without hesitation. They got married three months later – a small registry office ceremony with immediate family and a few friends present. The reception was a slap-up meal at the local Indian restaurant and a big party in the upstairs function room that lasted well into the wee hours. And just like that, they were husband and wife and Lucy still loved him as much today as she did back then. And some days she couldn't believe how lucky she was.

Lucy knew he still felt the same about her, but she also knew he was upset because she wouldn't talk to him about what was on her mind. They had always talked about everything. Every problem. Every idea. Everything. He tried to bring it up in conversation more than once, but she either denied there was a problem or deliberately changed the subject.

I wish I could tell you, Charlie. I wish I could tell you about these dreams of mine and about the people in them. They're both frightening and fascinating. We could laugh about it and wonder what's going to happen next in the story that's playing out in my head every night. But it worries me. That's why I'm going into town today. Not for groceries or things we need for the house. Not even to drink wine with Claire, although we'll probably do that. I'm going to find out what this is and why it's happening to me.

I wish you could come with me and sit beside me. Hold my hand and keep me safe. But you wouldn't understand. If I don't understand it, what chance is there you would?

He looked up from his scrambled eggs. 'Yeah, go. There's nowt urgent for you today. And please send another e-mail reminder to the bloke about the kitchen worktops and tell him if he doesn't get his finger out, we'll go elsewhere. We need them here and fitted by the end of this week so the tiler can start on Monday.'

'That's one of the things on my list.'

'Have you enough money? Need some?'

'Nah, I'm fine. Most of what I want to order is online so I'll use my card and I've enough cash for anything else,' Lucy said as she put on her coat and checked the contents of her bag – purse, phone, lipstick, tissues, kitchen sink. *Yep. All there.* She tucked a strand of hair behind her ear and looked at him. 'Speaking of money… how is Auntie Ethel these days?'

This was their code for – do we still have enough money to finish this house or will it bankrupt us?

'The old girl is hanging in there,' Charlie told her.

'Good,' Lucy looked thoughtful. 'So, in that case we could –'

'No! Lucy, for the love of God, no more soft furnishings. Seriously, if I have to look at one more throw or set of scatter cushions I *will* start killing the hostages!'

'We need curtains. Claire and I are going to look at curtains today.'

'Okay, I can accept we need curtains,' he said.

'And maybe one or two cushions because they have to match the curtains.'

'Arrrrgh!' Charlie covered his face with his hands and rocked back and forth.

'Okay, I'll see you later and I promise I won't buy any more scatter cushions. Throws however, are a totally different matter,' she told him, laughing as he continued to rock back and forth.

'Say hello to Claire from me and enjoy yourselves. Seriously though, have a good shopping trip.'

'Don't worry, if there's wine involved, we will.'

'I don't doubt that,' Charlie replied with a knowing grin.

Lucy spied her husband watching her from the kitchen window as she walked through the gate onto the lane towards the main road. She gave him a cheery wave as she hiked her bag up onto her shoulder. The bus would be along in about ten minutes and Claire would be waiting at the next stop. Charlie didn't know she had a doctor's appointment at ten-thirty and that was the real reason for her trip into town. Claire had insisted she make it, after Lucy had told her friend about her constant dreams. Now she was about to tell her doctor about them.

'I know it sounds daft, and I'm probably wasting your time, but I can't stop dreaming,' Lucy said as she sat down in the chair opposite the doctor in the examination room.

The doctor was an Asian woman around the same age as herself, maybe a little older. Lucy had seen her around the village but had never met her professionally until now. For a moment Lucy couldn't help wonder how the word 'daft' would translate, but when she heard the doctor's thick North Yorkshire accent, she decided the woman knew exactly what it meant.

'And I mean really dreaming. I can see colours. I can taste and smell things. I can feel heat and cold. I can follow the sequence of events and everything. It's like when I close my eyes at night, I immediately wake up somewhere else. Like I'm somebody else and I'm living a life there.'

'Tell me some of the details,' the doctor said, as she scribbled something down on her notepad.

'Well, in a recent dream, he taught me to snorkel and then scuba dive. We were on this little speed boat and it was a lovely sunny day. I think we were somewhere in the Mediterranean. Cyprus springs to mind. He showed me what to do – how to put on the tank and breathing techniques, and all that stuff. I was nervous and a little afraid of the water, but he was a good teacher and I ended up learning to scuba dive. This is in the dream. I can't scuba dive in real life, but I'm a good swimmer and not at all afraid of the water. Which was weird because in the dream I was afraid. Then in another dream, he turned up on the doorstep after he'd disappeared for ages. Two or maybe three weeks. At first, I mean in the first dream, he told me he was in the import and export business. But I wasn't so sure about that. Then, this time, he claimed he was a civil servant and did diplomatic work. But he wouldn't elaborate on what he actually did.'

Lucy paused as she remembered the details. This man, whom she didn't know, told her – no not her, the woman in her dreams – about his family – his daughter and his dead wife and brother. All the while evading her questions about what he did for a living.

'This was your husband who taught you to scuba dive?' the doctor asked, interrupting her thoughts.

Embarrassed now, Lucy looked down at her hands in her lap. 'Um... no. He is... I really don't know who he is. He's Israeli. Or so he says. But I don't know anyone from Israel. And in an earlier dream he said the scars on his shoulder and thigh were bullet wounds from his days in the Israeli army.'

Lucy paused as she watched the doctor frantically scribbling. For all she knew the woman could be writing her memoirs or a grocery list.

'I'm not sure, but I think he might be a spy or a secret agent.' *Oh God, she'll have me locked up now, for sure.*

The doctor paused momentarily in her scribbling and looked at Lucy over the rim of her glasses.

Well, that got her attention.

'Do you read a lot, Mrs. Wilson?'

'Um, yes. A bit. Why?'

'What sort of literature do you read?'

'Well, calling it literature is probably stretching it a wee bit. I usually go for whatever's on a 'two for one' deal in the paperback and magazine section in Tescos. But I love the Jack Reacher books. And that bloke who writes about the cop called Thorne. He's really good. Crime dramas, stuff like that. And I really enjoy biographies. But I don't read as much as I used to. I don't have the time these days.'

'What about television?'

'Yes, we have a television.' *What is it with me and these ridiculous answers today?*

'I mean, do you watch a lot of television in the evenings?'

'Sorry. Yeah, I watch TV sometimes. Not a lot now. You see, we bought a house a while back and it needs a lot of work and we're doing the bulk of it ourselves. We're working until late in the evenings. By the time we've had dinner and a shower or a bath, we're kind of knackered, so we end up going straight to bed.'

'Okay. When you do watch television what kind of programmes do you watch?'

Lucy thought about it for a few seconds and gave the doctor a wry look. 'Whatever happens to be on when I sit down in front of it and manage to stay awake. If Charlie – that's my husband – gets the remote first, then it's usually football or rugby. That's okay. I enjoy a good match too.'

'Do you watch anything specific? Such as horror movies or murder mysteries or spy dramas?'

'Yeah, sometimes, but I don't make a point of watching them. Like I said, if Charlie is watching a match, I often end up watching it with him.'

'Do you smoke?'

'No.'

'Have you ever smoked?'

'No. Well, yes. I smoked for a few years in my teens. All my mates smoked and it was just something we did. I gave it up because I couldn't afford it.'

'So, you don't take any nicotine replacement products?'

'No.'

'Do you take any recreational drugs?'

'Of course not!'

'Do you drink alcohol?'

'Well, sometimes I like a glass of wine with my dinner and then maybe one or two when I'm relaxing in the evenings. Only small glasses though.' Lucy had no intention of telling her that it was more likely to be three or four large glasses.

The doctor scribbled some more, then set her pen and notepad down. 'I'd like to check your blood pressure and then I'll have the nurse draw some blood for a complete work up.'

Lucy sat there impassively while the doctor put the cuff on her arm and took a blood pressure reading.

'Is it okay?' Lucy asked pulling her sleeve down again when the cuff was finally removed.

'It's within the normal range,' the doctor informed her. She sat down again and stared at her computer screen.

She's thinking of having to type up all those notes she's had to scribble. I'm wasting her time and mine here.

Finally, the doctor seemed to come to a decision and reached for a thick prescription pad. 'Mrs. Wilson, you're a fit and healthy young woman and I'm confident your blood tests will confirm this. I'm going to prescribe a short course of mild sleeping tablets for you because I think you are suffering from stress and I believe that –'

'But I have no problems going to sleep,' Lucy said.

'Yes, I know, but it appears from what you've told me, you are remaining in what is called REM sleep. That's an acronym for 'rapid eye movement'. It's the stage of sleep you are in when you dream. The medication I'm prescribing for you will help you bypass REM sleep and prevent you dreaming. It isn't an ideal solution because this stage of sleep is when the brain... well, the best way to explain it... does the housework. It deals with all the various things it has experienced during the day and compartmentalises them in a healthy manner. Most dreams are just that, and we only remember disjointed fragments which is why they can seem strange. I suspect that because you are suffering from stress, your brain is compensating by making you experience pleasant things such as sailing and swimming in an attempt to relieve the stress you are under.'

'But they are so vivid. So detailed,' Lucy replied.

'That's because you are remaining in REM sleep too long each night. Your brain is unable to switch off because of the stress that I believe is due to your house move. Moving house is one of the most stressful situations an adult can experience in life. That, and divorce. I suggest you try these for a week or two, no longer than that, and you should find that you will be back to normal in no time at all. Also, reducing your alcohol intake considerably will help. Alcohol is a stimulant, so –'

'I thought it was a depressant. That it helps you sleep.'

'Depending on how much is consumed and a person's individual reaction, alcohol can have both sedating and stimulating effects. In your case, taking a glass or two of wine is not relaxing you in the evenings. In fact, it's doing the reverse. I would suggest a cup of warm milk instead. No tea or coffee as caffeine is also a stimulant.'

Lucy silently took the prescription and thanked the doctor. On the way out, she gave the nurse what felt like a gallon of her blood and handed her the urine sample she had been told to bring along with her.

She left quietly, not feeling particularly confident with the doctor's diagnosis.

Claire was watching for her from the window in the bar across the street and waved when she saw her coming out of the surgery. Lucy raised her hand in acknowledgement while she waited to cross the busy road.

'So, what did the doctor have to say?' Claire asked as Lucy parked herself in the chair opposite. Seconds later, Lucy caught the attention of a passing waitress. The teenager, sporting spiky black hair streaked with pink, a nose stud and a bored expression, placed two menus on the table. She rattled off the various specials on offer then took their order for two large glasses of wine – a Pinot Grigio for Lucy and a Cabernet Sauvignon for Claire.

Claire and the waitress both grimaced when Lucy requested ice in hers.

'Okay, so every now and then I like ice in my wine. It's not illegal,' Lucy growled.

'Come on, what did the doctor say?' Claire reminded Lucy of her question.

'She told me I was suffering from stress. Then she gave me a prescription for sleeping pills and told me to lay off the wine. Like that's gonna happen!' Lucy snorted in disgust, taking a look around the small wine bar. It was busy for this time of the day, but then it was one of the most popular in this part of town. She had been here several times with Charlie and it was one of their favourite places to eat.

'Ah yes, stress – the all-new, trendy catchall for every ailment,' Claire exclaimed. 'No matter what you have, they tell you you're suffering from stress. Back in me mam's day, you were told to get over it and get on with it. And of course, she's toeing the health service/government conspiracy theory line that alcohol is the big bad evil...'

Claire paused as the waitress brought the wine to their table and asked them if they were ready to order.

'Yeah,' said Lucy. 'I'd like the linguini with smoked haddock, please.'

Claire shook her head slowly from side to side, in a silent eenie-meenie-minie-mo gesture as she tried to make her mind up. 'I'll have the pan-fried... no, wait. I'll take the Thai seasoned chicken breast. Oh, and two more glasses of wine, please. Thank you.'

The waitress quickly scribbled down their orders and left them to resume their conversation.

'Trust me,' Claire continued. 'In a few years when they've frightened everyone so much, we've all become tee-total, they'll realise they're losing a fortune in taxes and they'll tell us wine is the new superfood.'

'Well, it is a superfood,' Lucy said. 'It's made from grapes, so it's one of your five-a-day, isn't it?'

'Too right,' Claire said and they clinked their glasses in agreement. 'Do you want another one?'

'No. I'm good for the moment.'

'So, what did she think about your wild dreams?' Claire asked, taking another sip of her wine. 'Did she want you to go into all the saucy details, about how well he looked in his swimming trunks and how sexy he was?'

'Nah, she just looked at me as though I was nuts, which I probably am. And I don't think he's sexy. He frightens me and I hate the fact that I dream about him, whoever he is, every single night. I love Charlie and this feels like I'm cheating on him.'

'Dreaming isn't cheating,' Claire told her.

'I know. But it doesn't seem right somehow.'

'Is he really that sexy?' Claire asked.

'I suppose he is. I hadn't really thought about it that much.'

'Yeah, right!'

'I haven't. Anyway, whether he's sexy or not isn't the issue. It's the fact that I dream every single frigging night that has me worried.'

'I'll admit that is a bit strange,' Claire nodded.

'Not only is it strange, but when I'm dreaming it's like I'm in the mind of another woman who is living this life. She is the one shagging the Israeli guy not me, but I'm the one feeling jealous. Admittedly, she hasn't gotten around to shagging him yet but it's only a matter of time. I hope,' Lucy giggled. Then her face grew serious. 'But I'm the one who is watching – more than watching – I'm the one experiencing her life in my dreams. That's a bit unfair, isn't it?'

'When you put it like that, yeah. You know, it sounds a bit like a virtual reality movie or something. Have you mentioned it to Charlie? Without going into all the gory details, obviously.'

'God, no! I couldn't.'

'I wouldn't. Charlie is a honey but I don't think he would get this, if you know what I mean.'

Lucy nodded. 'The doctor says I'm having too much of something called REM sleep – that's the stage when someone dreams. And it's supposed to be good for the brain. But, in my case, it's lasting too long and that's why I'm remembering my dreams in so much detail. She said most people dream every night but they only remember fragments because this REM sleep mostly occurs a while after you fall asleep, then at different periods through the night and then before you wake. She reckons if I take one of the sleeping pills every evening for a week or so it will prevent me going into REM and I'll stop dreaming.'

'Oh, I read about this somewhere, REM sleep is when the brain sorts itself out. But it's normal and healthy and not having it isn't good.'

'Well apparently, having too much of it isn't good either.'

'So, are you going to try the sleeping tablets?' Claire asked.

'I don't know. Probably. Maybe. I'll think about it. But I'm not going to give up my wine in the evenings!'

Chapter 11 - Lucy's Dream

Still holding Jennifer's hand in his, Ilan stopped and swung her around to face him. They had left the noisy taverna and made their way down to the beach where they had walked for ages along the water's edge. The air was warm and a full moon hung low in the night sky, lighting their way.

The meal had been delicious. Ilan had ordered kleftiko – an oven-baked lamb dish – and he raved so much about how good it was Jennifer quickly realised it was his favourite. She selected the dolmades simply because she had never tried them before and the thought of eating stuffed vine leaves sounded interesting. Concerned she might be disappointed, she took a tentative nibble and found them delicious.

The good food, the wine, and his charming company, combined so perfectly she was walking on air. She didn't want to ever lose this feeling.

Yet Jennifer detected a tension in him. It was subtle and she almost missed it, but it was there – a current running underneath the surface in parallel with the light-hearted conversations that had made up most of the evening so far.

'You seem very serious tonight. Is something the matter?' Jennifer asked.

'There's something I need to discuss with you,' he told her.

'That sounds ominous.'

Ilan laughed but there was no humour in it.

He seems nervous. What is wrong with him?

'Seriously Ilan, what is it? What's wrong?'

Ilan took a deep breath and it was obvious to Jennifer he had come to a decision. His eyes, in the moonlight, were black circles. For a moment, he was a stranger and she did not know him. A shiver ran down her spine.

'I have something to tell you.'

'Okay. What?'

'I am a Mossad officer.'

His voice was low, almost a whisper, like he was telling her a secret. Which he was. But at the same time, he said it with conviction. And more than a little pride, Jennifer noted. It was an announcement. A statement of fact. And now that it had been spoken aloud, it was out there and it could never become unspoken. Jennifer knew his whole world hinged upon the next few seconds and her reaction to his words. He held her hand tightly, and she knew he was afraid to let it go in case she would disappear into the moonlit night.

Jennifer let out a long, slow breath, almost a sigh. She tore her eyes away from his face and gazed out at the water, watching the reflection of the moon dancing on the waves. It was such a beautiful evening.

'I know,' she told him.

'You know?' he asked, incredulous. 'How do you know?'

'Well, I didn't know for sure, but it crossed my mind a couple of times. I mean, the way you tend to disappear for weeks on end. How you never give me a straight answer when I ask about where you go and what you do. It did make me think you might be a spy. Or a criminal. I was actually leaning more towards you as a criminal, so you can imagine how relieved I am.'

Ilan stood there in silence. Surprised but also relieved by what she had said.

Jennifer put her arms around his neck and kissed him gently on the lips. 'Now that you've got your great secret – with 'secret' being the operative word here – off your chest, are you... are we okay?'

Ilan's eyes met hers and, in the light of the full moon, she could see once again the mischievous humour dancing in them. 'I am somewhat offended that you would think I am a criminal.'

'Get over it,' she told him with a laugh as she let go of his neck. She reached for his hand and they resumed their walk along the shoreline. They were heading back towards the taverna and the rowdy laughter and music that still poured from it, disrupting the stillness of the night air.

'Did you consider me to be a good criminal?'

'What? Do you mean good as in a competent and successful evil mastermind, or good like Robin Hood? To be honest, I never thought it through to that extent. Are you a good secret agent?'

'I consider myself very good at what I do.'

'So, is it really all tuxedos and martinis – shaken not stirred – and women dressed in skimpy clothes with suggestive sounding names? Women who look like bimbos but turn out to be dangerous spies? And Aston Martins that fire lasers out of their headlights?'

'Do you know anything at all about the intelligence services?' he asked sarcastically.

'Well, obviously I've watched one or two spy movies, and I really loved those spy dramas like Spooks and 24.'

'Trust me Jennifer, it is nothing whatsoever like the movies or the television.'

'So, no supercars then?'

'I have never driven an Aston Martin in my life, but I know a guy who knows a guy who had a second cousin who drove a Ferrari once,' he grinned. 'But seriously, Jennifer what I do is more... run of the mill. And it is not unlike the civil service. There is a lot of... paperwork involved.'

'But is there any really cool spy stuff? Like fast cars with laser guns and tape recorders hidden inside women's bikini tops? Or is that all a myth?'

'I think you watch too many movies,' he told her, amusement and exasperation in his voice.

'I'm serious Ilan. Now you've told me, I'm intrigued and I want to know more.'

'Jennifer, this is not something I am willing to talk to you about, for obvious reasons.'

'Don't you trust me?' She frowned. Then what he said dawned on her.

'Oh,' her eyes grew wide. 'Oh. I see.'

'Exactly.'

'Plausible deniability is the expression, isn't it?'

'It is.'

'I suppose I could google Mossad.'

'Yes, you could.'

'Do they have a website?'

'You should google it to find out.'

'Will I be arrested if I do?'

'No. It is a website. Anyone can look at it.'

'Cool,' she smiled.

The taverna was less noisy than it had been earlier. The party crowd had either called it a night or moved on.

Ilan steadied her as she shook the sand off her feet and slipped into her sandals.

'Do you want another drink?'

'No. I have a better idea,' she replied with a smile. 'Let's go.'

They sat in silence in the back of the taxi during the short journey from the taverna back to Jennifer's apartment. There was no need for words. The chemistry between them spoke its own silent language. Ilan held her hand in his but didn't attempt to kiss her. She didn't need him to. Not yet. She needed him to come home with her and make love to her. He wasn't tired and neither of them were drunk, so there was no reason not to. There were no more excuses. It was what they both wanted and the time was right.

He had finally told her the truth about what he did. She suspected all along he worked for Mossad, but she was relieved he finally trusted her enough to tell her. Now they could take their relationship a stage further. In the direction she wanted it to go.

Once inside her apartment, Jennifer hesitated, unsure of the mechanics, unsure of the basic moves that would take them from the front door to her bedroom. The distance suddenly seemed so much longer now.

Ilan pulled her close to him. His lips found hers and as he kissed her, she felt his strength and his desire. It matched her own need for him.

'Bedroom?' he asked, whispering into her ear.

'Back there. The door on the right.'

He didn't pick her up and carry her.

Oh, that would be too corny.

Instead, he took her by the hand and gently led her towards the bedroom. She walked beside him. No need for resistance. It was what she had wanted for so long.

Jennifer got to the bed first and pulled him down onto it beside her. Ilan's mouth quickly found her throat then travelled up to her lips. He claimed them as his property.

It wasn't long before she found herself prone on the bed and his tongue was tracing a gentle circle around her navel. He planted a trail of light kisses from there up to her bra. Then he paused and seemed to consider this area but decided to return to it later for more detailed exploration.

At some stage he had removed her T-shirt along with her jeans and underwear, although she had only a vague memory of him doing so, and now with a deft movement of his fingers behind her back, her bra disappeared. She suspected some of her items of clothing had suffered irreparable damage in his haste to rid her of them. She didn't care.

She was naked and vulnerable before him and right now this was exactly what she wanted.

'Please,' she whispered. 'I need you now, Ilan. Please.'

'Not yet,' he told her. He nuzzled her neck and gently nibbled her earlobe while his hand caressed her breast. 'I want to savour you. Discover you.'

He did just that and she was climbing the walls by the time his hands and lips and tongue had savoured and discovered every inch of her. Touching her, and tasting her, and stroking her. And all she could do was lie there. He wouldn't allow her to move, to touch him, swatting her hand gently if she tried to do so. He wanted to be in control.

'Please Ilan, please,' she begged.

He slid his hand between her legs and his mouth found hers again, his tongue and his fingers working to the same rhythm. She was more than ready for him and she whimpered against his lips, arching her back to meet his hand as it worked it's magic on her. She didn't want to come yet, not until he was inside her, but he wasn't leaving her with much of a choice as he brought her closer and closer to the edge.

Damn, he is good.

Then he stopped, suddenly and abruptly, leaving her hanging there. Her eyes flew open in amazement. What was he playing at, tormenting her in this fashion?

'Ilan? What the...?'

He was positioned above her. Smiling. Was that it? Was he merely playing with her? She was tempted to slap that smile off his face.

'Just a moment,' he told her. 'You probably haven't noticed but I'm still wearing my jeans.'

She had been so busy concentrating on him removing her jeans and T-shirt and underwear – although removing them wasn't quite the correct term for it, shredding them was more appropriate, in his haste to get her naked – that it never occurred to her to rip *his* clothes off.

Ilan rolled off her onto his side of the bed.

I'm already calling it his side of the bed.

He lifted his arms and pulled his T-shirt over his head, threw it onto the floor then lay back down again and raised his hips. He quickly unzipped his jeans and worked them down to his ankles then kicked them off. They joined his T-shirt somewhere on the floor.

He was about to do the same with his boxers when Jennifer sat up and stopped him with her hand. 'Let me help you with that.'

'Be my guest.'

Playing him at his own game, despite her need for him, Jennifer took her time. Slowly inching the boxers down a little bit, she made a striptease of it for her own pleasure and for his torment. He groaned when he realised what she was doing but made no move to take over, or to hurry her.

She slid her fingers underneath the waistband of his boxers, stroking and gently pulling the dark hair, circling the area from his navel to his groin, moving lower then hesitating and then almost as though she had forgotten what her original aim had been, she worked her hand up to his chest and began all over again. This time she did it with her lips.

'Neshama, please,' he whispered.

'Not yet. I want to take my time and savour you first,' she told him, throwing his own words back at him.

He gave her a look, but he knew that with his teasing of her, he had brought this on himself. He closed his eyes and surrendered himself to her.

Jennifer sat up and smiled and he knew he was in trouble when she straddled him.

She caught his arms at the wrists and pulled them up over his head, holding them in place with one hand while she lay along the length of him and kissed him long and hard, her tongue probing his mouth, her teeth catching his lip and pulling gently but firmly enough to make him groan. He tried to take control of the kiss but she pulled away and slowly shook her head.

'Behave,' she warned him.

With a shrug of his shoulders, he lay still and gave in to her once again. She resumed her oral exploration of his body and its reactions to her.

Her tongue traced a path from his mouth, planting tiny kisses on his throat and neck, across to his shoulder where she paused for a moment then pressed her lips against the old scar. He pulled his hands free from her light grip above his head and stroked her back, knowing that the scar distressed her.

She moved from it down to his chest where her tongue circled his nipple, and she worked from right to left for a few moments, playing with him and enjoying the strong pulse of his heartbeat against her cheek.

She ground her hips on top of him. He was hard and his breathing was ragged as she moved rhythmically against him, the boxer shorts a barrier between them. They needed to go.

She lifted herself off him and slid the boxers down his thighs as he raised his hips to assist her. She quickly removed them, dropping them onto the floor to join the increasing pile of assorted garments.

For a moment Jennifer could only stare in appreciation at him lying there beside her.

Ilan laughed gently and rolled his eyes at, what he thought was, her hesitation. He pulled her down onto her back, raising himself up on his arms over her. He stopped.

'What are you waiting for?' she asked as she parted her legs in invitation.

No further prompting was needed. Ilan reached down to his jeans on the floor and removed a condom from the pocket.

'There's more in the drawer,' Jennifer told him.

'Good,' he grinned as he tore open the foil.

He positioned himself as she lifted her hips towards him. She cried out in pleasure as he entered her, slowly at first, almost hesitantly then, as she put her arms around his neck, he drove himself fully into her. Hard and fast.

She moaned as he filled her. This was what she wanted. What she needed.

Locking her legs around him, Jennifer's mouth found his again and her fingers gripped the hair at the back of his head. She found his rhythm and made it her own and they were perfect together, working as one. She arched to meet him as he pounded himself into her.

She was close to orgasm now, and he felt she was near as he thrust faster and harder. He abandoned her mouth and found her left breast, sucking hard, matching the movements of his mouth to his thrusts. She moaned, her mouth against his shoulder, wanting to bite him, to tear into his flesh, to mingle pain with pleasure as she climbed higher and higher towards the ending.

She cried out his name as wave after powerful wave engulfed her and he seemed to go even deeper inside her. Then one last powerful thrust and he came hard and fast, forcing himself to match her continuing orgasm. She cried out and her legs trembled as they held him inside of her, refusing to let him go until she was completely finished.

Ilan collapsed, breathless and exhausted, on top of her. Their bodies were slick with mingled sweat and their hearts pounded in unison.

When she thought it was safe to move again, Jennifer cupped his face in her hands, lifted his head and looked into his eyes. 'What the hell was that?'

'That was a small taste of what you can expect from me,' he told her with a grin.

She arched an eyebrow. 'Every night?'

'Of course. Maybe even a couple of times a night, if that is what you desire.'

'Yeah, right.'

'What? You did not enjoy it?'

'Nah, I was bored out of my head. I mean, come on!'

'Hmmm, I suspect you may be a difficult woman to please and that I may have to rethink my strategy.'

'Please don't change a thing. That was beyond perfect. I don't think I have ever come so hard in my life.'

'Did I score ten out of ten?' Ilan asked as he rolled off her to lie beside her. He slipped his arm underneath her and pulled her to him in a gentle embrace.

'I'll have to say yes. In fact, you exceeded ten. I gave you some bonus points – mainly for skill and stamina – but one or two simply because I like you.'

Jennifer laughed as he punched the air in victory.

'I do have one regret though,' she said.

'You have? What?'

'I can't believe we waited so long. If I'd know it was going to be this good...'

'We have to make up for lost time. Yes?' Ilan said as he nuzzled her neck and his hand began to caress her again.

'Oh, yes!'

Chapter 12 - Jennifer's Dream

It was his warm breath on her bare shoulder that wakened her, pulling her up from the depths of sleep. A smile crossed her lips as the memories of their passionate lovemaking came flowing back.

Thought I'd feel a bit sore down there after all that. How come I don't?

Thinking about their lovemaking aroused her once more and she found herself wanting him again. He was still fast asleep and she turned around to face him, to reach for him.

Lucy screamed to see a stranger lying in bed beside her.

Charlie sat bolt upright, blinking in confusion. He turned to his wife. 'Lucy? What's wrong? What is it, love?'

Lucy leapt out of the bed and stared at him as she let out an ear-splitting, terrified scream. Her body was rigid. Her arms held tightly in front of her in a defensive posture.

'Stop it!' Charlie yelled as he grabbed her and shook her. 'Lucy! Can you hear me? Stop it. Stop it now!'

Eventually his voice reached her. The screams died away and she blinked and looked around her. Her eyes met Charlie's. Seeing the concern and the fear in his eyes, she covered her face with her hands and burst into tears.

'Lucy? What's wrong? Are you ill? What is it, love?'

Lucy shook her head.

'Then what is it? Tell me, please.'

Despite his pleas, all Lucy could do was sit on the edge of the bed and sob into her hands. Charlie couldn't get through to her. He was concerned and angry at her reaction and his inability to help her. He threw up his arms in frustration and stormed out of the bedroom, slamming the door behind him.

When he left, Lucy hurried into the bathroom and locked the door behind her. She sat down on the floor, crouching underneath the wash hand basin with her back pressed against the bath panel. She drew her knees up to her chest, folded her arms on her knees and buried her head in her arms. There she hid. Not only from her world, but from the world she inhabited in her sleep. Thinking about Charlie and the dreams brought more tears. They spilled from her eyes, dripped onto her legs and rolled down her thighs.

This is all wrong. This is not normal. It wasn't a dream. I was there. I was there, in that woman's body. I was in Jennifer's body. I was there in that bed making love to Ilan. I felt him touching me. Kissing me. Penetrating me. I felt him inside me. He aroused me and I wanted him so badly. And I felt myself come.

It was not a dream. It was not a dream! But he kissed so good. Charlie couldn't kiss that good to save his soul. Oh, god, what am I thinking? It was so real.

Her tears finally subsided and she crawled out from under the sink and pulled herself slowly to her feet. She turned on the cold tap and splashed water on her face then glanced at herself in the mirror. Her haunted eyes, red and puffy from crying, looked back at her but that wasn't her concern. It was what happened last night and the dark circles underneath her eyes that bothered her the most.

I sleep like the dead all night so why do I look so tired? And feel so tired?

It was not a dream.

It was not a dream.

The words repeated over and over in her mind.

Well then, what was it?

There was no answer. At least not one that the face in the mirror was prepared to give her.

Lucy squirted toothpaste onto her tooth brush and slowly, mechanically brushed her teeth, rinsing and spitting several times to wash away the memory of those kisses. She took a washcloth, soaked it in cold water and held it to her face for a moment or two. Back in the bedroom she selected an old pair of jeans and a T-shirt. She got dressed slowly then spotted her favourite cardigan hanging in the wardrobe – the one she wore when she was sad and needed to feel comforted. When there were no arms around her to comfort her. She pulled it on, wrapping it around her and, with a heavy sigh, went downstairs to face her husband.

It was not a dream.

It was not a dream.

She found him sitting at the kitchen table, engrossed in his thoughts. He didn't look up at her when she walked in.

'Do you want toast and marmalade?' Lucy asked. Maybe he would take her offer as an apology.

'No.'

'There are eggs and some bacon and sausages in the fridge. I could make you a fry if that's what you want?'

'No.'

'Cornflakes?'

'No.'

'Porridge?'

'No.'

Lucy sighed. 'Some coffee then?'

'Yeah.'

She put a spoonful of instant coffee into each mug, added boiling water from the kettle and a splash of milk. She added sugar to Charlie's. It was tempting to chuck in an extra spoonful in the hope it might sweeten his mood a little, but she knew that was pointless. She stirred it and set it in front of him on the table.

Charlie cupped his hands around the mug. He didn't drink it, nor did he look at her, preferring to stare into the coffee, as if it alone held all the answers.

'Charlie, I am so sorry,' she said and reached for his hand.

He snatched it away as though her touch burned him. 'What is wrong with you?'

Surprised by his hostility, Lucy stared at him. 'Nothing. There's nothing wrong with me.'

'Oh, don't give me that again, Lucy. I'm sick to the back teeth of you saying 'nothing' all the time. I want an answer from you. A proper answer this time.'

'Honestly, I'm telling you the truth. There is nothing wrong with me.'

'Is there someone else then?'

'What?'

'Are you having an affair?'

'Of course not! Charlie, how could you even think that?'

'What do you expect me to think?'

'Charlie please, I would… could never want anyone else. I can't believe you would even think that of me.'

Charlie looked at her and his angry gaze broke her heart.

If only I could tell him.

Tears filled her eyes and threatened to spill over.

'I'm sorry,' he said grudgingly. 'I didn't mean it. I'm worried about you, Lucy. You've been so quiet and withdrawn for ages. Is it the house?'

She shook her head. 'No, I love the house. You know that. You always joke about how I rave on and on about it, how I want to do this and make that, and how I write up a list every Sunday evening of what I plan to do each week and how I can't wait until we move in. You know that, Charlie.'

'Then what was all that shit when you woke up? You screamed at me as if you didn't know me or I was a monster of some kind!'

'For a second or two I thought you were a monster. A zombie to be precise,' she told him. The idea appeared from nowhere. Out loud, it sounded insane but maybe, just maybe, he would believe it.

'Yeah, right!'

'I'm serious Charlie. I was having this dream where you and I were on a beach somewhere, and it was dark and we'd made love. Really, wild, crazy sex. In fact, it was really fantastic sex.'

It was not a dream, the voice in her head told her but she pushed it away, willing it to shut up. That wasn't exactly how it had happened. Ilan, the man in her dream who wasn't Charlie, had finally told her he was a Mossad agent. Then they had gone back to her… Jennifer's… apartment and the wild, crazy sex had taken place. But Charlie didn't need to know those details.

'Then the moon came out from behind a cloud,' she continued, caught now in the narrative of the lie. 'The next thing I knew, you were turning into a zombie and you were coming at me to kill me. I started screaming. Which is something you tend to do when there's a zombie coming at you. And that's when I woke up. I'm sorry, but it scared the living daylights out of me.'

'A dream? Seriously?' Charlie glared at her. 'So, is that why you were screaming at me?'

She could tell he was still angry with her but it seemed to be lessening. 'Yeah. It was so vivid. It was great at first – the sex on the beach – and then it turned into a nightmare. I've had a… few weird dreams lately.'

'What sort of dreams?'

Lucy looked at him. Nothing on this earth would persuade her to tell him the details of this other life she was living every night when she closed her eyes. In the first place he wouldn't understand. Of that she was convinced. And right then, as she stood on the brink of telling him at least some of it, she realised part of her – a deep, secret, disturbing part of her – enjoyed it.

It was not a dream. You have a brain tumour. Or you're possessed. Or you're going insane.

Fuck off. It was a dream.

It wasn't quite the best of both worlds, but it sure as heck was close. It was real enough to her that every night she was living in this other place, as another person. Jennifer had a career she loved, which was more than Lucy could say about her crappy job. She was comfortably well off, and she had Ilan.

This sexy Israeli was the reason she didn't dare tell Charlie. He was the reason she could never tell Charlie. Not even Claire, who knew most of the details, didn't know how she felt about him.

'I don't really know,' Lucy lied. She knew, and she remembered every small detail, but she would never divulge that fact. 'Most of the time I can't remember them. You know when you wake up, and for a split second you remember a dream, then suddenly it vanishes, and you remember having the dream but you can't remember anything at all about the details of it?'

'Yeah, I suppose I've had a few like that,' he replied, still not entirely convinced by her explanation. 'Not that I dream all that much, though.'

'I don't either, normally, but lately I seem to be dreaming a lot more. I don't know why.'

It was not a dream.

Charlie took a mouthful of coffee. Lucy watched him, relieved that his anger had dissipated. He was rarely brought to anger. But whatever it was that she was going through – and the attitude that went with it – was affecting him. She had to figure out a way to change that aspect of it.

In the end, Charlie beat her to it. He got up from the table and approached her slowly, shuffling his feet and dragging one leg behind him. His arms were raised in front of him and his hands were bent like claws. He moaned in his best zombie accent as he shuffled towards her.

He looked so funny that Lucy started laughing. A giggle at first, then she couldn't stop herself. She howled and covered her mouth with her hands. Doubled over, almost choking, the tears began to stream down her face. She was laughing so hard it was beginning to hurt.

Her laughter was infectious and Charlie could no longer hold his gruesome pose. He grinned as her laughter took more and more of a hold of her and he found himself laughing along with her. Joining in with her, as she stood in the middle of the kitchen, bent double with her hands pressed tightly against her ribs. He put his arms around her and they held on to each other and they stood there, laughing together.

This is my reality. This man here in my kitchen, with his arms around me and laughing his head off, is the man I love. Ilan isn't real. It was just a dream.

'A zombie eh?' he asked when their laughter had finally subsided. 'You couldn't have made me into a sexy vampire or something?'

'Nah, sorry,' she said, tearing off a square of kitchen roll and using it, despite its rough texture, to wipe her tears away. 'I don't have any control over what I dream about.'

It was not a dream.

Piss off.

He put his arms around her waist and pulled her close to him. Her eyes were red and puffy but this time from tears of laughter and, as far as he was concerned, she looked beautiful.

'What do you say we take today off from working at the house, go for a long hike and then a nice lunch at that new pub you told me about last week?'

'Which one?' Lucy struggled to remember the pub he was talking about.

'The new pub you told me about last week?'

'Yeah, I know that but I can't think which one now.'

'Blue door? Big flashing Guinness sign in the window? Tasty-sounding menu?'

'Oh yeah. Got it.' Lucy nodded.

'Do you fancy it? A day off, a bit of fresh air and a nice leisurely lunch will do us both the world of good.'

'I don't know Charlie, I have so much stuff to do on my list. It'll throw me off for the rest of the week if I take a day off now. We do want to be finished and into the house by the end of July, don't we?'

'One day won't hurt. We could both use a day off.'

'Won't this hold us up?'

'We'll catch up.'

'Yeah, well okay.'

Lucy finished her coffee, rinsed the mugs under the kitchen tap and placed them in the dishwasher. She glanced out of the window – the sun was shining, the early rain had cleared, and it promised to be a beautiful day.

'Do you want lunch down at the pub or do you want me to make up a picnic for us?' she asked.

'The pub,' he answered without hesitation.

Three hours later, Lucy was huffing and puffing by the time she sat down on a large boulder to catch her breath. The last few hundred metres of the climb had been much steeper than she realised. Charlie was behind her and she reached for his hand to pull him up the last few steps and onto the boulder beside her.

'We made it,' she wheezed. 'I wasn't sure we would.'

'Yeah.' Charlie could hardly speak for gasping. His hands on his knees, he kept his head lowered until his breathing became slightly easier. 'You think you're fit until you try something daft like this.'

'I think I'm gonna give the Himalaya hike a miss this year,' she informed him in mock seriousness.

'Probably for the best,' he replied, still gasping.

They fell silent for a while, catching their breath and taking the time to appreciate the views.

'Speaking of the Himalayas,' Charlie began. He put his arms across Lucy's shoulder and pulled her close to him. 'Do you fancy going away for a week somewhere? Not the Himalayas, obviously. But somewhere. I was thinking of some place nice and warm with great beaches. Maybe Greece. Or what about Cyprus? I was there years ago with a bunch of mates and it's lovely. Great beaches and the people are really friendly.'

'No.'

'No? No to what?'

'I don't want to go there,' she told him with a determination in her voice that told him she meant business.

'Where?'

'To Cyprus. I don't want to go to Cyprus.' Lucy's blood ran cold at the thought of a holiday in Cyprus.

What if Jennifer and Ilan really exist?

It was not a dream.

The stupid thought refused to go away.

Or is it stupid? What if Jennifer and Ilan really exist and they do live there in Cyprus? What if I run into her – this woman called Jennifer? What if I meet Ilan? What if he knows me and smiles at me and he wants to –

'Why not?' Charlie interrupted her thoughts. 'It's lovely there and a break would do us the world of good. Recharge our batteries, so to speak. Plus, it would be fun. I don't mean right now while we're working on the house, but I was thinking about later when we're settled in. Maybe we could go in September while the weather is still nice?'

'I don't want to go to Cyprus,' Lucy said. There was a determination in her voice that made him look at her. It was telling him she meant what she was saying. She was giving him an emphatic no to his suggestion of going to Cyprus.

'Well, it doesn't have to be Cyprus. We could go to Greece or Spain or Portugal. The south of France, even. Wherever you fancy. You can choose.'

'I don't want to go anywhere, Charlie,' she told him. 'I'm happy here. I can't wait until we move into the house, and I'm really looking forward to finishing all the decorating. Yes, believe it or not, I am looking forward to that! And I can't wait to start furnishing it. But, most importantly, I can't wait until I'm living in it with you. That's better than any holiday.'

'I know, but we could –'

'I'm serious Charlie. Even if you took me to the most luxurious beach resort on the planet for a five-star holiday, I wouldn't be able to relax and enjoy it because in my mind I'd be at home in our house. Maybe next year?'

'Well, if that's what you want, okay then.'

'It's what I want. Now, let's sit here a while and get our breath back, I mean, appreciate these views,' she grinned and planted a kiss on his cheek. 'And then head down to the pub for lunch. Because I am *really* starving now.'

Chapter 13 - Lucy's Dream

'You are very quiet,' Ilan said. He stole a glance at Jennifer as he drove. 'What are you thinking about?'

'Um, nothing much,' Jennifer replied, trying not to sound evasive. 'About the houses we've already seen.'

In truth Jennifer was thinking about Lucy's disturbing mental meltdown during last night's dream. She didn't *want* to dwell on it but it wasn't something she could forget in a hurry.

And why is she lying to Charlie so much? Mind you, I'd be reluctant to tell Ilan about some of the details of my dreams too. But would I lie to him deliberately? Hmmm, if I was shagging someone else in a dream yeah, I probably would.

'Well?' Jennifer asked. She put her thoughts away for now and returned to her reality as they pulled up on the road opposite the fourth, and last, of the properties on her list. 'What do you think of this one?'

Ilan shrugged, 'I like it. I think.'

'Oh, try not to sound so enthusiastic,' she joked.

'It is a house,' Ilan said. 'As long as it is correctly built and fully functional what is there not to like?'

'That's not what I meant. Do you think it will be comfortable? A nice place to live in? Somewhere to call home?'

He shrugged his shoulders.

Jennifer sighed. 'Some help wouldn't go amiss, Ilan.'

'What's wrong with the apartment you are living in now?' Ilan asked.

'Because the lease will be up soon. And I want a place of my own. And I want you to help me look for one.'

Although Jennifer felt she could happily live in either of the two houses they had already viewed, the tightened line of Ilan's jaw told Jennifer he was not impressed by them. The third one was okay in his opinion, but she hadn't liked it so she discarded it and then he insisted she forget about the two he disliked. This was the last house on her list and it seemed she was running out of options. This one was definitely the best, according to the brochure, but it was also the most expensive and she was concerned that, financially, it would be out of her reach.

Ilan reversed into the paved driveway. Jennifer looked around her. The drive was large enough for two cars, three at a push, and there was a double garage. The house itself was set on the side of a hill and overlooked the small village, which she discovered had a fair-sized supermarket, pharmacy, two restaurants, a café and three bars. There was also plenty of office space available for rent at reasonable prices.

Tony, who had kick-started her career in Cyprus, had encouraged her to go out on her own. His support had been vital and he was the first client to sign up with her. Several had followed and a more spacious office than the one she was currently renting was a necessity.

Jennifer was already taken with the village and hoped the house would be what she was looking for. The price was a problem though. It was unlikely, but maybe the owners would come down a little.

Or I might win the lottery.

She checked the label on the bunch of keys the estate agent had given her and took the brochure out of her bag. Opening the car door, she smiled at Ilan. 'Shall we go and have a look?'

'Of course,' he said as he switched off the ignition.

As they walked to the front door, Ilan casually slid his arm around her waist. The house was larger than it looked in the brochure and Jennifer was pleased to see that from the outside it was well-maintained. She unlocked the front door and in they went.

Jennifer's eyes widened in wonder as she stepped inside and found a modern, stylish open-plan house. Light and spacious, it was a haven of calmness and comfort. The stark whiteness of the walls was balanced by the rich, dark pine wood work and earthen tiled floors. She glanced at Ilan and could tell from his wide-eyed expression and his low appreciative whistle that he was also impressed.

Hand in hand they explored the house. Three bedrooms. The master included an en-suite with a high-quality walk-in shower. Ilan nodded in approval and Jennifer smiled at the gleam in his eye when he remarked that the shower was big enough for two.

'Yeah, I noticed that too,' she told him with a leer.

This bedroom had doors leading out to a terraced area. Ilan frowned at the doors and frowned even more when he examined the locks. 'These are too flimsy,' he grumbled. 'You might as well not have any locks for all the good these will do.'

'Well, it probably wouldn't be too hard to have more secure ones installed.'

He nodded and chewed thoughtfully at his bottom lip.

'What?' Jennifer asked.

'Nothing. Some thoughts running around in my head.'

'About this house?'

'Mmm.'

At least he's thinking about it. That's more than he did with the others.

They spent a few more minutes looking around the en-suite and the bedroom. Ilan seemed to be paying particular attention to the built-in wardrobe and, for some reason unknown to her, the walls behind the unit. Impatient to see the rest of the property, Jennifer went ahead and checked out the other two bedrooms.

'This would make a good office, yes?' Ilan nodded, suddenly appearing behind her as she looked into the smaller bedroom.

'Possibly,' Jennifer replied, although the notion of working from home had never appealed to her and it didn't factor into what she wanted and needed in a house.

Still, I probably will work from home occasionally so an office would be a good idea. For me anyway. Ilan doesn't exactly need an office, large or small.

The main bathroom housed a cast iron bath and another walk-in shower. The fixtures and fittings looked expensive and Jennifer's heart sank in the knowledge that it was very likely she would not be able to afford this house.

The kitchen took her breath away. Well-designed, good quality and spacious, it was perfect. The white goods – dishwasher and fridge – were included in the sale and the utility room off the kitchen housed the air-conditioning and a double drainer sink. A washing machine and tumble dryer were also part of the purchase.

On the wall near the door, Jennifer noticed controls for an alarm system. She pointed it out to Ilan who nodded approvingly.

The living room was perfect. Large with the same earthen tiles on the floor, and the walls were painted white. The woodwork was finished in the same dark, natural pine.

Two large glass doors led out to the terrace. Jennifer unlocked them and stepped out and fell completely and irrevocably in love with the house.

Underneath her feet were natural sandstone tiles. A low-lying wall in similar material surrounded the terrace. To the right, the wall was high and offered a sheltered and partially shaded area where five large terracotta pots stood. Three held various plants, their foliage green and vibrant against the sandstone. The other two were empty and Jennifer imagined jasmine or some other scented flowers growing there.

She could picture herself sitting there in the evenings with Ilan beside her. He would be relaxed and content while he sipped a whiskey. She would be enjoying a very cold glass of wine and a gentle breeze would waft the scent of the jasmine around them.

To the left, the wall blended upwards and became the side wall of the double garage. In this area, there was an outdoor clay oven and a bricked barbecue where Ilan could cook to his heart's content. All it needed, like the rest of the house, was some furniture and two people to live in it happily ever after.

Jennifer walked over to the wall. It was waist high and she could see the town below and the views beyond. They were breath-taking. But she sighed sadly. It was out of her reach. It could never be hers.

'Nice,' said the man of few words as he appeared at her side. He draped his arm across her shoulders and pulled her close to him.

'Me or the view?'

'Both,' he told her and planted a kiss on her cheek.

'It really is a nice view,' Jennifer agreed as she turned around to look at the house once more. She loved it.

'I've seen enough,' she told him. 'Let's go.'

They drove back down the hill towards the centre of the town and Jennifer spotted a bank and a post office she hadn't noticed earlier.

Everything I need and want is right here, including Ilan. It makes it even more perfect.

She remained silent while Ilan drove around a few times until a car pulled out of the last remaining parking space across the road from a small café.

'I need coffee,' he explained as he quickly reversed the BMW into the slot before anyone could steal it from him.

'Good idea,' Jennifer replied.

Ilan carried the estate agent's brochure with him as they dodged the traffic to cross the road. The café was almost full of customers this time of the day but a couple of tables remained unoccupied. Jennifer nodded in the direction of an empty table and they quickly made their way to it. A waiter appeared instantly and they ordered coffees, a cappuccino for Jennifer and an espresso for Ilan, plus two slices of baklava.

Ilan studied the brochure once more while they waited for their food and drinks. Then he looked at her with a smile.

'What are you thinking about?' he asked.

'Ah, I love the house, Ilan. I know I'm earning good money, but this is still above my budget. It's everything I want but...'

'You need a place of your own. Yes?'

'Yeah, and this is perfect. The house is outstanding. I think my favourite part was that terrace but I also loved the kitchen and the bedrooms... oh hell, I'm in love with all of it. And this village is adorable. But I've been doing the maths, Ilan, and the mortgage would be hard. I mean, really hard. I'd be investing every single Euro I have and there'd be nothing left over.'

Jennifer looked despondent. 'I can't manage it. No matter how I try to juggle my finances I don't have that sort of money. I might as well forget about it and keep looking for something I can afford.'

Ilan nodded but didn't say a word as he continued to leaf through the brochure. He seemed fascinated by it. Finally, he set it down on the table and looked at Jennifer. He studied her while she finished her slice of baklava.

'I could get fat eating this,' she told him. 'I think I'm addicted to it. I love it.'

'Ani ohev otach.'

'I beg your pardon?' Jennifer raised an eyebrow as she carefully set down her fork and, puzzled, looked at him.

'I did promise I was going to teach you some Hebrew.'

'Yes, you did. What does it mean?'

'It is a common phrase in any language, but not one that should ever be said in jest. Or taken lightly.'

'Okay then. Translate it into English for me.'

'Ani ohev otach is Hebrew for I love you.'

Surprised, Jennifer could only stare at him for a moment. Then she smiled at him. 'Say it again.'

'I love you.'

'No, say it in Hebrew.'

'Ani ohev otach.'

Her heart was thumping in her chest. 'Is this merely a language lesson or are you trying to tell me something?'

'I am trying to tell you that I love you. I will say it to you in whatever language you prefer. Would you like to hear it in French? Or would you like me to say it in Spanish? Russian? Greek? I can also say it in Arabic, naturally.'

'Naturally,' she echoed him.

'No, I think I will say it again in English so that you understand me completely. I love you, Jennifer Scott. I am very much in love with you and I want to spend the rest of my life with you.'

Jennifer froze. A declaration of love usually had her running for the hills, the remainder of the relationship taken up with figuring a way to wriggle out of his arms, and out of his life.

Yeah. You need to run! Forget the coffee and the baklava. Grab your bag and get out of there!

Why?

You're asking why? What sort of question is that? You know why. This leads to marriage and commitment and babies. All the things you dread. Get out of there now!

What if I don't want to?

What the fuck? Why?

Because I think I'm in love with him.

Don't be stupid. Didn't you hear me? Marriage? Babies? Get out while you can!

'Jennifer?' Ilan frowned at her silence.

'I love you too,' she said, the words spilled out of her mouth before she finished her mental argument.

Ilan smiled and exhaled the breath he had been holding.

'Your timing could have been better though,' Jennifer told him. She sighed and looked away, her gaze taking in the small square and the surrounding buildings. It really was a lovely little town.

'I know. I'm sorry.'

She touched his face with her hand. 'Don't worry about it.'

'No. You're still sad. What is wrong?'

'Oh, I'm sorry. I was thinking about the house again. I love it but, like I said, I won't be able to afford it. I wish I could put it out of my head, but I can't.'

'Perhaps we should purchase it together,' Ilan said. Then his phone rang. It danced as it vibrated on the table between them. 'Excuse me, I must answer this.'

He grabbed the phone from the table and answered the call and his face darkened as he listened to the speaker on the other end. He rose to his feet and rushed out of the café onto the street below.

'He loves me,' Jennifer muttered under her breath, and glanced at the brochure again.

And I love him. And between us we could afford this house.

She sipped her coffee and watched Ilan on the pavement below the café. He was too far away for her to hear what he was saying but she could easily read his emotions from his body language. He stood with one hand in the pocket of his jeans and the other holding the phone to his ear. He seemed shocked, frowning at whatever he was being told by the person on the other end of the phone. Then he became agitated, pacing back and forth on the footpath, barely speaking and Jennifer could see that he was listening intently.

Ilan took the phone away from his face and rubbed his eyes with his other hand. His distress was obvious. He glanced around him, a quick look up in her direction, but without any acknowledgement of her presence on the café terrace where he had left her. He paced some more and then seemed to reach a decision. The stiffness in his shoulders told Jennifer that whatever it was, it was an important decision.

Finally, the conversation came to an end and Ilan slipped the phone back into his pocket. Jennifer knew him well enough to read his emotions as he looked heavenwards almost in despair, then rubbed his eyes as though weary and his shoulders slumped as if in defeat. His gaze travelled up to her sitting on the balcony of the café and smiled up at her. It was a smile that was full of love and adoration but tinged with sadness.

He briefly disappeared from sight as he made his way back into the café. A few moments later he was back and sitting opposite her.

'I am sorry but I have to leave,' he told her.

'What's up?' Jennifer asked. She raised an eyebrow and kept her voice as casual as possible.

Ilan frowned. 'All I can say is that someone who works for me is in trouble and I have to go and find her.'

'Her?'

Her? Of course, it would be a her.

'Yes. She is an operative and I cannot forsake her. I owe my life to her on many occasions.'

'Can you tell me where you are going?'

'I have to go to Cairo.'

'Will it be dangerous?' she asked.

'Probably not,' he replied.

'That doesn't reassure me very much.'

'I know. I am sorry.'

'When do you leave?'

Ilan checked his watch. 'I have a couple of hours until I leave for the airport. I have time to take you back home first.'

'Okay. Let's go then,' she said as she rose to her feet, slung her bag over her shoulder and headed out of the café to the car, leaving Ilan to pay the bill before following her outside.

Silence reigned on the drive back to Jennifer's apartment, both of them lost in their individual thoughts. It took a little under twenty minutes to drive the distance from the café to the apartment, but it was only when he parked outside her front door that he asked her if she was okay.

'Yes,' she sighed. 'I'm okay. I mean... hell, I don't know what I mean.'

'May I come in?' he said as he rummaged in the BMW's glove compartment then slipped something into the back pocket of his jeans.

'Of course,' she told him.

Once inside, Ilan closed the door behind him and caught Jennifer by the hand. He pulled her into his arms and held her tightly. She leaned against him and began to speak.

'Shhhh,' he quietened her, his lips brushing her mouth gently. He kissed her forehead as he inhaled the faint coconut scent of her shampoo. 'I need to hold you. I want to remember all of this, all of you, when I'm away from you.'

'I don't want you to go, Ilan.'

He pulled away from her, holding her at arm's length as though putting up an invisible barrier between them. Necessary, because without it, he would be tempted to remain with her.

'I must go. You know that.'

Do I? Is it really your work that's taking you away? I sort of believe you, but...

Jennifer lifted her head and looked into his eyes, memorising his face, his expression, knowing it could be ages before she would see him again.

'Will it always be like this?' she asked. 'You running off on a whim, leaving me here alone for weeks on end?'

'It's hardly on a whim. But no, it is not normally like this. This sudden... development demands my attention, and naturally, my presence. I must attend to it as quickly as possible.'

She sighed. 'Okay, I understand. I think.'

'I do love you, Jennifer.'

'But you love Israel more?'

'That is such a loaded question, neshama. I love my country very much and I will do all I can to protect and defend her. As much as I love you, Jennifer, there will be times when I must put Israel first, above all else. This is one of those times. Does that make a difference?'

'No. I do understand. I don't like it, but I understand.'

'When I am here, I will love you with all my heart and soul. When I'm away from you, I will put that love on hold until I return.'

His arms encircled her again, holding her tightly to him. Jennifer remained silent.

'Is what I do so wrong?' he asked.

'No. I never said it was wrong. That thought never even occurred to me,' she smiled. 'I'm simply not very good at sharing.'

Ilan laughed. 'I will have to teach you to share.'

She punched him lightly on the arm then her face grew serious again as she stepped away from him and walked into the kitchen area.

'Now, about the house,' Ilan followed her into the kitchen and took a can of Coke out of the fridge. He popped it open and took a long drink. 'I very much want us to purchase it together. It's ideal. Hardly anything needs to be done to it other than better locks and furnishing it, which I know you will do exceedingly well. You could even put some of your Scandinavian canvases on the walls,' he grinned. 'Naturally this will allow me to purchase a large television for the living room so I can watch football matches all day.'

'Naturally,' she replied. 'How large?'

'Large. Very large. You will believe you are in the stadium,' he grinned and drained the last of the Coke from the can.

'But seriously Jennifer,' he set the empty can down on the table and reached for her hand. 'I love the house as much as you do. Provided you want to live with me this makes sense. You do want us to be together? Yes?'

'Of course, I do,' Jennifer nodded.

Is that the closest I'll get to a proposal? Not very romantic but that's okay. I'm not all that into romance anyway.

'Good,' Ilan continued. 'I very much want us to be together. Tomorrow, I want you to telephone the estate agent and tell them you wish to buy it at the price the seller wishes. Then I want you to stall the procedure as much as you can until I return home.'

'How do I go about that?' she asked. 'I don't even have enough for a deposit. I could probably ask my dad for a loan, but even then –'

'You do not need to borrow money from your father,' Ilan said and pulled his chequebook out of his back pocket. He took a pen from a jar of assorted pens and pencils she kept on the worktop and began writing a cheque. 'I want you to lodge this into your bank account and use it as a deposit on the house.'

'You want me to go ahead and buy it? Without you here?' she stared at him.

'Yes. If necessary. I would love to be there with you when we buy it together but that may not be possible. So, I want you to do it. But try and stall for as long as you possibly can.'

He signed his name with a flourish and tore the cheque out of the book. He handed it to her.

Jennifer stared at the amount written on the cheque in horror. 'Oh, for fuck's sake Ilan! I can't take this. It's too much.'

She tried to hand it back to him but he folded his arms in refusal.

'Where did you get that sort of money?' Suspicion flared in her.

'I have genuine business interests here and in Israel.'

'I can't take it.'

'You must. I insist,' he told her. 'We can buy this house. We both love it and we can make it our home. I only ask that you put it solely in your name.'

'Is that legal?'

'Yes, of course.'

'Why put it in my name only?'

'For the simple reason that I may not have returned by the time you sign the contracts. We can easily change it later.'

'Are you sure about this, Ilan?'

'Yes, neshama. I am sure,' he kissed her. 'I have to go in a few minutes but before I leave there is one other thing.'

'What is it?'

He watched her carefully for a moment then held out his hand to her. 'You may not like this but give me your phone please.'

Jennifer frowned but did what he asked.

Ilan took the phone, opened it, and quickly typed in some numbers. 'I am adding two people to your contacts. The first number is for Amiel. I have known him for many years and I trust him with my life, so I know I can trust him with yours. The second number belongs to Chana – you met her briefly when I took you to the embassy dinner in Nicosia last September. You will love her. She is a very funny lady but also very professional.

They will be your family liaison contacts and either of them will assist you and advise you, and if need be, contact me on your behalf.'

'Family liaison?' Jennifer asked.

'Yes. It was approved some months ago.'

'Approved?' she parroted him.

'Your security checks came back clear and I was given permission to –'

'Security checks? Permission? What the fuck?' Jennifer glared at him.

'I am sorry if this upsets you, but I had to submit an application of intent regarding a relationship – a serious relationship. It is standard procedure. You had to be vetted and cleared before I could continue, to determine that you were not from another agency and were intending to –'

'Bloody hell!'

'I had to, Jennifer. Please understand.'

'I do. It makes sense. But how did –'

'I took copies of your driving licence and passport. They were checked and came back clear. You are exactly who you say you are. We also ran background checks on your family and friends, discrete checks I must add, and they also came back clear.'

'Well, that's good to know,' she said, a little sarcastically, taking the phone back from him and slipping it into her bag.

'You must understand, Jennifer, if this was only a casual affair…'

'What?'

'I can assure you that it is not casual on my part. I love you and I want to spend the rest of my life with you. But the nature of my work entails that my superiors had to be sure of you. I was sure but it had to be confirmed.'

'Did you doubt me? Even at first?'

'No, never. But they had to be sure.'

Jennifer took a seat on the sofa, confused by the conflicting emotions she was feeling.

'I'm sorry. I don't feel completely comfortable with this, Ilan.' she told him.

'I had no choice,' he said.

'I do understand and I accept that it had to be done but I wish you could have told me.'

Ilan took her hands in his. She glared at him but already she could feel her anger dissipating.

It makes perfect sense. He's an operative of a security service and it's only natural that anyone he became intimate with should be checked out.

It also showed her, and his bosses, the depth of his commitment and, in that respect, she was glad. He did love her and was prepared to spend the rest of his life with her, and he had to do this to ensure that would happen.

He could have walked away without having to deal with all the red tape needed so he could be with me.

But right now, it was a lot for her to process.

She could see the questioning look on his face and the relief in his eyes when she smiled and leaned forward to kiss him. His lips met hers, gently at first, then more firmly, with passion and yearning.

'When do you have to leave?' she whispered.

'Unfortunately, I have to leave immediately. I'm already running late.'

'So, I can't persuade you to take me to bed for half an hour first then?'

'I am afraid not,' he stood up and pulled her to her feet, keeping his arm around her waist as he walked towards the front door.

'I will see you soon,' he kissed her lightly on the lips then walked out the door.

Jennifer watched him as he drove away. This would be the ideal moment for the car to break down, as it usually did. But no, the engine sounded strong and healthy as it carried him away from her.

The sky was darkening as evening drew near and she watched the car's tail-lights until she could no longer see them.

With a sigh, Jennifer closed the door. Back in the kitchen she retrieved a bottle from the fridge and poured herself a large glass of cold, white wine. It was an expensive bottle of Pinot Grigio that Ilan bought a few weekends ago. One he enjoyed now and then, he told her. They never got around to drinking it together.

Well, we won't be drinking it together now.

It probably should have been savoured and enjoyed slowly in good company. But Jennifer gulped down more than half of the glass like it was the cheapest supermarket plonk. She was drinking out of necessity this evening rather than pleasure. And in the faint hope she would drink enough to ensure a deep, dreamless sleep. She refilled her glass and carried the bottle into the bedroom.

Just for tonight, the house wasn't important and just like Scarlett O'Hara in the old movie, she would think about it tomorrow.

Chapter 14 - Jennifer's Dream

Lucy snuggled under the duvet, making the most of the cosy warmth and the luxury of those few extra minutes before her busy day began. Before the new carpets could be fitted in the living room and in two of the bedrooms, she had woodwork to oil and it had to be done early to ensure it was dry. The fitters promised to be there by eleven but, in reality, they would show up around lunchtime, have a cup of tea and a good natter before even thinking about laying a carpet. They were skilled, but preferred to work at their own pace. Not surprising really, both men were well into their sixties.

While she waited for Charlie to bring her a cup of tea, Lucy's thoughts turned to Jennifer and Ilan. In her dream last night, Ilan finally told Jennifer he loved her. Lucy was delighted and eagerly looking forward to seeing how it would develop.

It no longer seemed weird knowing a total stranger's thoughts and emotions almost as well as her own. The terror she felt when she first began dreaming had diminished and left in its wake curiosity and interest.

'Why not?' Claire had asked her one afternoon over coffee. 'I'd be afraid. Well, concerned at least.'

Lucy had taken a sip of coffee as she thought about her friend's question. 'Because they're only dreams. I don't know why I'm dreaming this life with these two people. I never, ever dream about anything else now. But it doesn't matter. They can't harm me. They're not nightmares and they don't frighten me. In fact, I look forward to them. Jennifer is a lovely woman and Ilan is not only handsome and sexy, he is a very nice person. Their relationship is going well and I'm happy for them.'

Lucy paused and smiled. 'I feel I know her. I know almost all her thoughts and what she is feeling. I know all her likes and dislikes. And I learn more about her every night when I go to sleep.'

'You should write a book,' Claire had said.

'I doubt it would be interesting. It is to me, on a personal level, but it's hardly best seller material.'

Although tempted, Lucy refrained from telling Claire that Ilan was a Mossad agent. She felt it would be a betrayal of trust. He had insisted that Jennifer must never tell anyone so, by extension of his command to Jennifer, she kept this information from her friend.

Lucy was happy for the pair of them and delighted when Ilan suggested they buy the house together. It made perfect sense if Jennifer couldn't afford it but, more importantly, they belonged together as a couple. She hoped Jennifer would agree to his suggestion. It didn't bode well for them when he suddenly had to leave, but surely Jennifer understood.

But God, that bombshell he dropped! He gave her those phone numbers then told her she'd passed the security checks! Poor Jennifer. What an awful situation, to be hit with this just after he said he loved her. They have so much to discuss. They need to be together right now. God, what if something happens to him?

'A penny for them?' Charlie asked as he handed her a large mug of tea and climbed back into bed beside her, managing not to spill any of the contents of his own mug in the process.

'Just planning the day ahead,' she said and blew gently on the scalding hot liquid before taking a delicate sip.

'Yeah, we have lots to do today. Are you excited about finally moving in?'

She grinned at him. 'What do you think?'

'I think if you were really excited, you'd have been up and dressed hours ago!'

'It's only six-thirty in the morning! Give me another five minutes to finish my tea and then watch me spring into action.' She took his hand in hers. 'Seriously, Charlie I am so looking forward to this. Don't get me wrong, I've been happy living here these past few years. This house served its purpose for us, but it never felt like home. It's as if we've been waiting, no that's not correct... it seems the stars aligned in the right way to bring us to the house we've always wanted. Just like they have for...'

Fuck! I almost said Jennifer and Ilan.

'Just like they have for...?' Charlie looked at her quizzically.

'Um... I mean... a couple of years ago we couldn't even dream of owning a place like this. And when your business started to take off, we talked about moving, but never made any plans. Then your aunt left you all that money and you found the house on the internet. Like I said, it's as if the stars aligned perfectly in our favour and everything fell into place at the right moment for us.'

Charlie watched her for a few moments, a confused frown on his face

'Come on. There's a ton of work to do and lying here in bed won't get it done!' Lucy said, reluctant to allow Charlie to question her words. She gave up on drinking the hot tea, threw back the bedcovers and climbed out of bed. She gathered up an old pair of jeans and a sweatshirt and headed for the bathroom leaving Charlie sitting on the bed, more than a little mystified by her.

An hour later they were on the road, out of the small town and travelling through the countryside. Only a few miles from the house that, by this time next week, would become their home. The weather was dry, but dull and cloudy – the sun well hidden behind the thickness of the clouds – and rain was forecast for later. But even with the dark, gloomy weather, Lucy could only see the beauty surrounding her. She had learned, over the weeks of travelling to and from the house, to appreciate the spectacular views. The many occasions when they had been stuck behind a tractor on the narrow roads gave her plenty of time to appreciate these views.

Every day she discovered more of the wonderful beauty in the delicate nuances of colour and shade in this harsh, yet breath-taking, landscape. Not for the first time she imagined herself with a sketch pad, capturing the scenery before her. *Aye. If only I could draw.*

They turned onto the lane. It was their lane now. With its potholes and dry-stone walls on either side, covered in brambles – the fruit already ripening. Lucy was looking forward to picking blackberries and making jam. She hadn't the foggiest notion how to make jam. *I'll google it. It can't be that hard.*

There was an apple tree laden with fruit in the back garden which meant apple and blackberry crumble – Charlie's favourite. She had also discovered a pear tree and a plum tree that, unfortunately, the wasps adored.

As the house appeared before them, Lucy's heart soared. The very image of the house – their house – almost made her cry with joy as it reached out and welcomed her home.

Almost all the renovations inside were complete but they still had plenty of work to do outside; levelling the ground, laying topsoil and finally planting a lawn. This task would take them several weeks and once that was completed, they could decide what to do with the driveway. Charlie wanted to tarmac it but Lucy fancied gravel.

'Gravel costs less but it's more work,' he had told her. 'Keeping the weeds at bay for one thing.'

He had insisted that they needed a properly tarmacked drive and he had almost won Lucy over until someone mentioned that the harsh weather in the wintertime was hard on tarmac. The potholes that appeared in the nearby roads every year bore witness to this fact and he was slowly leaning more in favour of Lucy's gravel driveway.

She had done her best not to look too smug in the face of his retreat but secretly she was delighted. It was what she wanted all along, but she had managed to turn it around and make it appear his own idea.

They parked in front of the house and once inside, Lucy stored sandwiches and a carton of milk in the fridge. It was her turn to drive home later so she added some beer for Charlie to enjoy with his lunch.

Before she started work, Lucy looked around the finished kitchen. It was all new and gleaming and she smiled as she thought about where she would place things like the kettle and the microwave. And which cupboards she would use for plates and other crockery and which would be best suited to store tinned foods and such.

She poured the linseed oil into an old jam pot and unwrapped a new paintbrush. Charlie had already started work upstairs and she could hear live commentary of a local rugby match on the radio. A match they both probably would have gone to if they hadn't been decorating today. He was painting the second of the three spare bedrooms. Other than the carpets, the master bedroom and dressing room were complete. As was the en-suite bathroom. The new curtains were still in their wrappings and would be hung once the carpets were down.

The living room was big and square with four large windows that would get sunshine from morning until late in the evening, allowing plenty of light in from every direction. The large stone fireplace would soon house an open fire and once the carpet was fitted, they could bring in the furniture and hang the curtains. Then the room would remain untouched until they moved in.

It was a lovely room, but Lucy's favourite was still the smaller one beyond the kitchen. The one with the glass doors that led onto the paved area in the back garden.

Maybe not as fancy as the patio – sorry terrace – in the house Jennifer wants but mine is just as nice.

This was the room with the exposed stone walls and the fireplace that took up most of one wall. More importantly, this was the room that now held her wood-burning stove. Small enough to not be overpowering with its heat output, but powerful enough to make the room warm and cosy, it fitted nicely into the fireplace. As a bonus, it boosted the hot water supply.

The walls were now a warm, sandstone shade with dark-coloured solid wood for flooring. There were heavy curtains on the windows and doors. A leather suite, and a colourful rug on the floor. Large candles on top of the fireplace, scatter cushions and a television on a unit in the corner, made the room cosy and snug.

The last item Lucy added was a coffee table she found in a local charity shop. It had needed restoration, so she sanded it down to the bare wood and stained it a dark oak colour that complemented the various tones of wood in the room. Two coats of beeswax polish for the finish and it looked expensive and new.

Lucy had no idea where this love of working with wood came from and more than a few people had complimented her on her skills. Now, she found herself wondering if there could be a money-making craft business in it. She had even eyed up one of the smaller outbuildings as a potential workshop.

When they tested the stove to make sure it worked properly, the room lived up to the nickname they'd given it: 'The Snug'.

All the room needed now was a cat curled up in front of the fire. Lucy was determined to get one soon, despite Charlie's half-hearted protests. He wanted a dog but there was no reason not to have both. A neighbour informed her, when she enquired about kittens, that his farm cat was pregnant and if she wanted one, she could have the pick of the litter once they were weaned.

Oiling wood wasn't the hardest work in the world, but after a while it became mind-numbingly boring. Lucy had learned not to quit for a break when she got bored. If she did, it was hard to motivate herself to start again. The trick was to continue at a steady rhythm, on autopilot almost, and let her mind take her wherever it wanted to go. Usually, it took her to her most recent dream.

She replayed it over in her mind, searching each word and action for hidden nuances and feelings. For a while now, she had known Jennifer was head over heels in love with Ilan. It was nice to hear him saying that he loved her too.

One thing she did pick up on was Jennifer's concern about the depth of Ilan's commitment to her. His first commitment would always be to his work. Work that frequently took him away, sometimes for long periods. And it was dangerous. She had googled Mossad and other well-known intelligence agencies such as the CIA in America and MI5 here in the UK. Or was it MI6? One dealt with domestic stuff and the other international, but she had forgotten which one did what.

Then it occurred to her that maybe she shouldn't be reading this kind of thing on the internet. What if they knew she was reading it? She had logged off quickly and ignored her laptop for a few days until the fear of a knock at the door some evening had subsided. She had laughed at herself for her foolish paranoia.

The few websites where she had read about Mossad and all the other agencies, before her paranoia overcame her, made it painfully obvious that Ilan's work came with a high element of risk.

Anything could happen to him and Jennifer is all alone, worrying and not knowing if he's safe or not. It'll be hard for her. I couldn't live like that. Can she? Is their love for one another strong enough to endure it? Time will tell.

Lucy had long since stopped worrying about the dreams. They were a part of her life now. But it did get a bit weird at times. It was as though she was there, in Jennifer's body and it wasn't a problem when Jennifer was cooking or swimming or doing any one of the everyday things she did. That was okay. It was the sex and the general intimacy that was disturbing. Lucy didn't consider herself prudish – an explicit sex scene in a book or a movie didn't shock or offend her. If anything, she enjoyed it. And she could hardly call herself a prude considering some of the things she and Charlie got up to. But the intimacy she witnessed – experienced was maybe the better word – with Ilan and Jennifer was downright embarrassing.

It's a bit like walking in on friends having sex and being asked to join in!

That was exactly how it felt when she dreamt her way through their passionate love-making.

But aside from the sex, it was the intense detail in all aspects of Jennifer's life that Lucy found both disturbing and fascinating.

Whatever Jennifer was doing, Lucy experienced it. If Jennifer was in the shower, Lucy felt the warm water on her skin. If she was driving, she felt the breeze and the heat through the open car window. She could smell coffee and freshly baked bread in the café where Jennifer went every day for a cappuccino and a croissant.

Not just physical things either. She sensed Jennifer's frustration when a design didn't work out the way she hoped it would. Or her boredom when Ilan was watching football on television. Or her joy when one of the timid kittens finally plucked up the courage to allow her to touch it.

She could feel the warmth of Ilan's arms around her.

She could feel the ache in Jennifer's shoulder when it was going to rain, and she knew Jennifer had broken it playing hockey at school and that was why it was so painful when the weather changed.

She could even smell the jasmine on the terrace in the evenings when Jennifer would sit out there to watch the sun setting.

She dipped her brush into the pot of oil and her hand froze as a thought occurred to her.

Maybe this is a dream. Maybe I don't exist and all this is a dream. Maybe I'm the product of someone's mind. Someone's nightmare. Or it could be the fumes from this pot of linseed oil are making you high, you silly woman!

She shook off her foolish thoughts and concentrated on finishing the door panel.

The thought lingered in the back of her mind, but she forced herself to ignore its niggling reasoning and then she sat back on her heels to admire her work. Another room was finished. She ticked it off her mental list and thought about what she was going to do with the other two downstairs rooms. The smallest was for ironing and storage, but she wasn't sure what she wanted to do with the larger one. The kitchen was massive so they didn't need a dining room and they already had two sitting rooms. The two large windows in this room gave it lots of natural light for most of the day, so it would possibly make a good office.

Maybe Jennifer will decide what to do with it since it's her dream. Do you hear me Jennifer? Some suggestions would be great!

A glance at her watch told her it was almost half past nine. Time for a cup of tea and a chocolate biscuit. Lucy got to her feet, wincing at the stiffness in her knees from kneeling for so long, and went into the kitchen to put the kettle on.

'The kettle's boiling,' she yelled up to Charlie. 'Come down and get a cuppa.'

Chapter 15

Three days since the accidents.

Her husband sat by her bed with his shoulders hunched as he leaned towards her. This sad vigil was all he could manage. He held her hand in his and stared at her face in deep concentration as though the force of his will alone could make her eyes open again.

'He looks so tired,' the nurses said as they discussed him among themselves, their voices hushed and tinged with sympathy. He was scruffy and unshaven, and they noticed the exhaustion etched into his face.

'Probably starving too,' they said, because he never touched the food – the snacks and the sandwiches, they left for him. He drank only the coffee. It was all he existed on since she had been brought out of surgery and taken up to the Intensive Care Ward.

'Coffee and hope,' they said as they nodded wisely. The diet of the desperate.

His right hand refused to let go – to let *her* go. Every now and then, he fancied she squeezed his hand. She was squeezing his fingers gently, at least in his imagination. She was telling him that she was still here, that she was still with him and she wasn't leaving him any time soon. This was what he believed.

His left hand was curled tightly into a fist. The knuckles white and paralysed by the terrible fear that coursed through his veins.

If she died ...

He forced the thought away, refusing to allow it to manifest itself in any shape or form.

Instead, he tried to replay over and over in his mind what the doctors told him about her condition, searching for something – *anything* – positive in those explanations regarding her injury, the surgery or the subsequent treatment she had undergone.

He considered himself to be an intelligent man, well-educated and well-read. But in his shock, he could barely understand what they had told him. Expressions such as TBI, he knew, stood for traumatic brain injury. But when they talked about a subdural haematoma, and the concern on their faces when they informed him that she had a GCS of only six, he was able to understand what they were saying on only the most basic of levels. It seemed as if his brain, like hers, had partially shut down. So great was his shock.

The doctor watched his reaction, his eyes narrowing as he tried to explain the situation. He must have realized this was not the right time, because he broke off mid-sentence, patted him on the arm and told him to be patient and to try not to worry.

'She has survived the surgery and we have done all we can for her. Now it's up to her.'

He took little comfort from the doctor's words.

They threw him out each evening when visiting hours were long over, permitting him the little bit of extra time to sit beside her because they knew he slept in his car in the staff carpark behind the hospital. Except that he *didn't* sleep. They knew this too, because they could see him from the window of the nurse's station up on the third floor. He sat there in the car, smoking and waiting.

When they opened the doors the next day to allow visitors in again, he was always first. His eyes met theirs and they could see the hope in them. A hope that was quickly dashed when they lowered their own eyes and it was this that broke him every time. It told him there had been no change.

He stank of cigarette smoke and stale body odour.
The nurses gossiped about him amongst themselves.
'He is so handsome,' they sighed.
'He is so sad,' they murmured with sympathy.
'He loves her so very much,' they agreed.

On the fourth evening the doctor finally told him to go home and get some rest. He protested but the doctor was adamant.

'There is nothing you can do for her right now. Listen to me. You need to go and take a shower. Make that a priority. Please,' the doctor told him. 'Then you need to eat something, and then you need to get some sleep. There's no point in making yourself ill. You'll be no help to her if you are ill.'

'I can't leave her,' he told the doctor.

'I insist. Shower, eat and get some sleep. Come back tomorrow afternoon and we will discuss her condition and prognosis further. In the meantime, we have your phone number and we will call you if there is any change.'

Chapter 16 - Lucy's Dream

Jennifer opened her eyes to daylight spilling into the room. As she came fully awake, she had the feeling that someone was in the room with her. Sitting near the bed. She sat up quickly, and glanced around, but she was alone and the sensation disappeared immediately.

That was weird.

Jennifer made her way into the bathroom, turned on the shower and stepped in. The hot water eased her hangover slightly. As she dried and dressed, she was still thinking about the dream and the creepy feeling she had awakened to. But she couldn't explain it.

As she walked into the kitchen, Jennifer glared at the empty bottle of wine sitting on the counter and cursed herself for drinking all of it. Ilan had forgotten his sunglasses and they were on the table. They reminded her that he was somewhere she couldn't contact him. She hated that part of him. The part that put country before love. Before her. But it was also the part she admired about him.

The sunglasses reminded her of everything they had talked about last evening. The house, his declaration of love and the fact his superiors had vetted her, her family and her friends. *Making sure I'm a suitable girlfriend.*

The cheque he had given her was the icing on the... S*hit! Where was it?*

She frowned. The amount had frightened her and she tried to give it back to him. When he refused to take it, she had put it... *Where? In my purse?*

She looked inside and gave a sigh of relief to see the cheque tucked behind two twenty Euro notes. It was disturbing to see it again. She quickly closed her purse and made coffee.

With a mug of strong black coffee, Jennifer powered up her laptop and, to keep herself from worrying about Ilan, thought instead about last night's dream.

Lucy was correct in what she was thinking. *How do I know what she is thinking?*

The details were as Lucy described. She herself had experienced aspects of Lucy's life in great detail. She remembered the work Lucy had done – the doors, window sills and skirting boards she had oiled. She could feel the paintbrush in her hand and she could even smell linseed oil in her nose. It seemed to linger even now, mingling with the aroma of the coffee. *And I'm getting all the sex, too.*

As she drank the coffee, Jennifer typed the name Lucy Wilson into the search bar. It was a common name, like her own, and several pages of Lucy Wilsons appeared on the screen. She narrowed it down a little by adding United Kingdom to her search and tried again. Adding Yorkshire to the search narrowed it some more. *Still too many. Maybe if I try Facebook.*

Jennifer logged onto her Facebook account and typed Lucy's name into the search bar. She found twelve Lucy Wilsons in the UK, five in Yorkshire. The first one was a silver surfer who bred budgies, liked horror movies, country music and motorcycle racing. She was widowed and had a suspiciously high number of similar-aged men among her friends.

Judging by the make-up, hairstyles and boozy party photos posted by the next two they were teenagers.

Jennifer looked at the next one and a shiver ran up her spine. *This is her! She's real! What does this mean?*

She enlarged the photo and stared at the face on the screen. The long, brown hair and the hazel eyes were too familiar for it not to be her. It was her. This was the Lucy Wilson she met every time she closed her eyes at night.

Jennifer's heart pounded in her chest as she clicked on the name and began to scroll through Lucy's posts. There wasn't much to see other than photos from when she updated her profile and cover pictures. The last one was a scene of a snow-covered tree.

Lucy Wilson had eighty-three friends. She checked the updated cover photo and saw that one of the friends who had 'liked' the photo was called Claire. She already knew from her dreams that Claire was Lucy's best friend.

There was little else to be gleaned from it, other than she had married Charlie six years ago and she was a primary school teacher – Jennifer already knew that, having dreamt her way through Lucy marking homework assignments – something she discovered both of them found very boring.

If Jennifer wanted to know more, she would have to send Lucy a friend request and Lucy would have to accept it. She moved the cursor over the 'Add Friend' link. It was tempting, and she almost clicked on it, but stopped herself at the last moment, not wanting to go down the route of interacting with this woman in the real world.

If it was the real world?

Lucy's thoughts came back to haunt her.

Up until fifteen minutes ago, Lucy had been a character in her dreams. She had not been real. Now here she was on Facebook. Or at least, someone *called* Lucy Wilson, who was a teacher, married to a bloke named Charlie, and had a friend named Claire, was on Facebook. It was not a hundred percent proof, but it was hard not to believe this was the Lucy of her dreams.

So, what does this mean? Is she real and I'm not? Maybe neither of us are? Maybe we are both the product of our dreams? No. That doesn't make sense. Are we the dreams of someone else then? Fuck. That's insane. I don't know about you Lucy, but I am real. I'm here in my kitchen looking at your Facebook page while I drink my coffee and ache for my boyfriend. This proves I'm real. But you are too. And that's the scary part.

Jennifer quickly closed the laptop.

Chapter 17 - Jennifer's Dream

Five days to go!

Lucy smiled at the prospect of spending a couple of days pre-Christmas with Claire and Gavin.

They were well settled in now – the house keeping its promise of shelter, happiness and so much more as it welcomed them into its embrace.

Summer had slipped gradually to autumn and then, literally overnight, winter arrived. It was a winter living up to the forecasts of being the coldest on record. Lucy, who preferred a harsh winter to an uncomfortably hot summer, loved every frosty morning and rainy day. The super-efficient, central heating boiler kept them warm and cosy. The open fire in the big room burned brightly and the wood stove in the Snug supplied extra hot water as well as extra heat. The house gave them warmth and comfort as they spent their evenings curled up on the sofa, secure in the knowledge that neither wind nor rain, frost nor snow could touch them.

Lucy glanced at her watch. Charlie promised he'd be home early, then Claire and Gavin were coming at eight. But, like Lucy and Charlie, they wanted to spend Christmas alone, this one being their first as a married couple.

'Hot sex in front of the tree. Lots and lots of hot sex in front of the tree – before the glow wears off,' was how Claire had described their plans for the holidays.

'That doesn't make sense,' Lucy had told her friend. 'You pair have been living together for ages.'

'Yeah, but we're married now,' Claire rolled her eyes.

'Some Scottish guy.' Claire's initial description of Gavin was deliberately vague and she was reluctant to divulge too much too soon. She did, however, delight in regaling Lucy with the more explicit aspects of her new squeeze. 'He's nuts, totally bonkers, but a frigging stallion in bed. So good in fact I think I'm in love. Yeah, I know what you're going to say – good in bed doesn't equal a lifetime commitment and the most wonderful penis in the world shouldn't be the main criteria but, fuck it Lucy, you need a starting point. Get him under the duvet, see how he performs and if he brings you breakfast in bed the next morning, add that to his points tally. That's what I did and so far, I can assure you it's great. In bed and for breakfast! Full steam ahead as they say. You'll see when you meet him.'

Charlie knew him from the pub.

'Gavin? Are you talking about the big Scottish bloke who works for the Forestry Commission?' Lucy nodded. 'Yeah, he's okay. Bit of a tree-hugger but then all those Forestry guys are. Nah, I like him. He's a stand-up bloke. I think Claire and him are well suited.'

Other than that, they had been kept in the dark for months about the crazy-but-sexy Gavin. He could be a serial killer for all they knew. Eventually Claire plucked up the courage to introduce him over drinks and snacks at her place one summer's evening. Charlie and Gavin had clicked immediately. Lucy sipped her gin and tonic as she admired his physique, nodding enthusiastically when Claire asked if she thought he was good looking.

From that moment on, the four of them were the best of friends and Lucy was looking forward to the evening so much.

She had kept it simple. A beef casserole in the slow cooker. Garlic bread to be warmed up in the oven and an apple crumble she would serve with brandy cream afterwards. There was beer and wine and a bottle of Scotch whiskey for Gavin.

Logs were set in the fireplace, ready to light and they had a cosy evening planned to kick off the beginning of the festive holidays in this lovely old farmhouse.

Now, I just have to decorate the tree, then I can relax with a glass of wine before I shower and get ready.

The tree was a massive fir and it had cost a small fortune. But when they saw it standing proudly in the hall, just beside the staircase, it had been worth the extra expense. Anything smaller would have been dwarfed in the large, open space.

Lucy checked her watch. Half past four and completely dark. The only light came from the table lamps and the tea lights burning in their holders in various places around the house. Although she loved the scents of cinnamon or sandalwood, they had a purpose other than decoration. The electricity went off on a regular basis during a storm and they had learned to keep a supply of candles, matches and flashlights handy. Charlie was still deciding whether or not to buy a diesel generator.

She wondered what Jennifer had planned for Christmas. *Will she go for the whole turkey dinner, mistletoe and a tree? Or ignore it completely because of Ilan?*

She knew Christmas was not part of the Jewish faith and she wasn't even sure how it was celebrated in Cyprus.

Lucy placed decorations on the tree – a robin here and a bauble there. A few more, then some tinsel and she stepped back to admire her handiwork. She thought about the two people she knew so well yet had never met. She wondered how she would feel if she met them. Especially Jennifer.

Would we get on? Could we chat for hours, comparing our lives and our likes and dislikes? Would we laugh at the same jokes? Have we similar taste in movies, and music, and literature? Would we agree or disagree on politics? Movies? Fashion?

Back in the summer, when Lucy wakened from the dream in which Jennifer had googled her name, she decided two could play the same game. So, one evening when she finished researching a project for her class, she typed Jennifer's name into Google and did what everyone does in the twenty-first century. She had a good rummage around in the life of the woman she knew only from her dreams. It took only a few clicks to find Jennifer's Twitter account, Facebook page and her design website.

Lucy read the reviews on the website and all of them were good. Jennifer had received five-star ratings across the board. She spent another fifteen minutes looking at the various designs – some conceptual and some actual home interiors that she had designed either from her own ideas or from the customers. *Nice, but not my cup of tea.*

Jennifer's Twitter account hadn't been used in ages. Her Facebook page was a mixture of personal and professional with more emphasis on the professional and it was linked to her website. Aside from a few landscape photos and one or two close-up photos of what she had ordered for lunch or dinner – mostly fish dishes – there were only old photos of Jennifer herself and certainly none of Ilan. It didn't take Lucy long to realise that Jennifer didn't give much away online with regard to her personal life.

A part of her would love to meet Jennifer. She remembered Charlie suggesting a holiday in Cyprus. She said no at the time, an emphatic no, but now when she thought about it, wouldn't it be the coolest thing in the world to go on a package holiday to Cyprus and meet them?

But meeting Ilan in person?

Tempting but probably not a good idea, considering what I know about him. And I'd probably blush and go weak at the knees if he flashed that smile of his.

Just one more little bird to attach to a branch. Maybe it's a robin, maybe not. I can't tell sometimes.

Lucy hung the last ornament and switched on the twinkling lights. She sat back on her knees to admire her handiwork.

'Bugger!' The tree lights flickered on then off, then on for a few seconds, then went off completely.

There wasn't time to fiddle with them, checking every single bulb for the loose one, but she did it anyway. Up the stepladder, working each bulb from the top until about halfway down, one seemed loose. She carefully tightened it and to her relief the lights came on again. Fingers crossed, they would remain on, twinkling merrily the way Christmas tree lights were supposed to twinkle.

Lucy sat down on the floor awhile staring at the lights as they blinked on and off. She was completely mesmerised by them. They reminded her of... something she couldn't quite put her finger on.

Something connected to hospitals maybe? Like the flashing lights on a life support machine, except there was no steady accompanying beeping. It really is hypnotic. It almost makes me want to close my eyes and just drift away.

She was so engrossed that she did not hear the front door opening and Charlie calling her name.

'Lucy? Hey, Lucy?'

She blinked and looked up at him with a smile. 'You're home early.'

'Early? I'm late. It's six-thirty. How long have you been sitting there?'

'A few minutes, that's all. The lights went out so I had to check every bulb until I found the loose one. I got them going again and I was watching to make sure they were okay.'

He caught her hand as she got to her feet. 'My God, you're freezing! Are you sure it was only a few minutes?'

'Well, maybe it was about ten or fifteen minutes,' Lucy replied then glanced at her watch. It read a quarter to seven. *How on earth did I sit here for two hours?*

It was as if she had fallen into a trance staring at the blinking lights. Once again, the nagging feeling something was wrong with her clutched at her mind.

She smiled at Charlie and planted a kiss on his cheek, refusing to give in to her fear. His arms slipped around her waist and he pulled her close to him into a tight embrace. Lucy rested her head on his shoulder and relaxed against him, his warmth surrounding her.

'Have we time?' she suggested, giving him a meaningful look.

'No. We need to shower and change.'

'Not even for a quickie? In the shower? We could save time that way.'

A gleam appeared in Charlie's eyes.

'Race you!' Lucy yelled and bolted for the stairs. A second later Charlie was hot on her heels, his hands on her hips, practically pushing her up the stairs. She peeled off her sweater and undid her jeans, almost falling as she kicked them off but Charlie caught her by the arm to steady her. She was down to her underwear off by the time they got to the bathroom. Charlie turned on the water and stripped off his own clothes. He kissed her as he undid her bra and helped her step out of her panties.

Lucy could barely see through the steam in the bathroom but she found her way into the shower and stood underneath the powerful jet, relishing the heat as the hot water cascaded over her body. Charlie stood behind her, his arms around her, pulling her towards him. He lifted her hair to one side and kissed her neck and shoulder, nipping and teasing, as his hands found her breasts, squeezing gently. She moaned in response.

Closing her eyes, Lucy pressed her hands against the tiled walls and gasped with pleasure as Charlie entered her from behind. It was hard and fast and she was forced against the wall as the water sprayed over them and the hot steam encircled them. His arms held her in place despite the slippery surface and his mouth nuzzled her throat and neck.

Her orgasm coursed through her, leaving her weak and thankful for Charlie's arms still around her, holding her up. She moaned in pleasure and turned around to kiss him.

'Happy Christmas pet,' he grinned.

'I beg your pardon?'

'That was your prezzie.'

Lucy glared at him through the steam.

'Well, you did say you wanted something different this year,' he shrugged. 'It was a toss-up between this and a gift voucher.'

'A gift voucher for how much?'

'Um, well I was tempted to push the boat out and buy one for a tenner,' he told her, still grinning from ear to ear. 'I'm ten quid up now.'

'Cheeky bastard! Get out of here so I can get showered and ready.' Shooing him out, she reached for the bottle of shampoo.

Lucy washed and dried her hair in record time. Some carefully applied make-up and, after a frustrating ten minutes trying on different outfits, she finally decided on a red top with a plunging V-neck, black leggings and the earrings Charlie bought her for her last birthday.

Despite the shower, sex, and the lost time in front of the tree, Lucy had a few moments to enjoy a glass of wine before the doorbell sounded the arrival of Claire and Gavin.

They were carrying a bottle of wine each and two wrapped Christmas presents. Lucy squealed like a pre-teen at a boy-band concert when she found hers contained a set of beautiful copper-coloured tea light holders. The other present was a bottle of expensive malt whiskey. Charlie did a near perfect imitation of Lucy's delighted squeal.

The evening had been great fun. After dinner, lots of alcohol was downed and the conversations varied from one topic to the next – the house and the work they had done, being one of the main topics.

Charlie disappeared upstairs just before one o'clock, yawning loudly and pleading exhaustion as he bade them goodnight. A short time later Gavin was snoring loudly on the sofa leaving Lucy and Claire alone to chat and continue drinking.

Claire decided this was a good time to bring up the subject of dreams, but Lucy shook her head.

'Some other time,' she told her friend.

'But are you still dreaming those same dreams?' Claire was nothing if not persistent.

'Yeah, I'm still dreaming about Ilan and Jennifer,' Lucy sighed and took another sip of whiskey. She really didn't want to discuss it, but there was no escaping Claire tonight. She wouldn't elaborate any further, however. In her opinion, they were friends of hers that Claire had never met and therefore she didn't *need* to know anything about them.

Claire switched tactics. 'Have you spoken to the doctor again... about the dreams? What about the sleeping tablets? Did they make any difference?'

'That was ages ago. I did try one, just after I got the prescription, but I still spent the night dreaming. All the next day I was groggy and half-asleep and I felt like shit, so I chucked them in the bin.'

'Didn't you see the doctor again and tell her the dreams happened every night and they were in sequence?'

'No.'

'Why not?' Claire sat up straighter on the sofa.

Lucy shrugged. 'Because they don't bother me any longer, and I didn't see any reason to talk to a doctor. I've told you before, and I know it sounds crazy, but I enjoy them.' *And what's even crazier is that I might not be sitting here having this conversation because Jennifer is dreaming it.*

A cold sense of dread ran down her spine and Lucy shivered despite the warmth of the fire.

'Okay, I get that that you enjoy them,' Claire said. 'But aren't you worried about what's causing them?'

Uncomfortable now, Lucy shuffled closer to the edge of the sofa before tucking her legs underneath her. She turned towards her friend and frowned. 'No, not really. I mean, when I went to the doctor, she checked my blood pressure and it was fine. And nothing weird showed up in any of the tests from the two gallons of blood the nurse sucked out of me.'

'Vampire Sue? Or was it the other one?' Claire asked.

'It was the other one, but she's becoming as bad as Sue.'

'Oh, I hate her. She's evil.'

'Isn't she just? Anyway, they couldn't find anything weird in my blood and I feel okay so, yeah, I'm not worried.'

'But maybe there's something wrong with your head – with your mind. Maybe its psycha – psychie – oh bugger – psycho...logical.' Claire got there in the end but she was having more and more difficulty pronouncing some of her words. 'Whoa! I think uh... I think I need to pace myself a bit.'

She set her wine glass down on the coffee table and stared at it as if it had bitten her.

'You're well into your second bottle, or is that your third one? I think it's a little too late to be starting to pace yourself,' Lucy told her.

'Yeah, I suppose that's true,' Claire picked up the glass again and took another mouthful.

Lucy's eyes narrowed. 'Do you think so?'

'About your head or about my alcohol consumption?'

'About me?'

'I dunno, Lucy, but maybe you should consider it. I mean, seriously, who dreams the way you do?'

'Well, she does, I think.'

'Who?'

'Jennifer. The woman in my dreams.'

'Aye. If she exists at all, that is. She could be a figment of your crazy-in-the-head imagination, like an imaginary friend or something. Or maybe you have some sort of personality disorder.'

'Ahh, gee thanks.' Lucy stuck her tongue out in response to Claire's suggestion.

'I'm just saying. Normal people don't dream someone else's life every night,' Claire took another mouthful of wine. 'Not every single night and not in the way you do.'

'So, you think I'm not normal?' Lucy asked, glaring at the woman she considered her best friend since primary school.

'Dear God, woman. I've never, ever thought of you as normal. Fuck's sake! I wouldn't be friends with you if you were normal. Your *kind* of crazy suits *my* kind of crazy!'

They clinked their glasses together in a toast to their friendship.

'Seriously Lucy,' Claire continued. 'I think you should talk to someone. Not a GP but maybe a specialist or expert of some kind who deals with sleep disorders. For all you know it might be a common enough occurrence within medical circles, but just not commonly known.'

'What would I tell Charlie? He knows nothing at all about my dreams. I couldn't suddenly announce that I was going to see a sleep shrink, or whatever.'

'You don't have to tell him anything. Just go. Make up some excuse to be away for a day or two.'

'Oh yeah, like that would work. He'd want to come with me.'

'Then we'll go. You and me. Tell him it's a girl's only weekend. Or, we could make it my hen party. I never had a hen party.'

'And whose fault was that? Running off to get married the way you did.'

'Yeah, well okay, it was on the spur of the moment. Gavin planned it all and didn't tell me. But seriously, we could go for a day or two and you could see a doctor and no one would know. That would work.'

Lucy rubbed the side of her head. Could there be something wrong with her? Could it be some undetected, hard-to-diagnose illness? Or some sort of psychological episode, or episodes? Whatever it was, it wasn't natural and maybe she should see someone about it. But who and where?

'I'll give it some consideration,' she said.

'Serious consideration?'

'Yeah.'

'Good girl,' Claire said and glanced at the clock above the mantelpiece. It read two fifty-five in the morning. 'Now, maybe we should seriously consider going to bed.'

'How are you going to waken Gavin?'

'I'm tempted to leave him here. I love him more than life itself, but his snoring makes me want to press a pillow over his face.'

'Get earplugs. And no offence Claire, but I really don't want the loveable big, noisy lump lying there drooling and farting on my new leather sofa.'

Claire sighed. 'Okay, help me get him at least half-awake and up the stairs.'

It was almost three-thirty when Lucy finally crawled into bed beside a gently snoring Charlie. Nothing at all like the loud thundering, rumbling noises Gavin produced. *And Charlie doesn't drool. Or fart. Well, not that often.*

Almost asleep, she snuggled against his back, wrinkling her nose at the smell of the cigars Gavin and he had smoked out on the patio earlier. *I hope he doesn't start smoking again.*

Chapter 18 - Lucy's Dream

By the time she had punched through the automatic options and reached a human voice on the other end, only to be put on hold, Jennifer almost ended the call. The number she had dialled was for the Israeli embassy in Nicosia.

She blanked out the awful music and stretched her leg underneath the desk to retrieve the pen she had dropped. She was still stretching for it when the music disappeared and was replaced by a voice in her ear.

'Um, hello,' Jennifer forgot about the pen and stood up quickly. 'I was wondering if it would be possible to speak to... Chana?'

'Who is calling please?'

'Hi. My name is Jennifer. Jennifer Scott. I'm a... friend of Ilan Ben-Levi.'

'Oh, hi Jennifer. One moment please. I will get Chana for you.'

On hold again, different music this time, but still as annoying, Jennifer clutched her phone in her hand and paced the floor. Calling Ilan's work was probably not the best idea in the world but, even if she couldn't speak to him, she needed to connect with him in some way. Lucy's notion, or rather Lucy's friend's notion, that there might be a medical reason for the dreams disturbed her more than she cared to admit. But there was nothing she could do about it at the moment and the best way to take her mind off it was to focus on Ilan.

The music disappeared and a familiar cheery female voice with an English accent replied. 'Jennifer! Hello! It is so lovely to hear from you again. How are you, my dear? Is everything okay?'

'Um... yes. I was wondering if you know when Ilan will be home.'

There was a pause at the other end before Chana spoke. 'I'm afraid I can't tell you that, Jennifer. Is there something I can help you with?'

This was the third time she had spoken to Chana; a woman she imagined as middle-aged, late fifties or early sixties possibly, and of small stature. She had an English accent, which Jennifer found comforting, and the stern, clipped voice of a school mistress moulded in the Miss Jean Brodie style. *Or she could be a Goth or an aging hippy for all I know.*

The first time she had spoken to Chana, Jennifer had been in a panic about the house purchase. Ilan was away and she was left to deal with it on her own. A crappy day, and a moment of weakness at the thought of buying a house she could not afford, forced her to try and make contact with him somehow. Just to hear his voice for a couple of minutes. She never thought it possible, but she tried anyway. And Chana told her to wait by the phone and she would try and have Ilan contact her. When her ringtone sounded, louder than normal it seemed, Jennifer yelped in surprise.

'Jennifer? Hello? Are you okay?'

It was him! Calling via satellite phone from somewhere in the world.

'Yes. Everything's okay. I love you and I miss you so much.'

She knew better than to ask questions about where he was and when would he be home.

'I --- be home ------- can.' The static caused Ilan's voice to fade in and out and Jennifer missed most of what he was saying. But she got the gist of it.

His words still broken by static, Ilan asked about the house and, just hearing his voice, vanquished her concerns. She told him it was going smoothly and would be theirs very soon.

'That --- great,' he said. 'I --- --- --- see --- and you. I love --- so ---' Jennifer managed to tell him the same before the call dropped out and he was gone. It had lasted less than a minute but it was enough. His voice alone lifted her spirits.

That had been a year and a half ago and since then Ilan had been back and forward several times. Sometimes away for only a week or so, sometimes longer. Then home until he was needed again. On one occasion he was only back for two days before he answered the phone during dinner and left immediately, grabbing a piece of chicken off his plate as he kissed her goodbye.

But this time he had been gone for over two months and Jennifer was worried about him. It was the notion that something had happened to him that had prompted her to phone Chana.

'Yeah,' Jennifer replied. 'I'm concerned about Ilan. It's been ages now and he usually isn't working for this length of time. Do you know when he's likely to be coming home?'

'I can understand your concerns, Jennifer,' Chana told her. 'I'm afraid I am unable to tell you much. But if it is any comfort to you, I can tell you that all is well with him and that he will be home as soon as he possibly can.'

Well, that's a bit of a bog-standard response.

'I'm relieved to know that, thank you. But when?' Jennifer thought she could hear what sounded like an exasperated sigh before Chana replied.

'I cannot answer that, Jennifer. I'm sorry.'

'I just want to know if he's okay. I want to know when he's coming home. I want him here with me because I want us to be together the way we'd planned.' *I sound like a petulant child. I want, I want, I want.*

'I'm sorry for bothering you, Chana. I'm just a bit... well, I just feel... so alone right now.' *Trouble is, I'm not alone. You see, there's this woman in my head...*

'I do understand. And you are not alone, trust me. I spoke to Ilan before he left for... work. He told me he loves you very, very much. I have never seen him so relaxed and at ease with himself. And so happy. All he could talk about was you. How much you mean to him and how much he is looking forward to spending the rest of his life with you.'

Another bog-standard response. Thanks, Chana.

'That's good to know. I do know he loves me, but it's nice to hear it from someone else.' Jennifer was proud of her own bog-standard response.

'Jennifer, please understand. What Ilan does is very important. He would be with you if he could. But at the moment he needs to be, well, you know what I mean.'

'I know. I do understand. I just get so lonely without him. When we bought this house, I imagined him here with me, maybe not all the time, but at least some of the time. I'm sorry for being such a nuisance. I just miss him so much.'

'You're not a nuisance dear,' Chana told her. 'You know you can phone me any time you want. For anything, even if it's just for a chat when you are feeling lonely.'

'I know. I really appreciate it. Thank you so much.'

Jennifer said goodbye to Chana and ended the call with a sigh. Even though Chana was only a voice on the other end of the phone it had been good to talk to her. The woman had been friendly and interested. But friendly and interested didn't help her all that much right now.

Lucy was fortunate in that she shared her life completely with Charlie, other than the hours when they were both at work. They were home together every evening and their weekends were spent doing normal weekend stuff together. They were a team and Jennifer wanted her life with Ilan to be exactly like that. But he was away somewhere, doing God knows what, and she was alone and missing him.

Okay. This is part of being in love with a… what do they call them? A spook. I'm in love with a spook and I'm gonna have to put up with shit like this. But I'm a strong, independent woman. I can look after myself and I don't need a man at my beck and call twenty-four/seven to help me change a lightbulb or paint a ceiling. Or keep me company for that matter. I have my own life and my career and if that's the way it must be then I'll love him when he's here and I'll wait for him when he isn't.

It sounded good in Jennifer's head. But when she looked around the kitchen and saw only one coffee mug sitting on the counter, loneliness engulfed her once more and left her feeling no better than she felt before her phone call to Chana.

Chapter 19 - Jennifer's Dream

Charlie held Lucy's hand in his as they walked up the path from the back of the house towards the hill. Carly, their two-year old black Labrador zig-zagged back and forth in front of them.

They had adopted Carly from the local animal shelter in January and it took her only a day or two to worm her way into their hearts and their lives. Lucy wanted a rescue and they looked at several, but were having difficulty making up their minds and the cuteness overload was becoming unbearable. Their choice had been narrowed down to three puppies when they spotted Carly. Staff at the rescue centre told Lucy she had been surrendered the previous Christmas as an abandoned puppy – dumped, shivering and terrified at the side of a busy road. A motorist had almost run her over but caught her and brought her to the shelter. A good home had been found, but the elderly owner had died in January. Unable to keep the dog themselves and, not knowing what else to do, his family had brought her back to the shelter.

The young dog was depressed and pining for her home. No one seemed interested in her in the three months she had been in their kennels.

'Everyone wants the pups. No one wants an adult dog, even an adult as young and as beautiful as Carly. It's such a shame,' the woman in charge of the shelter continued. 'She's one of our favourites. Well trained and such a loving, playful dog. Good with kids too, as she was used to the owner's young grandchildren since she was a small puppy.'

Carly had taken one look at Charlie and almost fell over herself greeting him. It was love at first sight for both of them and, after the home checks had been carried out and the paperwork signed, Carly became theirs.

The overnight frost was beginning to lift and the April sunshine gave a hint of warmth to the air though the frozen grass was still crunchy beneath their feet. Lucy smiled as she took in the views.

'What's that smile for?' he asked.

She squeezed his hand and smiled even more. Her eyes met his and her face broke into the biggest grin he had ever seen.

'What?' Charlie asked with a curious frown on his face.

'Claire's pregnant.'

'Wonderful. I'm delighted for her and Gavin,' Charlie said, giving her hand a gentle squeeze. 'So, I'm guessing you're looking forward to being an auntie, of sorts?'

'Well yeah, I suppose I am, but I'm not sure if I'll have much time because I'm pregnant too,' Lucy told him, suddenly blurting it out.

Charlie stopped walking and stared at her for what seemed an eternity.

He doesn't want it.

Lucy's eyes welled with tears, her emotions suddenly all over the place. Then, to her relief, Charlie grinned as he threw back his head and let out the loudest yell she had ever heard. Carly jumped and barked loudly, partially in fear at the sudden noise and partially because she could sense the excitement in her humans and had to be involved. She matched Charlie's yelling laughter with her barks until Lucy had to gently shush the two of them.

Charlie began a victory dance sending Carly off on another barking session. Then he stopped and looked at his wife. He was still grinning from ear to ear.

'Pregnant? You're really pregnant?'

'I'm really pregnant.'

With a grin, Charlie's eyes travelled down to his groin. 'Well played, big fella! Ya did me proud!'

Lucy felt the laughter bubbling up inside her and tried to force it into submission. This was a serious moment and it should be treated as such. They were going to have a baby and from this moment on they would be no longer a couple but a proper family unit. It would have been nice to be all grown-up and serious but, watching Charlie congratulating his penis, giving it the thumbs up and telling it how wonderful it was, being serious was impossible. Her laughter began slowly – a grin on her face that she tried to halt by biting the inside of her lips. Then it became a giggle and that was it. She couldn't stop. She laughed so hard she was doubled over, holding her ribs. Carly sat down and gazed in confused wonder at this human making such strange noises.

Lucy attempted to speak but couldn't manage it. She clutched Charlie's arm and held on for dear life. Her laughter was infectious and soon he was in the same state. They held on to one another until gradually their laughter subsided and their eyes met.

'Did you say something about Claire being pregnant?' Charlie asked jokingly.

'Uh, yeah. I think I mentioned it.'

'Copycat!'

'It's me that's the copycat,' Lucy told him. 'She beat us to it. Or rather she and Gavin beat us to it.'

'Our one might be younger but it will definitely be smarter and better looking,' he bragged.

'Aww look at you, the proud daddy already.' Lucy grinned at him.

'You don't know the half of it pet,' he pulled her close to him, wrapping her tightly in his arms and kissing her tenderly. 'I love you so much and I am so happy and proud of you. And me little swimmers!'

Tears of happiness filled her eyes as she stood there, while the warmth of the sunshine battled the cold wind that was blowing over the hills. She snuggled close to him, feeling his strength and love enveloping her, keeping her warm and safe. Lucy knew this was the happiest she had ever been in her life. This man, this place, this happiness was all she had ever dreamed of, and all she wanted in her world.

Chapter 20 - Lucy's Dream

With a cat-like stretch Jennifer opened her eyes and made the transition out of Lucy's life back into her own. She reached for Ilan but his side of the bed was empty. She needed to check on him but for a moment or two she was content to relax in the comfort of her bed.

Hmmm. Lucy is preggers. This could be interesting.

Pregnancy and motherhood had never been of interest to her and Jennifer could not feel any emotional resonance at Lucy's condition other than curiosity and concern about what, if any, effect it might have on her.

Am I gonna have morning sickness? Weight gain? Weird food cravings? If I do, how on earth do I explain it to Ilan?

Aside from that, it would be interesting in a detached way, to experience it through her dreams.

She remembered the boredom when friends regaled her with tales of their pregnancies. And from what she had been told about it, childbirth was an ordeal to be avoided at all costs.

She also remembered how she gradually parted company with several friends once they became parents. Women who, like her, had partied until the wee hours – often staggering home when the sun was coming up. Then it became nothing but babies, babies, babies and Jennifer's eyes glazed over as she fixed an interested smile on her face. Her brain turned to mush as her friends talked about nothing but their precious darlings.

They were so fixated on their little humans she had no other choice but to retreat before she went insane.

And retreat Jennifer did. They were happy. She was happy that they were happy. She just couldn't stand talking about babies and toddlers every time she met them. She gradually declined invitations, yet still maintained a casual friendship, keeping it distant enough to ensure she wasn't called on to babysit or to help at birthday parties. The very notion of doing that terrified her.

Thinking about it now that she was in a settled relationship with Ilan, she asked herself if she had changed over the years.

How would I feel if I was pregnant? In a state of panic? Or happy? Amazed at the thought of another human being – a perfect combination of Ilan and me – growing inside me? Would it look like him or me?

Jennifer lay in the comfort of the king-sized bed wondering how much different her life would be if she had chosen to go down the road of motherhood. Imagining what it would be like if she had one or even two children – a toddler and a new-born baby perhaps?

Well, for starters I wouldn't be lying here relaxing. I'd already be up from the crack of dawn feeding and dressing the little monsters.

Showering quickly, Jennifer slid into an old pair of jeans pulled on a vest top and made her way barefoot to the kitchen.

This is why I don't want kids. I can go barefoot all day without worrying about crippling myself on a Lego brick!

A banana skin and an apple core lay on the counter. *At least he's eaten something.*

She dumped the remains of the fruit into the recycling bin and spotted Ilan outside on the terrace, lying on one of the sun loungers. His eyes were closed and his head tilted upwards as he caught some early morning sunshine on his face.

Jennifer rapped the window to get his attention and indicated if he wanted some coffee. His thumbs up signal back to her told her he did.

While she waited for the coffee to brew, Jennifer opened her laptop and quickly checked her emails. She deleted the usual spam and fired off replies to the ones she needed to deal with. One from Tony with a couple of contracts she might be interested in and a reminder about dinner with Shirley and him the week after next.

'Yes, I'll speak to the clients and get back to you on it, and I have the dinner date in my planner. I'm looking forward to the evening.'

The next one made Jennifer smile. It was from an elderly Norwegian couple who had retired to Cyprus and commissioned her to decorate their new villa. The message was full of praise for her work and their delight at the finished product. Jennifer loved the part where they said they felt right at home, only much warmer. That always had been her goal and she was pleased she was achieving her ambition not only in hotels and resorts but also in private homes. They finished the email with a promise to recommend her to any of their friends who were thinking of moving to the island, and an invitation to dinner with them some evening that would be convenient for her.

She considered her reply and began to type. **'Dear Inga and Petter, Thank you so much for your kind words. I'm delighted you are happy with my interpretation of what you wanted in your new home. Please let me know what date suits you, as I would love to have dinner with you both and once again see the house in its finished state. Best wishes, Jennifer.'** Before she sent the email, she deleted the words – in its finished state – and replaced them with the more personal – **now you have moved in and made it your own.**

The next one was from her brother. A brief line saying he might come to visit this summer with the family.

'Yes, please!'

The last email was from her father. He was also considering a trip to Cyprus. Possibly in the summer to catch up with her, but also to watch the annual Cyprus Car Rally, and could she please put him up on the sofa for a week?

'Of course. I told you I have a spare room, didn't I? As for the rally, I'll get you a programme so we'll know where to go to watch the stages. I haven't been to a rally in ages and I've missed it, so I'll go with you to a couple of them. Ilan might too. I'll ask him.'

Maybe her father would take a look at Ilan's old car. It was on its last legs and needed some serious mechanical work done to it to keep it running properly, but he refused to trade it in.

He really loves that car. Maybe dad can keep it alive a little longer for him.

Ilan remained stretched out on one of the sun loungers when Jennifer stepped out carrying two large mugs of coffee. His eyes were still closed and he seemed to have gone back to asleep. Carlos, the ginger tomcat she had recently adopted, was stretched out along Ilan's leg. With a hiss and a snarl, he launched himself off Ilan's leg to run and hide behind the nearest plant pot.

'Right back at ya Carlos, you ungrateful little bastard,' she hissed back lovingly at the glaring cat and parked herself on the other lounger. Ilan opened his eyes, muttered a curse under his breath and rubbed his leg where the cat's claws had dug through his jeans.

'Todah,' he said, sitting up before taking the mug from her. He reached for the pack of cigarettes and lighter on the small table near him but changed his mind and took a sip of coffee instead. Jennifer noticed two butts already on the plate he used for an ashtray but he rarely smoked so there was no point in commenting. He would quit again in a day or two.

Although they were not as dark and angry now, the bruises on the side of his face seemed more pronounced in the morning sunlight. Yet she knew these were insignificant compared to the bruises and cuts on his abdomen and ribcage.

Normally Ilan came home reasonably happy and healthy. This time, for whatever reason, he was battered and bruised and would take a while to heal. But his mental recovery concerned Jennifer. This latest mission had taken its toll on him and it was her responsibility to guide him through the trauma he had suffered – the details of which he initially refused, despite her concerned questioning, to elaborate on.

But Ilan was not someone who enjoyed being taken by the hand. At the very least, he would permit her to quietly support him while he made his own journey. In other words, leave him alone and allow him to work it out for himself. Chana had told her this was always the best course of action and it was something she was quickly learning to do.

But it bothered her that he shut her out.

Initially Jennifer hadn't registered the degree of his mental and emotional trauma, so pleased was she to have him home. But the haunted look in his eyes and the weary, despairing slump of his shoulders, relayed a truth that he could not mask. The way he held her so tightly, as though he would be lost if he let her go, told her he was suffering from more than just the physical injuries he had received at the hands of his captors.

On his arrival home yesterday evening, Ilan embraced his wife at the door and shrugged off her concerned questions about the marks on his face. It was only later when he stepped out of the shower that Jennifer saw the other bruises.

'What happened to you?' she said, catching his arm and turning him around to face her.

'It's nothing,' Ilan replied, wrapping a large towel around his waist and attempting to make light of the situation. 'You should see the other guy!'

The knuckles of both hands were bruised and scraped. It was obvious he had fought back. But when she saw the full extent of his injuries, she realised this was a fight he had barely won.

'You need to see a doctor, Ilan. You might have broken ribs, or internal injuries.'

'No.' Ilan's voice was harsh. 'It looks worse than it is. I have already been attended to.'

'When?'

'When we were taken back to Israel to be debriefed. I was treated by a military doctor. My injuries are not serious, I promise,' he said with an attempt to reassure her. But she wasn't convinced and the worried look on her face told him she wouldn't be reassured so easily.

'Neshama honestly, they are bruises. They'll disappear in a few days and I can assure you I have no broken ribs or internal injuries. I am okay. I'm merely a little stiff and sore, but I'll recover.'

Reluctantly Jennifer let the matter drop. If Ilan wanted to tell her what had happened he would do so on his own terms, and in his own time

Jennifer had remained silent, biting her lip nervously while he dried himself, pulled on a T-shirt and baggy sweat pants and headed into the kitchen where he cracked open a bottle of whiskey. He poured out a large measure.

With the glass in one hand and the bottle in the other Ilan sat down on the sofa in the living room and began to drink. A long mouthful at first, drinking half the contents of the glass. He stopped and took a deep breath, almost a sigh, before proceeding to sip occasionally while he stared at the darkened television screen with no inclination to switch it on.

'Ilan, please...' Jennifer sat down beside him. She felt she had to try again. 'Tell me what happened.'

He poured another whiskey and reached for her hand squeezing it gently. The physical connection between them seemed to be helping, or maybe it was the whiskey, and Jennifer could sense his body beginning to relax. He carefully shifted his position on the sofa so that he was partially facing her. He took another long drink of whiskey and Jennifer wished she had poured one for herself.

'Things... went... wrong,' he said, forcing the words out. His mouth was a grim line and his eyes narrowed as he remembered. 'We were compromised and we became... trapped. Some of my team, my people, were killed... then I was captured and...'

'How many were killed?' Jennifer asked, surprised he was talking about it.

'Two. And two were badly wounded. One of them died later, so in total we... I... lost three.'

'What happened? What went wrong?' she asked.

'No matter how much you plan,' he said. 'No matter how much detail you go into – you go over and over every possible scenario from conception to resolution – sometimes you cannot allow for simple bad luck. That's all it was. Simple bad luck.'

'How did you get away?' Jennifer reached for his glass and took a sip of the burning liquid then handed it back to him.

'When we failed to report in, our exfiltration team realised something was amiss and came to retrieve us. They managed to recover us, but they… lost two of their own in the process. Too many deaths occurred,' Ilan told her as he briefly closed his eyes and Jennifer saw a glimpse of how much he was suffering at the losses.

'I am so sorry Ilan. Did you know them well, the ones who were killed?'

'Yes. I have worked with them on many occasions.'

Words became useless and they sat together silently. Ilan in memory of the comrades and the friends he had lost and Jennifer thinking about how close she had come to losing *him.*

'If you had died,' she asked eventually. 'How would I have known?'

'Someone would have contacted you.'

'Would it have been Chana?'

'Yes. It most likely would have been Chana.'

He carefully put his arm around her, trying not to wince in pain in the process. 'I didn't die Jennifer, so the point is moot. I've no intention of dying.'

'But you could have.'

'But I did not,' he told her. 'I need to explain. I'm not normally involved in operations such as this. The work I do is more… behind the scenes… sometimes more covert. But on this occasion… a visual identification was necessary and I was the only one in a position to do it. I had to be there. Do you understand?'

'I think so. Yes.'

Satisfied, he nodded. 'I think it's bedtime now. I've told you more than enough, probably more than I should have. Would you mind if we do not speak of it any more tonight?'

'Yeah, okay. But are you going to be okay?'

He nodded and reached for the bottle of whiskey but Jennifer stopped him with her hand. With a look he asked for more. Jennifer considered it for a second.

He really shouldn't. But I want a drink too. And if I leave him to it, he'll drink the whole bottle.

'Let me get some ice and we'll both have a drink. Celebrate your home coming.'

She jumped up and made her way quickly to the kitchen where she filled a tumbler with ice cubes and got a glass for herself. Ilan poured two hefty measures and added the ice. They drank slowly and quietly, both lost in their individual thoughts. Despite everything, Jennifer was just glad to have him home. That was enough for now.

'I am glad to be home,' he told her, as though reading her mind.

'I know,' she replied, touching her glass to his in a silent toast. The ice cubes tinkled as they swam around in the amber liquid. Jennifer took a sip, savouring the taste. The burning warmth of the whiskey and the cold ice against her lips.

We'll get through this. He'll be fine in a day or two and things will get back to normal. He could have been killed but he wasn't. I'll take that as a win.

Jennifer finished her drink and stood up. She took his hand in hers and gently pulled him to his feet and led him down the hall towards their bedroom, thankful to have him home.

That talk last night was good for him. Now here he is sunbathing on the terrace, almost as if nothing happened. Almost.

'Did you feed the cats?' she asked, sipping at her coffee, still unsure how much he wanted to talk. He was gradually becoming the man she knew. But he still had some distance to go and she knew she had to tread carefully with him.

'Yes. Well, I fed the two at the door. The others – I presume there are others – have not appeared yet.'

'It's okay. They usually show up later.'

'How many are there now?'

'Um, I'm not sure. Four possibly. Yeah, about four. Or maybe six. And a lovely little black kitten that only showed up last Tuesday. She's a female, I think, and very young. As soon as she's ready I'll catch her and make an appointment with the vet to have her spayed.'

Ilan laughed out loud. He knew she was joking. They only had two regular cats, plus the kitten. The other two showed up twice a day for food then disappeared again immediately.

Hearing his laughter, Jennifer felt her heart brighten. He was slowly coming out of the black mood of despair and grief that surrounded him.

'You do love your strays, my darling,' he said with a smile.

'You're the stray I love the most,' she said giving him her best leer and mentally crossing her fingers. He threw back his head and laughed and she breathed a sigh of relief. It was a genuine laugh this time, full of the humour she had come to know, and love so well.

He's going to be okay. His bruises will heal and, more importantly, his grief will find its own place in his heart. It'll probably remain there for a while, but he'll get through this.

Chapter 21 - Jennifer's Dream

'Charlie! Get up here! Now! Please!' Lucy yelled from the bathroom.

At the sound of her voice Charlie stopped dead in his tracks, the opened jar of coffee in one hand and a spoon in the other.

He had left Lucy in her dressing gown, brushing her teeth and admiring her swollen belly, to make her a cup of tea and a slice of toast with a banana and some cheese on it. Bananas and cheese had recently overtaken salted peanuts and strawberry jam in the craving ratings.

'Just be thankful she isn't into Mars Bars, barbequed ribs and fishcakes. On the same plate!' Gavin had told him with a shudder as they compared pregnancy notes one afternoon when they escaped to the pub for a much-needed pint.

'Charlie! I need you up here! Right now!' Lucy shrieked more loudly this time.

He would have heard her from a mile away never mind the kitchen. She had encountered either an axe-wielding serial killer or a little spider. Knowing Lucy, it was most likely a little spider.

'Yeah. I'm coming.' He put the lid back on the coffee jar, switched off the kettle and ignored the two slices of bread that popped up in the toaster. He took a small tumbler from the cupboard, tore off a square of kitchen roll and went upstairs to her aid. Maybe he could rescue the spider before she slammed a heavy book down on top of it.

He discovered neither a murderer nor a spider hiding in the bathroom. Just Lucy in her dressing gown, her eyes wide and filled with tears that threatened to overflow and spill down her face.

'What's wrong?'

'What's that for?' Her tears seemed to vanish as she pointed to the tumbler and the kitchen roll.

'I thought you'd found a spider.'

'And you were going to kill it with a square of kitchen roll?'

'No. I was going to catch it and put it outside,' he replied.

'Spiders do not deserve to exist,' she told him. 'Anyway, there isn't a spider.'

'So, what were you screaming about?'

'I think I'm going into labour. And I wasn't screaming.'

'Yeah, right,' he burst out laughing.

'I'm deadly serious Charlie. I'm in labour. The baby is on the way.'

He saw the look of fear in her eyes and his heart began to hammer in his chest. This was it. They were having a baby! He was going to be a father. He felt the weight of responsibility settle on his shoulders and he took a deep breath. There was no going back now.

'Right then. All right then,' he clapped his hands together with a smack then rubbed them in a let's-get-on-with-it gesture. He glanced around the bedroom until he found what he was looking for. The dark blue overnight bag that contained everything Lucy reckoned she needed for going into hospital. A couple of changes of clothes, her fluffy slippers, toiletries, make up, hairbrush, and two paperback books – a particularly gruesome murder mystery and a well-thumbed one called 'Childcare for Dummies'. She called it her 'how to' book, even though Claire, who was now the proud and happy – although continuously exhausted – mother of a two-month-old baby daughter, had told her to chuck it in the bin.

'There is no such thing as a 'how to' book when it comes to having a screaming baby in the house,' Claire informed them. 'We read almost all the baby books ever printed and we thought we knew everything. We did in theory. But nothing, nothing at all, can prepare you for the awful, exhausting reality of it.'

Gavin had agreed. 'I never knew weans could yell so loudly and at such a high pitch. It's like they're being murdered.'

Charlie picked up the bag. The weight of it surprised him. What the hell did she have in it? He knew better than to ask her.

'Right then,' he said. For the first time in nearly three years, he wanted a cigarette. He forced the thought away.

'Right then.' He knew he was repeating himself, but he suddenly found himself to be almost in the grip of a panic attack and, as a result, his vocabulary had forsaken him. Lucy stood there making no indication that she was planning to go anywhere, anytime soon. She seemed rooted to the floor.

'Lucy? Hey, Lucy?' He waved his hand in front of her eyes. Eyes that were two round saucers. She blinked a couple of times, then looked at him.

'I can't Charlie. I can't do this. I've changed my mind.'

'You've what?'

'I've changed my mind. Seriously, Charlie let's get another dog – a puppy. Or maybe a couple of alpacas. Or chickens. I don't want a baby. I want free range eggs every morning. Honestly, I've changed my mind. Let's get some hens instead.'

'It's a bit late to change your mind, love,' he said, although he was thinking the very same thing. Chickens would be easier to look after.

She whimpered in pain and clutched her stomach as a contraction reminded her there was no going back. No changing her mind.

'Oh shit. Charlie, this is really happening!'

'Okay. Right then. Let's go.'

Lucy took a step towards him, and then she remembered she was naked underneath her dressing gown. 'I need to get dressed first.'

'Throw your sweatpants and a T-shirt on. That's all you need. Do you want me to help you?'

'No. I'll manage. Go and bring the car round to the front door and switch off the tumble dryer at the mains, and the dishwasher too.' She was paranoid about leaving things switched on when they were out of the house. 'You might have to come back up and help me get down the stairs, though.'

Fourteen hours later an exhausted Lucy was still swearing like an old drunken sailor. She cursed the staff in the ward. She cursed everyone she had ever known right back to her primary school days. She cursed every actress who had given birth on television and made it look easy. She cursed Claire for phoning to see how she was doing.

'I'm fucking dying here! You told me this was a doddle, you bitch!' She screamed into the phone that Charlie was holding to her ear.

Claire quickly wished her good luck and said she would call her later. 'When you're feeling better, and er… up for a chat,' she said and quickly ended the call before Lucy could unleash another volley at her.

Lucy cursed the fact that men didn't give birth and, most of all, she cursed Charlie for 'getting your leg over and knocking me up, you evil bastard!'

A nurse quietly asked her if she would like some more pain medication.

'Of course, I want more fucking pain medication!' she snarled. 'Give it to me! Right now!'

She caught Charlie's eye and glared at him. 'What are you looking at?'

She was getting ready to physically attack him but one of the nurses got Charlie's attention and indicated she wished to speak to him. Charlie prised his hand out of Lucy's death-like grip and spoke quietly to the nurse.

'Is she okay?' he asked.

'She's fine,' the nurse told him. 'But the baby isn't quite ready to come out yet.'

'When will the… um… when will it, you know… happen?'

'It won't be long. Look, why don't you go and grab a cup of coffee for a few minutes. She seems to be taking it out on you and she might calm down a little if you were out of the room. Get a coffee and come back in about half an hour.'

'Look, I'm sorry about Lucy. I think she swore professionally in a past life and she's reliving some of it again.'

The nurse burst out laughing. 'It's nothing we haven't heard a hundred times before.'

'Maybe I'll bring an exorcist back with me,' he said, imagining green vomit and Lucy's head rotating full circle on her neck, like in the old movie.

The nurse laughed again and pushed him out the door towards the coffee machine.

Three hours later their beautiful daughter came kicking and screaming into the world. Although exhausted, Lucy was completely and overwhelmingly in love with her. She was also back in love with Charlie again – much to his relief.

Chapter 22 - Lucy's Dream

Jennifer cautiously opened her eyes, afraid for a moment that the dream had been real.

Oh God, that was awful. The pain! Why on earth do we go through that!

Yet, despite her horror at the process, she felt an unexpected wave of love and adoration for the tiny, screaming bundle Lucy held in her arms.

Ilan was beside her with his head propped up on one arm. He watched her intently, his other hand rested lightly on her hip.

'What were you dreaming about?' he asked.

She half turned to face him, enjoying the touch of his hand on her skin as it moved to explore her. As though he had forgotten what she felt like from the night before.

'What makes you think I was dreaming?'

'I was watching you while you were sleeping. Your eyes moved back and forth underneath your eyelids. It's called rapid eye movement and it...'

'I know what it's called,' she told him.

'The way your eyes were moving I'd guess you were having an extremely intense dream. Yet your body was completely still. That's not normal.'

'Okay, yes, I was dreaming,' she admitted.

'About me, I hope,' he smiled as his hand found its way to her breast.

'No Ilan, it wasn't about you,' Jennifer frowned and pulled away slightly. 'Do you want to hear something really weird?'

'Now you have me intrigued. Tell me.'

She sat up in bed and adjusted the pillow propped up behind her back. 'It was strange. I dreamt that I was giving birth.'

Surprised, Ilan tilted his head back in a questioning look. 'Do you want children? You have always said you didn't. Have you changed your mind?'

'What? God, no! I don't want kids. Ever!' *Especially not after that!*

'So, this was merely a dream?'

Jennifer was amused to see how relieved he looked.

'Why do you not want children, at least not any more than the one you have? Your daughter?' she asked.

He shrugged his shoulders. 'When Nurit was born she was premature and we almost lost her. My wife was pregnant when we got married. Yeah, I knocked her up. It was a – what do you call it? A shotgun wedding? Jewish style. We were engaged and planned on getting married sometime in the next year. But we were married within a week. Then Nurit was born early and it seemed she was going to die. Every day we watched her in that incubator, fighting desperately for her life, and we thought every day would be her last. Then she grew stronger, a little bit at a time, and we permitted a little bit of hope into our hearts.'

He smiled at the memory.

'She was a fighter – still is. And then one day the doctors told us we could take her home. The first time I held her in my arms… the love I felt for her was so powerful it frightened me. So much that I knew I could never go through that again. I love my daughter with all of my heart, she has grown into a fine young woman and I am so very proud of her, but she's the only child I will ever want or need.'

He pulled her close to him and she rested her head on his shoulder. 'I love you Jennifer. I want you and I need you and I love you with all my heart and soul. You are all I want in my life. I have no need for children to make us complete.'

'I'm glad,' she told him. 'I'm happy that it's just the two of us.'

'Of course, we always have the cats,' he said with a smile. 'Our lives wouldn't be complete without your stray cats.'

'Oh, yeah. Our furry children,' she laughed.

'Tell me more about your dream?' Ilan said, getting back to the subject that Jennifer would have preferred to avoid.

'It's not only one dream.'

'What do you mean?'

'Well, I've been having this recurring dream for ages now. I think it started roughly around the time you and I met – maybe sometime afterwards. I can't remember exactly when. And I think I told you about it at the time but you've probably forgotten. It was a dream about an old stone house in England, somewhere in Yorkshire maybe, and this couple who had bought it.'

'It sounds intriguing and yes, I vaguely remember you mentioned it at the time. I can't remember the details. But then you never said anything more about it so I never thought about it again.'

'I think I only mentioned it once in passing to you. But since then, I've been dreaming every night about that house and about the two people who live in it.'

'Okay, now you have me intrigued. But stop. Don't say anything more until I make coffee.'

Ilan threw back the bedsheet and climbed out of bed. He pulled on his jeans. To Jennifer's delight and distraction, he remained shirtless.

'Do you want coffee?' he asked.

'Yes please, but I'll get up too.'

She threw back the covers and swung her legs out of the bed. She dressed quickly in a pair of jeans and one of Ilan's old army T-shirts.

Before Jennifer could sit down at the table Ilan carried both mugs outside and parked himself at the small table on the terrace. He pulled a chair out for Jennifer and patted the cushion for her to join him.

The kitten, still nameless but part of the family now, watched them from the top of the wall behind the jasmine plants. Jennifer had the toy water pistol close to her and wouldn't hesitate to use it if the kitten peed in the plant pot.

'She has to learn that my plants are not litter trays,' Jennifer explained.

'Okay, tell me about your dreams?' Ilan resumed his interrogation.

Jennifer tried not to squirm. 'There really isn't a lot to tell. I keep having this dream. I think you would call it a recurring dream? Although a recurring dream tends to be the same... this one is more... more like a series.'

'Go on.'

'It's mostly about the couple in the house I told you about. They're married. He's a builder and she's a primary school teacher, although she only works part-time now – three days a week, I think. Anyway, his aunt died a while back and left him a considerable sum of money and they used it to buy this beautiful old stone farmhouse out in the country – in the Dales. That's a part of Yorkshire.'

'I know where it is.'

'Their names are Charlie and Lucy, and for ages now every night when I go to sleep, I dream about them. And all my dreams were about the house and work they did and how much they enjoyed it and loved their new home. Pretty bloody boring, if you ask me, but they were happy.'

'But you told me you had a dream in which you had given birth?'

'Yeah, I did. Oh God, that was seriously weird! In the last few dreams, Lucy has been pregnant. I've dreamt all the morning sickness, and the weight gain, and the baby clothes shopping. Then last night she gave birth to a baby girl. In the dream, I mean. They have a couple of names in mind, but they haven't decided yet. They wanted to name her Lily after a favourite aunt of Lucy's. But her friend, Claire, named her own daughter Lily, so now they need to choose another one. They're thinking of calling her Amy, but they haven't made up their minds yet.'

Jennifer stopped and sipped at her coffee. *I'm sitting here telling Ilan about these two people as if I know them.*

'Are these dreams in sequence? I mean, is it a continuing narrative?' Ilan interrupted her speculation.

'Yes.'

'Are you sure you don't know her – from your childhood, or university perhaps? Or is it possible that you know her from some other part of your life in England?'

'No. Definitely not. Until I started dreaming about her, I didn't even know she existed.'

'Does she exist? Are you sure she's not merely a figment of your imagination?'

Jennifer frowned and shook her head.

'No. I mean she exists within the dream,' she hesitated, 'but I'm starting to wonder if maybe she really does exist.'

'Why do you think that?' Ilan asked her.

Because I Googled her. I looked at her Facebook page and I almost sent her a friend request. And I don't think I want you to know this.

'I'm not sure, she said. 'I believe she exists.'

'That's not the same as *knowing* she exists.'

'I know that, Ilan. Look, she seems real. That's all I know for sure. I know her thoughts and her feelings and I have followed her life for ages now.'

'But this occurs only in your dreams?'

'Well, yes. But I know every detail. Normally in dreams you only remember fragments. These are different.'

'How are they different?

'It's hard to explain but it seems that when I go to sleep, she wakes up. Then she goes to sleep when I awaken,' Jennifer said as she looked at him. 'I know that doesn't make sense because we're not in opposite time zones and it's not an exact day and night thing. It's more like she takes over as soon as I fall asleep and I assume the same happens when she goes to sleep. But I'm aware of everything she has done that day, although it skips forward in time so it's not every day of her life. And I also think she's aware of me.'

Ilan shook his head. 'No. This isn't possible. It's merely a similar dream you have experienced over a few nights and your belief that it's sequential is merely another part of the dream. Do you not agree?'

'I never thought of that,' she admitted. *And I don't believe that for one minute.*

'It makes more sense. Yes?'

'Okay, yes. It makes more sense when you explain it that way. But it's hard to believe that it's all been one dream.'

'Is it possible neshama, that it's connected to this house? I mean that perhaps you were experiencing some anxiety over buying it with me, and about settling here on a more permanent basis? With me?'

'No! Of course not! This house is perfect. I love it so much, and I love you with all my heart. Please don't ever doubt that.'

'I don't doubt you,' he said.

'So, you really think it's only one dream?' Jennifer asked. She needed to hear him tell her again. She needed to believe it herself but she wasn't sure she could.

'I honestly can't imagine it being anything else,' Ilan replied.

Jennifer nodded in agreement. His calm reasoning made the likelihood of only one dream seem so much more plausible. But, still...

'So, you won't worry any more about it? Yes?'

'Yes. You're right, of course. I'm being daft.'

You don't get it, Ilan. And I don't know how to explain it to you. It's not just one dream. It's every bloody night. I'm living this woman's life through my dreams. And this woman is living my life in her dreams. And it is disturbing. Very disturbing.

It was time to change the subject.

'I have no work planned today. What do you want to do?' she asked.

Ilan sipped the last of his coffee, set the mug on the table. 'I think we should do something that involves swimming. That would be very cool.'

Chapter 23

Four days since the accident.

The alarms startled Charlie out of a fretful doze. He opened his eyes and jumped to his feet. Something had happened. Something terrible. Frantically, he spun around to find the source of the noise. It was coming from the monitors, attached by cables to Lucy. He glanced at them as they blinked and flashed an array of numbers and symbols that made no sense whatsoever to him. But he knew enough to know that something was very wrong. That something was wrong with Lucy! He took her hand in his and called out her name but she didn't respond or react in any way.

'Lucy. Lucy. Wake up darling. Please wake up.' He clutched her hand in both of his, lowered his head and pressed her palm to his lips. Her flesh was cool against the warmth of his. He waited for a response. For Lucy to stroke his face with her fingertips. For her eyes to open, see him and smile at him. But none of this happened.

It was like she didn't exist anymore. Lucy was merely a body. A body that lay on a bed surrounded by cables and tubes connected to machines that pumped air into her lungs and kept her heart beating so blood could carry oxygen around her body and keep her alive. Keep that damaged brain flushed with oxygen in the vain hope that it might just fix itself and she would wake up and smile at him.

But she didn't. She just lay there. No amount of blood or oxygen pumping through her body changed that simple fact. Everything that Lucy had been – his crazy, fun-loving wife and best friend – was now reduced to a body lying, unmoving, in a hospital bed. Would he ever hear her giggle when someone, usually her, let out a loud fart? Would he ever cringe with embarrassment when she would let loose a string of swear words when something annoyed her? Would his heart ever swell again in his chest when he listened to her teaching the girls a silly, made-up song?

Something in his soul told him that he wouldn't.

The implications of this gripped Charlie's heart and the awful fear of losing Lucy seemed to squeeze the life out of him.

A nurse rushed in and killed the alarm and Charlie found the silence to be almost as terrifying as the beeping. Despite his frantic questions, the nurse refused to answer him and deftly shoved him out of the room. She pushed him back against the wall to allow the crash team unfettered entry as they rushed in. They shut the door behind them and someone closed the blinds.

Charlie stood there alone in the corridor. He could only imagine the flurry as they battled to find out what was wrong with his wife.

She was dreaming about the blackness again. It surrounded her. Viscous blackness that engulfed her and it pulled her down into its murky depths. She knew she would drown if she didn't waken and escape from the deathlike grip it had on her.

If only she could escape from it. She had to try. Something told her that her very life depended on it.

But how?

With all her strength she attempted to rise. To push through the blackness and up into the light. She had to get away from it.

'NO!'

A voice. From somewhere. Where? Who? Someone was nearby.

She turned her head from side to side but there was only blackness.

'Who's there?' she demanded.

Her voice sounded strange. Raspy. Unrecognisable. It felt as though something was stuck in her throat. She tried to clear it. Coughing and retching, trying to swallow.

I need to wake up. Something's blocking my throat. Choking me. I need to sit up. Open my eyes and wake up.

'Don't wake up,' the voice warned her.

'Who are you? Where are you?' she said.

'I'm here, by your side. You know who I am.'

'Then help me. I need to get out of here. I'm trapped and I need to you to help me.'

'No,' the voice in the darkness replied.

'What? I don't understand. Please help me.'

'I can't,' it told her.

'Why not?'

'Because if I help you, you'll waken up.'

'Who are you?'

'You know exactly who I am.'

Charlie stopped pacing when the door opened. The doctor's eyes met his as he walked towards him.

'What happened?' he asked.

'It seems Lucy began to wake up,' the doctor told him. 'We've noticed some strange brain activity and it indicates she is dreaming, and she was possibly trying to wake up from a dream. But, in this instance –'

'That's good? Isn't it?' Charlie interrupted him, jumping on the fact that if Lucy was merely asleep and dreaming then she was going to be okay.

'Yes and no,' the doctor said. 'In fact, Lucy appears to be in a heightened state of REM sleep. Do you know what that is?'

'Um, I'm not sure,' Charlie replied.

'It… well, it basically means in the stage of sleep when someone dreams. Lucy is constantly dreaming. Possibly caught in a nightmare and trying to waken up from it. This really shouldn't be happening considering the amount of sedation she has been given. On the plus side, it means she's fighting to stay alive. But she is not ready yet. Her injury is severe. We had to operate to remove a haematoma, a blood clot, that had formed when she hit her head. But the mere act of removing it is not enough. So, in layman's terms, while any damaged brain cells don't heal, other cells around the area can take over their function. This takes time. While she remains in a medically-induced coma, the surrounding cells will go to work. Do you understand?'

'Sort of. I think so,' Charlie replied. 'Will she be brain-damaged?'

'I'm sorry Charlie, I can't answer that at this stage.'

'So, what happens now, doc?'

'We've temporarily increased her sedation, put her in a deeper coma, to ensure this does not happen again until the healing takes place. Then we'll gradually lower it and bring her around at a measured pace. Under our control.'

'What happens now?' Charlie asked.

'For now, all I can tell you is to go home and spend some time with your daughters. We'll contact you should anything change.'

'This is serious, isn't it?'

The doctor placed a hand on Charlie's shoulder and gave it a gentle squeeze. 'It is, I'm afraid. But Lucy is young and strong. There's still hope. Don't give up on that. Don't give up on her.'

Unknown to Charlie, another man was about to receive similar news in a hospital in Tel Aviv.

With a slight nod of his head, the doctor invited Ilan into his office. Reluctantly he did so and took a seat in front of a large, cluttered oak and leather desk that dominated the small, but spacious office. The table looked out of place in the modern room.

The doctor took his own seat at the other side of the desk and lifted a bundle of files, placing them on top of a filing cabinet behind him, to clear away the barrier of paperwork between them.

The doctor was a small man with a full head of grey hair, a goatee beard in corresponding colour, and grey, or perhaps very pale blue, eyes. It was hard to tell from behind the rimless spectacles he was wearing. Whatever the colour, they radiated quiet intelligence and compassion, as he peered over the rims of his glasses like he was examining a rare specimen.

'I must say you look somewhat better in appearance than you did when I spoke to you the day before yesterday. It always amazes me what a shower, some decent food and a night's sleep can do to lift and rejuvenate both body and spirit. Don't you agree?'

It was a rhetorical question, and Ilan answered it with only a frown and a slight nod of his head.

The doctor studied the screen in front of him, scanning the notes quickly as he realised Ilan was impatient to hear what he had to say and had no time for small talk. He cleared his throat.

'As you already know when you and Jennifer were brought to the hospital in Larnaca, she had regained consciousness. She was alert and talking and insisted she felt fine so, once she was given a check-up, both of you were flown home to Tel Aviv. In hindsight, this was a bad decision. But, didn't Jennifer insist she was fine?'

Ilan nodded.

'If she had been admitted for observation, the subdural haemotoma would have presented itself and she could have been treated more promptly. By the time she arrived in Tel Aviv, she was displaying some of the classic symptoms – headache, nausea, confusion and drowsiness.'

'Then this was my fault. If I hadn't insisted that we travel immediately to Israel, Jennifer wouldn't be in this situation,' Ilan said.

'It is not your fault. You were not to know,' the doctor told him. 'When she collapsed and you brought her here, and told us she had struck her head in a car accident, we suspected a brain bleed. The CT scan confirmed that the sudden blow to Jennifer's head had resulted in the tearing of the small blood vessels that run along the surface of the brain. The blood collected between the layers of tissue – the dura and the arachnoid. As it accumulated, the pressure on the brain caused swelling and this was the cause of the symptoms she presented with. And this took time to develop. You couldn't have known there was anything wrong when you left Cyprus. Do you understand?'

'Yes.'

'Because we were now aware of the severity, an immediate craniotomy was preformed to access and remove the haematoma and to reduce the pressure on the brain. This was successful. Jennifer was then placed in a medically induced coma to allow healing to occur. We have been gradually reducing this. Tests have shown that there is brain activity, but this seems to be elevated above normal, and –'

'What do you mean – above normal?' Ilan asked.

'I mean that she has been showing increased brain activity not normally associated with a medically induced coma, which is quite puzzling because it suggests that she is… well, dreaming. In fact, Jennifer appears to be in a permanent state of continuous REM sleep. Do you know what that is?'

'Yes. Go on.'

'Her response to external stimuli to gauge reaction has been, at best, minimal. There is very little response to pain and sound. However, she does have brain activity and we can take that, at this stage, as a positive. She is also still heavily sedated, but we are reducing the sedation gradually and well… it is still early in the game.'

Ilan glared and was tempted to shout that his wife was not a game but he held his tongue as the doctor continued.

'In the coming days, we will continue to monitor her closely as we attempt to bring her back to a wakeful state.'

'And then what?'

'I think we should take it one day at a time,' the doctor said.

His mind bogged down with worry, Ilan left the hospital, with its plain halls and patronising staff, to get a drink somewhere. A nurse advised him of a bar just a couple of blocks away.

The day outside was hot – dry, dusty heat – but he was cold. So cold, he was almost shivering, and he inhaled an entire cigarette in the five-minute walk to the bar. When he got there, he took a seat and ordered a large whiskey. No ice, no water.

Ilan downed the liquid, grimacing at the bitter taste it left in his mouth as it burned its way to his stomach. He craved another cigarette and nipped outside to where all the world's smokers were banished. He lit up, inhaled deeply, smoking the cigarette in record time. He went back inside to take up his position on the same barstool and ordered another drink. But the whiskey couldn't warm his cold heart or soul. Nothing could. The doctor had told him everything and nothing.

Chapter 24 - Jennifer's Dream

Charlie was channel-surfing when Lucy walked into the room, a mug of rum-laced hot chocolate in each hand. He glanced up at her and raised his eyebrows as she handed him one of the steaming mugs.

'Yeah,' Lucy whispered. 'They're both asleep. Finally. Fingers crossed they'll sleep right through the night.'

'I hope so. I could do with a full night's sleep. We both could.'

'They're just excited about going back to school tomorrow,' she told him.

'The joys of having two kids now, eh? Where are the years going? Here, sit down and put your feet up,' he patted the sofa beside him, screwing up his face in a grimace when he realised what he had done.

For a moment they were silent as they remembered how Carly, their beautiful Labrador, had loved to snuggle up on the sofa between them in the evenings, her chin resting on either Lucy's or Charlie's leg.

Lucy felt tears well up in her eyes as she thought about the much-loved dog, and her tragic death while playing in the garden. She had spotted a rabbit, dropped her toy, and chased after it. In her excitement and determination to catch the rabbit she ploughed into the hedge and impaled herself on a sharp branch. She had been killed instantly.

To hide her tears Lucy opened the glass door of the woodstove, stoked the fire and added a couple of logs.

Slippers kicked off; Lucy joined Charlie on the sofa. She curled her legs underneath her and ran her hand lovingly across the seat cushion, feeling the luxuriousness softness of the leather as she snuggled close to Charlie.

The chestnut colour suited the room perfectly. Between the warm glow from the stove, the warm colour of the leather and the red candles burning in glass jars, the room had a comfortable cosiness that belied its size. The girls were fast asleep and everything about the evening was perfect – everything apart from the dog-sized empty space on the sofa and in their hearts. They would fill it soon, but not yet.

'We should consider getting another dog.'

'No. Not yet,' Charlie replied gruffly. 'It's only been six weeks and two days.'

'Remember a while back you asked me what I wanted for my birthday,' Lucy said as she hastily moved away from a subject still too sensitive to put into words.

'I remember asking what you wanted, but I don't remember what you said,' Charlie replied, settling lower into the sofa. 'What do you want for your birthday?'

'I didn't say anything because, at the time, I couldn't think of anything. Now I can. I'd love a camera, Charlie. I want a good quality digital one – not one of those 'point and shoot' ones like I already have – but a proper digital SLR.'

'Okay,' he said, his voice non-committal.

'I looked at the prices and yeah, they are expensive. They average around three or four hundred quid with whatever accessories you want on top of that. But I was thinking, if you combine it with my birthday and Christmas present and I put some money towards it myself then it wouldn't be too expensive.'

'Why?'

'Because it's too much for you to buy on your own,' she told him.

'No, I mean why do you want a camera?'

'Do you remember the craft fair I went to back in July?'

'Um, yeah. Sort of. Why?'

'Well, I noticed a couple of the stalls were selling photographs, some printed onto canvas so I had a look through them. Some were very good but, even with my little point and shoot camera, I can honestly say I've taken better photos, and I started thinking…'

'That's always a bad sign.'

'Ha, ha. You're funny. Not!' Lucy punched him gently on the arm. 'Anyway, I was thinking about maybe trying to do something with photos on canvas myself. I spoke to a guy who makes them and he said he could do a good deal on different sizes if I ordered in bulk. He said, if I was interested, I could try a few first and see if they sell – to test the water, so to speak.'

'Why not put them on canvas yourself?' Charlie suggested. 'It would save you some money by cutting out the middleman.'

'I don't have a clue how to do that.'

'You could learn. It's not rocket science. Honestly, Lucy, if it's something you fancy doing, you might as well do it properly. I'd be happy to renovate one of the outbuildings and turn it into a workshop for you. Just look into how you'd actually do it, and the cost of materials and everything.'

'You think I should?'

'Yeah, why not? You have an eye for a good photograph. Remember your work colleague's wedding we went to last year and you gave her a photo album with photos you took of the wedding? She said it was a damn sight better than the wedding album they paid for! You could also do stuff like that – weddings, christenings, funerals… okay, probably not funerals,' he grinned. 'But you know what I mean.'

'I'd thought about that too, although I prefer landscapes and I'd really love to try my hand at macro photography. There's a photography course beginning in the community college next month and I'm thinking of signing up for it. It includes printing onto canvas now that you mention it. It's two hours two evenings a week, for six weeks. You could manage the girls, couldn't you? If you're okay with me going?'

'I'm okay with it. No reason not to be okay. You know we'll be fine.'

'It's something I really want to do, Charlie. I'm bored with teaching. I mean, I can still do it on a part-time basis like I did before, but if I could make a success of my photography, then maybe I could do that full-time instead. If we can afford it, that is.'

'We can afford it and you don't have to sell it to me. I'll get you the camera for your birthday, but you'll need to be with me because I wouldn't have a clue what to buy. And I'll sort out a workshop for you.'

'You da best, baby,' she told him with a smile.

'Of course, you'll have to repay me.'

'No problem.'

'What had you in mind?' he asked.

'Well, I suppose I could do the washing up all on my own for a week. Or, maybe I could do this…' she leaned closer and whispered into his ear.

Charlie's eyes widened.

'Does that work for you?' Lucy asked.

'Yes. Definitely!'

Chapter 25 - Lucy's Dream

Jennifer stood at the window and watched the snow as it fell in large, gentle flakes. *Lucy would love this. That course she took a while back was interesting and this is exactly the sort of thing she would want to photograph.*

The closest ones, big and featherlike, took on an orange hue in the glow of the nearby street lights.

Oh, they'd be perfect to photograph, wouldn't they Lucy?

From the hotel window Jennifer could see the roof tops of the nearby buildings. Berlin took on a unique beauty, blanketed in a gentle covering of pristine whiteness. She looked down at the streets, empty of all but the hardiest souls. Heads down and shoulders hunched against the cold, they hurried to wherever they were going.

Ilan stood behind her, his arms around her waist, and his chin resting lightly on her shoulder. She was thankful for the warmth in the hotel room as she enjoyed the relaxing, peaceful, display of the falling snow.

'It's beautiful,' she whispered, almost afraid to break the magical spell.

'You are beautiful, neshama,' he said.

She turned her head to smile at him.

'Thank you. And thank you for bringing me here.'

His arms tightened around her and he kissed the back of her neck. She leaned against him and basked in the sensation of his body against hers. The feel of his lips, and the happiness she felt, not only in his arms, but also in his company. It was a happiness she prayed would never diminish.

'Hatihyi ishti?' he whispered.

Jennifer froze.

'Did you hear what I said?'

'Yes,' Her voice was quiet, almost fearful, and all thoughts of Lucy's blossoming career flew out of her mind.

'Do you understand me?' He turned her around to face him.

'Yes. My Hebrew is very good now, thanks to you. It's actually better than my Greek.'

'Are you going to answer my question?'

'Oh, Ilan… I'm sorry. I don't know what to say to you.'

'Well, the obvious answer would be either *ken* or *loh*. Yes or no. I was hoping you would say ken. What's wrong?'

Jennifer took a deep breath. 'There's nothing wrong. I just don't know what to say to you.'

'You do not wish to marry me?' His expression told her he was both disappointed and shocked.

'No, it's not that. I would love to marry you. I would love to be your wife. It's… well, you know I'm not that crazy about getting married.'

He pulled back from her and went to the minibar and poured a glass of whiskey. From his closed expression, Jennifer knew he was disappointed with her answer.

'Do you need time to think about it?' Ilan asked. 'If that's what you need then I'll give you time. All the time in the world.'

'Please don't get all sulky with me,' she told him. 'I don't see why we need to get married. I love you and you love me. We have a wonderful life together. What's wrong with the way we are now?'

'Nothing,' he replied.

'Good. Now pour one of those for me and we can spend the rest of the night pretending we're married.'

Ilan stared at her for a moment before opening the minibar and making her up a vodka and diet coke. He handed it to her.

'Todah.'

'Bevakasha,' he replied, his tone still clipped. More disappointed than angry.

'Don't be upset with me Ilan. I just don't think we need to be married.'

'I think we should.'

'Why?'

'I want you to be my wife. I want us to be together legally, spiritually and in every way.'

'I do understand.'

'Do you?'

'Yes. I would love to be your wife,' she said as she took a small sip of the ice-cold liquid. 'But I don't want to go through the process. If we could suddenly flick a switch and be married then I'd be more than okay with that. But a wedding, with all that pomp and ceremony, and me having to be the centre of attention? I'm sorry, but even a small ceremony would freak me out. I like what we have Ilan. Why do we need any more? Why do we need to make it legal?'

'I have my reasons.'

'Pension benefits?'

'That is, of course, a consideration. But my reasons for wanting to marry you encompass so much more than that. Naturally, if anything should happen to me, I want you to be safe and secure and being married ensures that, but –'

'Something happening to you is not something I want to dwell on, if you don't mind. Yes, I know there are risks in your line of work. I've learned to accept that and I try not to worry about you. But being married wouldn't change that.'

'I know. But I would still like you to be my wife, Jennifer. I want to marry you because I love you, because I consider you my soul – my neshama. My everything.'

She took another mouthful of vodka. 'Let me think about it, please. Let's enjoy this week here together and I'll think about it. I'll probably say yes, but for me it's a big decision, so please give me a few days.'

Ilan nodded. Jennifer could tell it was not what he had wanted to hear.

'So, what were you saying about pretending to be married?' he said with a smile as he reached for her, taking her into his arms.

'Uh, yeah, like all married couples – not tonight darling,' she said as she ducked out of his embrace.

His face fell and Jennifer laughed as his forlorn expression.

'I'm joking,' she told him.

She caught his hand in hers and pulled him towards the bed. He gulped down the whiskey and pretended to resist at first then gave in to her. Her lips met his as their need for one another caught up with them.

Afterwards she felt herself drifting off to sleep in the circle of his arms. There was no other place she wanted, or needed, to be.

The pale morning light spilled into the room as Ilan yawned sleepily and sprawled on the bed, tired but content. Jennifer was seated in front of the mirrored dressing table. She smiled as her eyes met his in the glass, remembering their passion from the night before. She put the finishing touches to her make-up then turned her attention to her hair, still wrapped in a small towel.

'Why did you have your hair cut short again?'

Jennifer set the dryer down and picked up a jar of styling wax. She scooped out a small amount and rubbed it into her palms.

'For this very reason,' she said as she held up the jar of wax. 'I can dry it and style it in about five minutes.'

'I liked it longer,' he told her.

'I know you did, but this is easier to maintain, especially in the summer when I'm in the water so often. But even now in the winter… well, it's just so much easier to look after. Don't you like it?'

'I didn't say I don't like it. I *do* prefer it longer but this style also suits you, so I also like it.'

Ilan watched as she used the wax on her palms to style and give shape to her hair – spiking it up at the back and sides and parting her fringe down on either side in a way that framed her face and gave her an impish, mischievous appearance. He wanted her again.

His eyes met hers in the mirror.

'What?' She tilted her head with a quizzical expression on her face.

'Come back to bed.'

She stood up and walked towards the bed, a smile on her lips. As she approached him, she hooked her thumbs into the waist of her panties, slowly slipped them down and kicked them off where they fell to the floor.

Ilan threw back the bed sheet as she approached him and offered himself to her as she straddled him.

Later, as she lay in his arms, he asked her what her plans were for the remainder of the day.

'I'm starving, so breakfast first would be a good idea.' She looked at her watch. 'Although we might be too late for breakfast now. The snow has stopped and I'd really love to go sight-seeing. And tomorrow some shopping. Definitely shopping. What do you want to do?'

He smiled and stretched then pulled her closer into his arms. 'I could easily stay right here.'

'I dunno, Ilan. I think you'd get bored all on your own,' she told him with a straight face.

'Sight-seeing it is then.' Ilan sighed dramatically, got out of bed and went to take a shower.

'Can you hear that?' Jennifer frowned.

Still damp from the shower, Ilan pulled on his underwear and jeans then looked around the room for his black woollen polo neck. 'Hear what?'

'I'm not sure. It's a steady beep, beep, beep. But faint.'

He listened for a moment or two. 'I don't hear anything.'

'Well, I can hear it. I can't place it but it is definitely familiar.'

'Describe it to me.'

'There isn't much to describe. I can hear a steady beep, beep, beep that's all. But I can't pinpoint where it's coming from. Sometimes it –'

'Does it sound like an alarm?'

'Not really. A little bit like a dodgy smoke detector, maybe. You know, when the battery is running down. Or, it's a bit like the warning sound a van or truck makes reversing. Whatever it is, it's really bloody annoying.'

'Can you hear it now, even as we speak?'

'Yes.'

Ilan stood still for a moment, his head cocked to the side as he listened. Then he walked over to the window, opened it and leaned his head outside. He listened for almost a full minute then stepped back in and closed the window.

'Do you still hear it?'

'I told you, yes. Why?'

'When did you first hear it?'

'I'm honestly not sure. I really can't remember but it seems to be there all the time. Sometimes it sounds more like an electrical hum – like the noise a fridge makes but mostly it's a beeping noise, and I hear it mostly in or near my right ear. Ilan, what are you thinking?'

'It's possible you might have tinnitus.'

'Yeah, sure. Isn't that what factory workers and such get when they're exposed to loud noise over many years? I've never been exposed to loud noise over a long time.'

'Classic eighties rock played at full volume on your car stereo could be described as loud noise exposure.'

'That wouldn't do it.'

'It might.'

'You play your car stereo just as loudly.'

'I drive a convertible. The noise is not contained and therefore causes less damage.'

'I don't think I have tinnitus,' she told him, kissing him lightly on the cheek before grabbing up her warm coat and her handbag. 'It's probably water in my ears from the shower. Never mind about it. Let's go and eat something, please.'

Chapter 26 - Jennifer's Dream

The glow from the laptop screen bathed Lucy's face in bright light. She twirled a strand of hair around her finger as she scrolled through the results of her search on vivid recurring dreams. The first link was an article on something called Lucid Dreaming which she had never heard of before. She read through it quickly. The gist of the article told her someone could become aware they are dreaming and, in time, learn to control what happens within a dream and how everything in that dream could seem real.

Is that what I'm doing? It can't be. While I can see, hear and feel what Jennifer is doing, I'm not controlling any of it. And I'm not in her life. I'm only observing it and remembering it when I wake up.

It didn't really apply to her situation. But it might still be worth reading the article properly and have a look through the dozens of related links when she had a bit more time. She decided to try a different approach and typed – **are dreams evidence of another reality?** – into the search bar. There were fewer items this time, but one article caught her attention. It sounded farfetched, but it was slightly more relevant to her situation.

Lucy began to read it.

It was the multiverse theory that states many universes exist parallel to each other. And in these other realities there was a copy or many copies of a person making all kinds of different decisions in different situations that later manifest in dreams, and that some of our dreams are really glimpses of events taking place in an alternate reality, or *many* alternate realities.

The next line made her heart beat faster in her chest. It read: **many Native American tribes and Mexican**

civilisations believed that dreams were a different world we visit when we sleep.

This could be me. This could definitely be me. And Jennifer.

There were dozens more articles, blogs and websites. Some of them delved into quantum physics and Schrodinger's Cat, and how it was both dead and alive while inside the box, and what it really meant – about how the cat is both dead and alive until someone looks inside the box and determines the reality, because the ability of observation is what influences the outcome.

Bugger. I get it, but it's way too deep for this time of the evening. And doesn't relate to me since I'm not a cat and I'm not in a box.

She clicked on another link. It was also about parallel universes and how our dreams are memories of those other infinite universes, and –

'Cup of tea, love?'

'Oh, yes, please,' Lucy said, as she minimised the search page and opened the folder that contained her latest photos before Charlie could see what was on the screen. He came around to her side of the desk and set the mug down beside her hand.

'Thank you,' she said.

'How's the course going?'

'I'm loving it, Charlie. It's so interesting and I've learned a lot from it. But the important part was learning how to print photos onto canvas like you said I should. It seemed impossible at first –'

'Not so much impossible as too much trouble, you mean?' Charlie nudged her elbow gently.

'Yeah, okay. A bit,' Lucy admitted with a grin. 'But then I got the hang of it and it's actually dead easy. Between the craft fair last month and that one last weekend, I've sold five large canvas photos and another twelve smaller ones.'

'Well done, pet. I knew you would. But my favourite is still the one you have hanging in the hall.' He pulled the other chair up to the desk and sat down beside her. 'What's that?'

'This? It's a photo of a flower.'

'It doesn't look like a flower to me.'

'It's the inside of a purple tulip. I did it for my class a while back and the tutor was well impressed. He said I captured the sexuality of it.'

'Eh?'

'Yeah, he's a bit of a tosser. I think he meant the reproductive organs. I don't know much about flowers, but I think this is where the pollen comes from. I don't get what he meant by sexuality though. Maybe he just likes looking at photos of a plant's naughty bits.'

'Seriously?'

'Forget him. This was part of my macro coursework. But I've been using an editing program I downloaded that uses filters and stuff so I can make it sepia – like an old photo – or black and white, like this.'

Lucy opened another photo of the same image but in monochrome.

'Uh, yeah. I sort of see what you're doing,' Charlie told her. 'Just not sure it's my cup of tea.'

'It's all part of the learning process. Because next week I have to concentrate on imagery rather than the actual photo. Last week it was all about how you look at what you are photographing and how light and surroundings affect it.'

'And what do you mean by imagery?'

'Well, I'm not completely sure, but I think he means I have to capture an emotion, a feeling, and use a selection of photos to tell a story.'

'How?'

'Buggered if I know, Charlie. Any ideas?'

Charlie took a mouthful of his tea. 'What else do you have?'

Lucy opened her photo folder and waited for him to look through the pictures displayed on the screen.

'I like that one. The tree with the setting sun behind it. Yeah, that's nice.'

'But I need to know why you like it.'

'Um, well. I like the darkness of it. The blackness of the bare branches and the trunk with the orange light – the sunset – behind it.'

'Why?'

'I dunno. It's eerie. A bit oppressive. The branches seem to be reaching forward towards me. It's a little bit creepy but that appeals to me in a certain way.'

'Why?'

Charlie scratched his chin as he studied the photograph, trying to explain what it meant to him. 'I dunno Lucy. It makes me think of – humanity and the planet and what we're doing to the earth. This tree isn't angry at us. It's sad… because it will die soon. Maybe not tomorrow, or next year, or the year after that, but it will die because of us. At least I *think* that's what I see.'

'Okay. That's good. Now what does this image tell you?' She clicked on the next photograph.

'Um, it's the same tree.'

'Yeah, it is. How does it make you feel?'

Charlie scratched his head as he thought about the photo, allowing his eyes to see the image while he concentrated on how he felt about it.

'Don't overthink it,' Lucy told him. 'Say what you feel.'

'Happier, I suppose. The tree is in leaf and alive. The sun is shining so it's spring or summer and naturally that makes me feel warm and fuzzy. It… um, it tells me that life goes on, or something. How did I do?'

'It's not a test,' Lucy laughed. 'It's something we did in class this week. We have to feel the emotion rather than see what is in the picture – how it makes us feel. What we think about it. What our imagination is telling us about it.'

A fig tree in Cyprus is what my imagination is telling me.

'Where is it?' Charlie asked.

'It's the tree in the field up behind Niall's farm. I go up there a couple of times a week and take different photos of it. Mainly because it's a lovely old oak and also because I want to take a series of photos of it over a year – all four seasons. You know, with snow and rain, with autumn colours and new growth in spring. With the sun behind it at dusk on a summer's evening and in front of it in early morning,' she took a sip of her tea. 'This is partially because I really like that tree but I also have to realise the concept of what appeals to someone viewing a photograph. Not just what is in the picture but how it makes them feel.'

'It all sounds a bit arty-farty to me,' Charlie said.

'Well, it is. But if it makes me a better photographer I can be as arty-farty as the best of 'em. Now, how does *this* make you feel?' Lucy clicked back onto the photo of the tulip.

'Uncomfortable.'

'Why?'

'It doesn't look like a flower. It's dark and creepy and I feel that I could be sucked into it. Like a black hole in a sci-fi movie.'

'What about this?' Lucy clicked on a similar image but this time it was the interior of a yellow tulip.

'Okay. That one makes me think of toast with lots of butter on it,' he said as he gathered up the two empty mugs. 'And now I'm hungry and I'm going to make toast. Do you want some?'

Lucy shook her head and laughed as he planned his escape to perfection. She was surprised he had stayed so long. As Charlie closed the study door behind him, she closed her photo folder, opened up her internet browser again and began to read the article on dreams and alternate realities.

An hour and a half later and still none the wiser, Lucy decided to give up. She yawned and stretched her arms above her head, to work the stiffness out of her shoulders, and looked at her watch. It was bedtime, so she powered down her laptop as she wondered what events in Jennifer's life she would dream about tonight.

Chapter 27 - Lucy's Dream

Jennifer linked her arm with Ilan's as they walked through Berlin's busy pedestrian area, ducking this way and that as they jostled with the bustling crowds. She breathed in deeply the rich aromas of coffee and freshly baked bread that sought to entice them into any one of the numerous cafes they passed by.

'Okay,' she said. 'Since we did the whole tourist bit yesterday and the day before, and I really enjoyed it, could we spend today shopping? Would you be annoyed if we did that today?'

'Of course not,' Ilan replied with a smile. 'I can think of nothing I would rather do.'

She stopped and unlinked her arm from his. She stepped away from him and gave him a suspicious look. 'You're being sarcastic, aren't you?'

Ilan's arms were outstretched in a questioning gesture that, along with his expression of denial, was delivered with a mixture of wide-eyed innocence and over-the-top disappointment that she would even think such a thing of him. He was so good at it she almost believed him.

It was the devilish twinkle in his eye that gave him away and Jennifer began to laugh quietly at herself for, once again, falling for his wicked sense of humour and at him for still being able to catch her out, even after all these years.

She reached for his hand, taking it in hers and squeezing it tightly.

'I love you so very much,' she told him.

'But not enough to marry me,' he said.

'That's not true, Ilan. I've told you. I just don't do weddings. I couldn't. The thought of it simply terrifies me. Anyway, wouldn't I have to convert to Judaism to marry you?'

'No. That's only for religious ceremonies. We don't have civil weddings in Israel but, for anyone who prefers not to have a religious wedding you can marry outside of Israel. For many Israelis, Cyprus is where they go and the marriage will still be recognised in Israel. Since you and I both live in Cyprus, it would make sense for us to be married there.'

'But we'd still have to have a wedding?'

Ilan rolled his eyes. 'Yes. That goes without saying. But it could be as big or as small a wedding ceremony as you want it to be. I would go along happily with whatever you prefer.'

'I'd prefer it if it were just you and me?'

'What about your family – your father and mother, and your brother and his family?'

'They wouldn't mind either way. Like I said, Ilan, I would prefer it if it were just you and me.'

'Seriously?'

'Yes, seriously. I honestly do not want a wedding. Not now. Not ever.'

He shrugged his shoulders. 'Okay then, if that's what you wish. I won't ask you again.'

'I didn't say no to getting married, although to be honest, I already consider us to be a couple with no need to make it – legal. I'm just saying no to a wedding. But let me think about it – mull it over for a few days. Please.'

He nodded. She could tell he wasn't happy with her answer.

She took his hand. 'Are you angry with me?'

'No. I'm disappointed, a little bit. As for being angry? I have no reason to be angry with you.'

'Then we are okay?'

Jennifer breathed a sigh of relief when Ilan pulled her close to him, embracing her in his arms.

'We're okay,' he told her and kissed her gently, his lips brushing hers.

She leaned into him, relishing the warmth of his arms around her on this cold day. She suddenly felt a yearning to be back in Cyprus, with its mild, comfortable winters. The yearning spread through her and tugged at her heart. Berlin was nice. It was fun. She was certainly enjoying the week, especially in Ilan's company, and she was glad she had allowed him to talk her into the trip. But the thought of going home all of a sudden appealed to her.

'Come on. You promised me some shopping,' she said, taking his hand and pulling him in the direction of the nearest shopping mall. 'Let's get it over with and we can get back to the hotel where it's warm and cosy.'

Less than two hours and a cup of hot chocolate later, Jennifer was bored. Shops in Berlin in the winter weren't exactly filled with the kind of clothing one would wear in Cyprus at any time of the year. It was a fact that Ilan had pointed out to her several times already.

Still, she had managed to find and purchase some make-up, a scarf, and a beautiful lacy bra and panties set which Ilan insisted on paying for, claiming he was the one who would benefit most from it.

Jennifer could tell that Ilan's interest was waning when she noticed him gazing longingly at the nearby bars and licking his lips in anticipation of either a cold beer or a large whiskey. He had been very patient up until now, but his patience was wearing thin. She was about to suggest they have a hot toddy and then hail a taxi back to the hotel – where they could relax by the indoor swimming pool and avail themselves of the spa room – when his phone rang.

He quickly fished it out of his pocket and stepped away from her to answer it. From what Jennifer could hear of the hushed conversation, he was speaking in French.

Jennifer tilted her head from left to right as she admired the heavy woollen coat in the window of a nearby store. It wasn't really suitable for the climate in Cyprus. But if they were to spend a lot of time travelling in Europe in the winter…

Just as she had almost convinced herself that she *really* needed the coat, Ilan finished his conversation and turned back to her.

'I am sorry,' he said. 'I have to… meet someone.'

'Ah, of course. More James Bond shit,' she said with a grin, wondering if he had arranged this to get a break from shopping with her.

'It will take me perhaps a couple of hours, three at the most. Will you be okay on your own?'

'Don't worry about me. Go do your spy stuff. I spotted a couple of shoe shops I want to check out and I can make my own way back to the hotel when I'm finished. If I get back early, I'll be in the pool or the sauna. Or most likely the bar. But I'll have my phone close by.'

'I'll call you.' Ilan held her close for a moment then planted a kiss on her mouth.

'Be careful,' Jennifer told him as he walked away.

Her feet aching, Jennifer placed the carrier bags on the floor, kicked off her shoes and sat down on the bed. She was thankful to be back in the hotel room and she reckoned it was time for a glass of wine, or perhaps a gin and tonic. She was massaging the aches out of her feet when her phone began to ring. It was Ilan.

She smiled in delight as she answered the call. It seemed he was finished early.

'Hi. Where are you?' Ilan asked.

'Back at the hotel. In our room. I got bored on my own so I'm back for either a swim or a gin. Probably both.'

'I need you to go out again. Go out onto the street at the front, take a left and then another immediate left and you'll see a pharmacy. I need you buy a small first aid kit. Nothing too big or expensive, but make sure it contains antiseptic cream or lotion, and if possible, one that also contains a local anaesthetic cream. Then I want you to find somewhere that sells a sewing kit.'

'I beg your pardon. You want me to buy a what?'

'A sewing kit. You know, a needle and some thread.'

'Is everything okay?'

'Everything's fine Jennifer. I'll explain when I see you and you can tell me how much money you've spent shopping.' His voice was light-hearted and joking. 'Can you get the items and meet me back at the hotel, please?'

'Yeah, I can do that. Look, if you don't mind, I'll skip the swim and meet you in the bar. I'm dying for a drink.'

'Good idea. I would very much enjoy a drink myself?'

'Are you sure everything is okay, Ilan?'

'Yes. I'm looking forward to having a drink with you. It would be nice if you bought me one for a change?'

Ilan ended the call.

Jennifer grabbed her purse and key card and hurried out. Something in his voice caused her concern. That, and the nature of the items he wanted. He was injured.

Obviously not seriously, or he wouldn't be laughing and joking with her, but still...

It took Jennifer no time at all to carry out her task. She got the first aid kit then noticed a shelf containing assorted travel items. It was there she found the sewing kit.

Within a few minutes Jennifer returned to the hotel. She went directly to the bar and took a seat, placing her bag of purchases on the floor beside her. Instead of a gin and tonic, she ordered a large glass of white wine.

Ilan was late. His phone call had been well over two glasses of wine and three chapters of her paperback ago. Jennifer frowned as she checked her watch for the umpteenth time. Just as she was about to phone him, he appeared almost out of nowhere at her side, startling her in the process.

'Dammit, Ilan! You frightened me! What kept you?'

As her heart stopped racing, Jennifer noticed that his face was pale and his left hand was wrapped in a blood-soaked handkerchief.

Oh, he's cut his hand. This is why he wants the first aid kit.

'I need to go up to the room. Can you buy a bottle of whiskey and bring it up with you?' Ilan gathered up her bag of purchases, peeked inside and nodded. There was a look in his eyes Jennifer could not interpret.

'What's wrong?' she asked.

Her question was met with the merest shake of his head. 'Nothing's wrong. Just get the whiskey and meet me in the room.'

Jennifer shrugged her shoulders, she knew not to question him too much in a public place, and quickly finished her drink. She watched Ilan as he made his way to the elevator then caught the bartender's attention and asked him for a bottle of Scotch. She charged it to their bill, grimaced at the inflated price, and made her way to the elevator.

Once Jennifer was in the hotel room, Ilan hung the Do Not Disturb sign on the outer handle and closed the door, making sure it was locked. He shrugged off his coat, set it down on the nearby chair, and took off his wool sweater.

Jennifer gasped when Ilan turned to her and she saw his side, covered in blood that seeped from a gash above his hip. Her hands flew to her mouth as she stifled a scream. His jeans were soaked from the waistband to his thigh and the red stain had spread out, darkening the fabric of the denim. This was why the handkerchief was soaked in blood. Not from his hand as she had thought.

'I'm afraid I've been stabbed,' he told her, a note of apology in his voice.

'What happened?' Jennifer managed to ask, her voice small and frightened. 'Was this something to do with who you were meeting?'

'No. That had already taken place. I was on my way back to the hotel and I saw two kids trying to mug an elderly man so I intervened.'

'Seriously?'

'Yeah. I pulled them off him and one of them stabbed me. When he realised what he'd done he ran away.'

Jennifer stared at him. 'Is this the truth Ilan?'

'Yes.'

'Let me see it properly.'

'It's not as bad as it looks,' he told her and lifted his arm to allow Jennifer a closer look. 'Just messy. And extremely annoying.'

Jennifer shuddered in horror. Her heart thumped in her chest and she whimpered, unable to speak. She could see the wound with the blood congealed around it.

'I need a drink,' Ilan said.

He retrieved a small glass tumbler and cracked open the bottle of whiskey Jennifer had purchased from the barman. He poured the whiskey, filling the tumbler to the brim, raised it to his lips and gulped it down. All of it. He grimaced as the burning liquid travelled down his throat and into his stomach. But he filled the glass again only this time he set it down on the bedside table and turned to look at her.

'Please don't panic Jennifer. It's not so bad. I just need you to help me patch it up.'

'NO!' She finally found her voice. 'You've been stabbed. You need to go to a hospital.'

'I can't attend a hospital. You'll have to do it.'

'Do what?'

'It's not deep. More of a slice than a puncture wound but it needs to be closed. All you have to do is clean it and stitch it. Please.'

'No,' she said. She shook her head from side to side to emphasise her refusal. 'No. I can't.'

He took another drink of whiskey, spilling some as he gulped it down. Jennifer could see the pain etched on his face.

'You must.'

'I can't. I don't know what to do,' she said. 'This is insane.'

'I can talk you through it. Please Jennifer. I need you now like I have never needed you before. You have to help me.'

Hearing the plea in his voice, Jennifer knew in her heart she had to do this. But how? What he was suggesting – cleaning and stitching his wound – terrified her on an almost cellular level. She could hardly breathe and her heart was hammering in her chest. How could a simple winter city break, sightseeing and shopping, making love and having fun, turn into this nightmare?

Jennifer was not squeamish. Never had been. Once, years ago, she sliced through the fleshy part of her thumb with a steak knife while cooking. She casually, almost detachedly, rinsed it under the cold tap. After a close inspection, she debated with herself whether or not to go to the local emergency department. The thought of waiting, possibly for hours, to be seen decided the matter. It probably should have been stitched at the time – the ragged one-inch scar across her thumb bore witness to that – but it stopped bleeding and she wrapped a couple of band-aids tightly around it and forgot all about going to hospital. In time, it healed.

But Ilan had been stabbed. This wasn't an accident with a household knife. Someone had used a knife to deliberately stab him.

'Please, Jennifer.'

'No... I can't. I don't...'

Her tears began to fall. He reached out to her, placed his palm against her cheek and caught them with his thumb as they fell, wiping them away, imploring her with his eyes.

'You have to do this for me.'

'I don't know how.'

'Jennifer. Please.'

'I don't know. Will you talk me through it?'

'Yes.'

'Okay. I'll try.'

For Jennifer the next few moments were a blur as Ilan gathered up the first aid, the sewing kit and the bottle of whiskey. She followed him into the bathroom, still pleading with him to allow her to call for an ambulance.

'Or at least a doctor? Maybe the hotel has one on call?'

'No. Any sort of knife crime must be reported to the police. For obvious reasons I can't allow that to happen.' His voice was firm.

'But that needs to happen. Surely, you want whoever did this to you caught and punished?'

'He's already been punished for his crime,' Ilan said.

'What do you mean?'

'When I intervened and he tried to stab me I grabbed his arm and twisted it, which is why he only cut me. He dropped the knife and I kicked it into a sewer drain. I twisted his arm again. I think I broke it. He was nothing more than a kid and from his expression of pain and fear, I don't think he'll try anything so foolish again.'

Jennifer closed her eyes, imagining the scene and how easily it could have gone so horribly wrong. Ilan could have been killed.

'Now, I need you to concentrate Jennifer. Can you do that for me, please?'

She nodded.

'Okay. First, you have to disinfect the wound. I need you to run the tap water until it's as hot as possible,' he said and sat down on the edge of the bath. He placed the sewing kit on top of the small cabinet and the whiskey bottle on the floor beside him. 'Then take this towel, soak it in the hot water, and use it to clean as much of the blood away as you can.'

Jennifer did as he asked. On closer inspection she realised it was only a deep, long cut and not a puncture wound, but it still looked horrific. She washed her hands thoroughly and winced as she carefully cleaned the blood away. Most of it had dried although some still seeped out. She poured a generous amount of the disinfectant over it, repeating the process until Ilan begged her to stop. One more careful inspection and Jennifer sighed. She had hoped it wouldn't require stitching, but it was obvious even to her untrained eye she was going to have to attempt stitching it up. Every movement he made threatened to open it and then the blood would begin flowing again.

She opened the sewing kit and took out the thread and a needle. Her hands were shaking.

'Are you okay?' he asked.

'No. I'm fucking well not okay,' she glared at him. Not angry. But not pleased either. And very frightened. 'Ilan, I have no idea how to do this.'

'It's just like sewing two pieces of material together, or a better analogy – a Christmas turkey after it has been stuffed.'

I'm never eating turkey again.

Jennifer swallowed and tried to ignore the threatening wave of nausea.

'You have to pinch the flesh together with your thumb and forefinger,' Ilan explained. 'Insert the needle through one side, underneath the wound and out through the other. Then you pull the two sides together, but not too tightly because you need to allow for a slight flexibility so the thread won't cut through the flesh. It doesn't have to be neat and tidy. Just secure it so it can knit and heal. Don't worry. It will be easier than you think.'

He reached for the whiskey again, filled the tumbler to the brim, and took another large mouthful.

'I need to get drunk enough to dull the pain before you begin to stitch it,' he said in response to her frown.

Jennifer took the glass from him. It was about three-quarters full. She took a small sip, then another, and then drank down a larger mouthful.

'Sorry, but I think I need to get a little bit drunk before I do this,' she told him and her voice faltered.

'Will you be able to put the stitches in if you are drunk?'

'I'm not sure I could do it sober,' she replied and took another large gulp. She attempted a wry grin. 'It's not like I've ever done it before.'

'I'll talk you through it. Pour some of the disinfectant over the needle and the thread first.'

Jennifer washed her hands again, poured some of the disinfectant over them and over the threaded needle. She took a deep breath to steady her mind and her hands that were clean, but trembling. She pursed her lips, blew her breath out slowly and fought back the tears as she paused for one more deep breath. This time she held it as she tentatively placed the thumb and finger of her left hand above and below the wound just as Ilan had explained she should do. She pinched the two sides together then, took the needle in her right hand and pierced his skin, forcing the needle through his flesh.

The needle met resistance, and Ilan gasped at the new source of pain. Jennifer gritted her teeth and pushed the needle through and out the other side. The thread followed the path she had created.

'Do I need to do individual stitches?' Jennifer let out the breath she had been holding.

'Yes. Tie each one and then cut the thread.'

She looped the thread to tie it and, once it was secure, she cut the thread.

'Like this?'

'Yes.' Ilan's voice was barely audible.

Jennifer let out another long breath. It was both easier and more difficult than she had expected it to be. Ignoring the temptation of the nearby whiskey bottle and

Ilan's laboured, pain-filled grunts, she proceeded to complete the second stitch.

He told her it would take about six or seven. She had completed three. It seemed she had been on her knees by his side on the cold bathroom floor for hours. Her legs were beginning to cramp, and her shoulders ached from the tension. Her mouth tasted dry, like sandpaper, and she was still fighting the nausea.

She pierced his skin with the needle once again and bit her lip as he growled in pain. She knew she was hurting him and she asked him if he wanted her to stop for a little while.

'No. Finish it,' he said between gritted teeth. His face was white and beads of sweat dotted his forehead.

After what seemed an eternity of pain for him and horror for her, Jennifer carefully pulled the thread through for the last time. Tiny teardrops of blood seeped through where the needle had pierced the skin. She wiped her own tears away as she watched the drops swell before her eyes. She stared at them and it seemed they were staring back at her.

'Do I need to trim the ends of each stitch, to keep them from catching on your clothes? Jennifer raised her eyes to his.

It took a while for him to answer. 'Yes. Do it quickly, please.'

She did what he asked, and with a sigh of relief, sat back on her aching legs, reluctantly inspecting her handiwork. It wasn't neat by any stretch of the imagination and it would probably leave an ugly scar, to add to the growing collection of scars on his body, but it looked as if it would hold so long as he didn't move around too much.

Her hands were shaking and suddenly Jennifer was exhausted. She wanted to crawl into bed and cry herself to sleep. But there was still work to do. Infection was the main concern. She had to disinfect it again and then apply the dressing.

'Now we must clean up,' Ilan said as she taped the dressing in place.

He took her hand and gave it a reassuring squeeze.

'Give me a minute,' Jennifer said as she pulled her hand out of his grasp and only just managed to lean over the toilet bowl before throwing up.

For the remainder of the afternoon and into the early evening Jennifer lay beside Ilan and watched over him as he slept fitfully. No blood seeped through the dressing and she took this as a positive sign. Infection however, was a concern and Jennifer had insisted he take two of the blister pack of antibiotics she found in her washbag. Left over from a throat infection she had last winter and almost past their expiry date, she hoped they would be enough to ward off any infection before it took hold.

She wanted to sleep herself, but her concern for him kept her awake, afraid to close her eyes even for a second.

Eventually he came fully awake and pulled himself up to a sitting position, carefully avoiding too much movement on his left side.

'No. You should sleep, Ilan,' Jennifer frowned as she sat up beside him.

'I feel better, but I'm starving and I suspect you are too. We should order room service.' He smiled and took her hand in his. 'Did you clean up in the bathroom?'

'Yes. It's probably not clean from a forensic point of view but it should be okay.'

'You are an excellent field medic, neshama.'

'I think I'll stick to my day job. I do not ever what to go through that again!'

'Neither do I,' he replied.

Some of the pallor had left his face and his eyes were brighter.

Jennifer swung her legs over the edge of the bed, reaching down for her bag as she did so.

'Take these,' she said as she handed him two non-prescription painkillers along with a bottle of water.

'I would prefer whiskey,' he said.

'I'm sure you would,' she replied with a smile. 'But you forced me to play doctor, and this is *so* not how I remember playing doctor when I was young. You have to abide by my rules and take your medicine when I say so.'

He began to laugh but stopped when the pain in his side told him that laughing wasn't such a wise idea. He took the pills she offered and washed them down with the water.

'So, what do we do now?' Jennifer asked.

'We eat. Then we sleep. In the morning we go home. I am sorry for ruining the remainder of your holiday.'

'I'm just thankful you're okay,' she took a deep breath and smiled at him. 'Oh, yeah, I almost forgot. The answer to your questions is yes. Yes, I will marry you.'

Chapter 28 - Jennifer's Dream

Charlie was having difficulty opening the bottle. Lucy watched him as he tried to unwind the wire that held the cork in place. She could tell he was annoyed with it and she crossed her fingers, praying he wouldn't get so frustrated he'd throw it at the wall and hand out cans of beer instead.

Finally, he managed to get the wire off. He twisted the bottle and used his thumb to push the cork out from beneath the lip. A spray of champagne followed in its wake. Everyone cheered loudly and held out their glasses for him to fill with the sparkling liquid.

Lucy smiled at her husband as he poured the champagne. He looked great in his new suit and not at all self-conscious as she thought he might be. He didn't do 'dressed-up Charlie' very often, but when he did the transformation was remarkable. She laughed as he worked the room, laughing and joking and bowing ceremoniously as he filled their glasses, even though it was only the four of them standing there.

Claire was stunning as usual in her favourite short, black, off-the-shoulder dress. For such a special occasion Lucy had decided to splash out on a new dress and she had chosen a similar style to Claire's, but she had gone for a deep red colour, in an almost metallic fabric. It matched the subtle highlights she now had in her hair.

The red highlights had been Claire's idea. She claimed they would complement the dress and Lucy, who had never coloured her hair in her life, had been a bit apprehensive at first but when she saw the effect in the mirror she had squealed with delight and wondered why she had never taken the plunge before.

Charlie loved them and told her they set off her eyes and that they looked fantastic in the light.

'It's like there's a gentle shimmering flame around your head,' he said with a smile as he whirled her around the kitchen. 'You look amazing.'

Now here she was, wearing her new red dress and with her new hairstyle, and to say she was a bit nervous was a massive understatement. Her hands were clammy and she was shivering, despite the warmth that surrounded her. Her heart was racing a mile a minute and she hadn't a clue what she was going to say to everyone this evening. Yet, riding alongside her nervousness was the notion that, just for tonight, being the centre of attention was the coolest and most exciting thing ever.

Charlie cleared his throat and raised his glass. Claire and Gavin followed suit.

'The taxi will be here shortly so before it arrives, I want to say a few words,' he said and smiled as his eyes met Lucy's. 'To my extremely beautiful wife. I have to say, seeing you standing here all dressed up to the nines, this is one hell of a transformation from the woman I usually see at this time of the evening. The Lucy I know would be lying stretched out on the sofa wearing her jammies and wrapped up in a manky old dressing gown. And she'd have a glass of wine in one hand and the TV remote in the other. Yes, you heard me. She often gets into her jammies *this* early in the evening.'

His remark was greeted with peals of laughter and Lucy stuck her tongue out at him.

'It wasn't all that long ago when she sidled up to me one evening and began nibbling my earlobe and tickling my neck. Naturally, I thought I was on a promise so I was ready to give her anything she wanted. Nudge, nudge, wink, wink as they say,' he grinned and waggled his eyebrows. 'Anyway, to cut a long story short, I did get my leg over that night and Lucy got the expensive camera she wanted. And that included all the accessories!'

He stopped and gave her his best leer. Lucy couldn't stop herself from blushing furiously while she laughed along with Claire and Gavin.

'Did you say *all* the accessories?' Gavin asked.

'Too right, I did,' Charlie responded. 'And believe me, it was worth every penny!'

'But seriously…' he paused until the jokes and the laughter had died down. 'I just want to congratulate her on this evening and on everything she has achieved. She's a wonderful mother to our pair of little rascals. She's a very sexy woman and the love of my life. And my she's my best friend. She's funny, smart and filled with an amazing zest for life. She's all this and much, much more, and now she has added another feather to her cap by becoming a recognised and highly sought-after photographer.'

He paused and looked at the floor for a second or two while he gathered his thoughts.

'This exhibition of Lucy's work we're going to is more than just a local event. A few days ago, her website went online and by this morning she had already sold seven of her pieces in Europe and in the United States – and for a good price I might add. So, can we all raise our glasses in a toast to my beautiful, darling Lucy, the boss of **Lucy Wilson Photography**. Cheers Lucy. You've gone viral, pet!'

The four of them clinked their glasses together and toasted her success and one by one Claire, Gavin and Charlie kissed her on the cheek and told her how proud they were of her and that she was amazing and her work was wonderful.

Words failed her and Lucy could only grin from ear to ear as she basked in their compliments.

Charlie held her tightly to him and whispered, 'I love you so much.'

It was perfect and Lucy felt as if she were dancing on the top of the world. She had dreamed of becoming a photographer since she was a teenager. But life, as it usually does, got in the way and she played it safe with a 'real job'. Now she was living her dream as a moderately well-known photographer on the brink of becoming world-famous.

It was perfect. Or at least it would be if only the bloody annoying beeping noise in her ear would go away.

'Let's go party,' Charlie whispered in her ear.

Next morning, Lucy groaned and blinked against the pale sunlight as it streamed in through a chink in the curtains.

Too bright. It hurts.

The party had lasted until almost four in the morning. Lucy had no recollection of getting into a taxi. She dimly remembered Charlie telling her that a mate of his was collecting them.

Lucy's brain seemed to be functioning on only the most basic level. She sat up slowly and her head began to spin. Enough alcohol had been downed over the course of the evening to keep a medium-sized distillery in profit.

Never again! Well... until the next time.

Steam rose in faint curls from the mug of tea Charlie had placed on the bedside table for her. He was probably as hungover as she was yet he still got up first to made her a cuppa. Lucy blew gently on it and then took a tentative sip of the hot liquid, thankful that she wasn't feeling nauseous. The tea was good. It made her feel a little better, more awake. But what she really needed was water – lots of water.

Lucy took another sip of tea and climbed out of bed, remembering her dream about Jennifer and Ilan as she dressed. And as she was remembering, it dawned on her that she wasn't really interested in what they had been up to. Right now, her life was much more exciting.

Charlie was sitting at the kitchen table nursing a large mug of strong black coffee. He was dressed in jeans and a tatty sweater. He was pale and dishevelled and could hardly keep his eyes open. He looked terrible.

'Good morning,' Lucy said with a rueful smile.

'What's good about it?'

'I know. I'm feeling poorly myself. Do you want a fry-up?'

'No. I'd only throw it up. I'll stick with the coffee. How are you?'

'I'll survive. I'm tired and I have a headache, and this annoying beeping noise in my ears.'

She switched the kettle on again to make another cup of tea and popped two slices of brown bread into the toaster. 'Thank God for Louise keeping the girls until tomorrow. Are you sure you don't want anything to eat?'

Charlie shook his head. 'Definitely sure. Did you enjoy yourself last night?'

'Oh, Charlie,' she replied with a smile that lit up her face. 'It was magic! You know, I was so nervous at first because I didn't know how things would go. I thought maybe everyone would laugh at some of the photos, especially the macro ones, you know, the close-ups. I mean...' she caught the toast as it jumped out of the toaster, placed both slices on a plate and smeared butter onto them. 'I was worried people wouldn't like them, but they were the most popular. Can you believe it? I sold most of them!'

'I know. I was watching you and I thought your eyes were going to pop out of your head with amazement. You sell yourself short sometimes, Lucy.' Charlie caught her in his arms and kissed her gently. 'You really are an amazing photographer, sweetheart.'

The evening had been a complete success, with more sales than Lucy ever expected, and it seemed people were not going to stop congratulating her for a long time to come.

She had wisely kept it both simple and local. However, both she and Charlie had been amazed at the interest in her exhibition. They hadn't known it at the time, but Claire had videoed all the exhibits and uploaded them to YouTube with a link to Lucy's website. It yielded a lot of interest, and buyers, on a much more global scale than she had ever anticipated.

'It's a little bit frightening,' Lucy said.

'How d'you mean?' Charlie asked.

'The way it's taken off so quickly. I never expected it to, and I never expected people would want to pay big money for some photographs I've taken. I keep waiting for someone to say this is all a big joke.'

'Lucy, love. You need to have more faith in yourself. Why wouldn't people want to pay good money for your photographs? They're genuinely amazing. You're very talented, sweetheart. Do not ever doubt that for a minute.'

Lucy smiled, basking in the glow of his words.

'I love you so much,' she told him.

'Good. Now get down off your pedestal woman and make me another cuppa!'

Chapter 29 - Lucy's Dream

Jennifer glanced up from her work as Ilan opened the study door and stuck his head in.

'Hey there,' he said.

'Hey yourself,' she smiled. 'Come in.'

'Do you want to go out for lunch?'

'You're bored, aren't you?' Jennifer asked.

'Somewhat. And hungry,' Ilan replied.

Jennifer wrinkled her nose and waved her hand over the desk she was sitting at. It was littered with drawings, scribbled notes and swatches of fabric. Even her laptop – open to a design program – sat there, somewhere, buried and ignored beneath all the paper and fabric.

'As tempting as that sounds, I'm really too busy.'

'Can't you take a lunch break? You've been working at that all morning.'

Ilan peered over her head, his hands resting lightly on her shoulders, and studied her sketches and notes. The drawings depicted rooms, a house plan and the layout of various items of furniture within the house and the rooms. Other than that, they made little sense, mainly because Jennifer's work held little interest to him. Jennifer preferred it that way. When she was working on a commission, she locked herself away in the study until she was finished or hunger lured her out.

'I know, and I'll probably be working on it all afternoon too. I'm getting nowhere at the moment. I can't seem to interpret what the buyer wants. It doesn't make sense. The colours will clash and it's gonna look terrible. And of course, I'll be the one who gets the blame when she realises, too late, that she doesn't like it.'

'Maybe a break would help,' Ilan suggested.

'It wouldn't. Listen. How about you go out and get something and I can prepare it here?'

'Are you sure?'

'I'm sure. I'll take a break then and we can have lunch on the patio. With wine, please. And we're low on cat food.'

'Okay, sure. And we can talk about getting married over lunch and a glass or two of wine.'

With those words, Ilan closed the door quietly and left Jennifer to her work.

She placed her elbows on the edge of the desk, cupped her face in her hands and stared at the laptop. It wasn't just her customer that was frustrating her.

Ilan hadn't mentioned getting married again, although sometimes Jennifer thought he was on the brink of talking about it. Then he would hesitate, look at her and say something else. Totally unrelated.

When they returned home from their disastrous trip to Berlin all those months ago Jennifer fully expected him to go into full 'wedding planner' mode and braced herself for an onslaught of ideas and suggestions on how they would spend their special day. But so far nothing. Until now.

If he has planned a big event behind my back, I will kill him while he sleeps.

Jennifer closed her eyes and rubbed her forehead. This had been on the cards since the moment she had agreed to marry him. Just after she had performed minor surgery on him.

I'll stall him. Tell him I'm too busy with work. It's not untrue. I have three big contracts coming up in the next two months. I really do want to marry him. I just hate the idea of having to plan something.

The other, and more immediate, distraction was Lucy and it was time she did something about it. With Ilan out of the house there was no time like the present.

Jennifer pushed her chair back and stood up. She paced the room and thought about what she wanted to say to the woman who haunted her dreams every night, and her thoughts every day.

Suddenly nervous, Jennifer wiped her hands on her jeans and looked around her. She took in the details of the room she stood in.

This is my life. My house and my world. Not in that old house with Lucy and her family.

She took a deep breath. 'Lucy? Hi. Um, I hope you can hear me. I think you and I need to talk.'

Chapter 30 - Jennifer's Dream

Lucy stepped out of the shower, wrapped a towel around her and used her palm to wipe the condensation off the bathroom mirror. Her reflection, through the steam, frowned at her because Jennifer had sent her a very surprising message.

In her latest dream, Ilan had nipped to the corner store. While he was out of the house Jennifer spoke to Lucy and told her she wanted them to meet. In a dream.

'Lucy, we need to talk about this,' Jennifer had said as she stood in the middle of her living room, her eyes fixed on a point up near the ceiling, as if Lucy was hiding in the attic. Lucy noticed how self-conscious she looked standing there talking out loud to an empty room.

'I think we have to try and figure out why this is happening to us and what we should do about it,' Jennifer said. 'And how we stop it. This isn't normal, Lucy. It might even be dangerous. Surely you realise that?'

While Lucy was happy enough to concede what Jennifer said was true, she had no idea what could be done to stop the pair of them dreaming about one another. She wasn't even sure she wanted it to stop. Jennifer's life was interesting. Not that her own wasn't, especially now her photography career had taken off. But Jennifer's was too. Lucy wasn't ashamed to admit to herself that it was a whole lot of fun to experience another person's life through her own eyes.

She had followed Jennifer and Ilan's wedding argument that afternoon as if she had been there. Ilan had pushed for at least some sort of ceremony and a celebration afterwards with a few of their closest friends and nearest relatives. Jennifer had stood her ground, stubbornly refusing to relent and had insisted that she just wanted to show up at the register office, make it legal and then go back home. She did not *want* a ceremony. She didn't want to wear a *wedding dress*, and she damn well didn't want a party of any kind afterwards!

Lucy laughed until tears streamed down her face as she remembered Jennifer's anger over the whole situation when she refused to speak to Ilan. That was bad enough, but then he tried to over-think her reluctance, claiming she didn't love him as much as she said she did. It was a claim that resulted in Jennifer hurling a coffee mug at him. It missed its intended target but dented the wall behind him before it fell to the floor in pieces. The argument showed no sign of ending any time soon when Jennifer blamed Ilan for the loss of her favourite coffee mug.

Then Lucy's dream skipped forward in time to the wedding.

After a week or two of constant bickering, Ilan gave up and told Jennifer, in no uncertain terms, they were getting married the following Wednesday morning, the eleventh of March at eleven o'clock. It was booked and it was up to her if she wanted to show up or not.

Jennifer had replied angrily that the date and time couldn't be more perfect.

'An armistice. Brilliant. More a cessation of hostilities than a wedding,' she had said.

Ilan had glared at her for a moment or two but suddenly burst out laughing as she stood there with a snarl on her lips, ready to launch another mug at him.

They did get married on the day, at the time he had arranged, and it was as quick and painless as it could possibly be. It had been the two of them and the necessary witnesses – staff at the registry office, commandeered at the last moment – and it had taken a little more than fifteen minutes. Despite her protests, Ilan insisted on buying her a wedding ring. It was made from white and yellow gold and inscribed with the Hebrew words – Ani ledodi vedodi li. Jennifer had cried when he translated the inscription – I am to my beloved as my beloved is to me.

Lucy had also cried.

It was moments like their wedding that Lucy enjoyed. And she couldn't deny she enjoyed the sex. *Does that make me a pervy voyeur? Probably.*

She thought about Jennifer's suggestion for a moment or two before making up her mind. Unsure of what it could possibly achieve, or if it was even possible, she decided she would agree to consider Jennifer's request.

But how would they go about it?

Cyprus was two hours ahead of the UK so Jennifer was normally asleep and dreaming before Lucy went to bed. From what Lucy had experienced since this connection began, there was a one-day time lag, meaning that Lucy dreamed what Jennifer experienced the day before. She could only assume the same delay occurred in Jennifer's dreams, but she didn't know this for sure. Maybe if they both fell asleep at the same time it could work, but she was going to tell Jennifer that, even if she could, she wasn't going to stop dreaming.

Chapter 31 - Lucy's Dream

'Ilan, can I ask you something?' Jennifer said as she frowned and chewed thoughtfully at her bottom lip.

She had settled down on the comfortable lounger with a glass of wine in her hand and Ilan was seated at the small table, where he was enjoying a large whiskey. The evening was still and the air around them was infused with the scents of the flowers. The sun had long since set and Jennifer could see a few stars beginning to appear in the night sky.

Maybe this isn't the right time. It's too perfect an evening, why spoil it?

She had arrived home exhausted and frustrated, thanks to a client who couldn't decide what he wanted, to find Ilan in the kitchen chopping onions and mushrooms. The vision her husband presented, dressed in black jeans and a black T-shirt, a tea-towel thrown across his shoulder lifted her mood considerably.

She had quietly set down her handbag, slipped off her shoes and planned to simply watch and admire him for a moment or two. For such a tall man, he was agile and confident in his every movement. Even in the kitchen.

Her culinary voyeurism didn't last very long. Without turning around or looking up from his onion-chopping, he informed her the wine was chilling in the fridge and that dinner would be ready in two hours.

How the hell did he know I was standing here? Obviously, he has some sort of spy super-sense. She was tempted to ask him about it, but she knew he would just laugh away her question.

Dinner had been perfect, as it always was when Ilan cooked. Jennifer rinsed the plates and loaded them into the dishwasher. Between them they tidied the kitchen then moved out onto the terrace to enjoy the rest of the evening. Three large glass jars on the ground near their seats contained candles and the light from them gave off a warm and comforting glow in the semi-darkness.

Jennifer decided this was the perfect time to ask Ilan the question that had been nagging her for ages. Or at least ascertain if he was open to answering her questions.

'Depends on the question,' he replied. 'If it's in relation to my work the answer will be no. But if it is about anything else then, of course, I will attempt to answer you.'

'Do you dream?'

Ilan cocked his head in surprise and looked at her. This was not the question he had been anticipating. A flippant reply was on the tip of his tongue. Along the lines of 'Yes, I dream of winning the lottery.' or 'I dream only of you.' But then he realised she was serious.

He shrugged his shoulders and frowned as he wondered where the conversation was going. 'Yes, of course I dream. Everyone dreams. Why?'

'Do you dream often?' Jennifer asked.

'I have no idea. Define often?'

'I suppose I mean every night.'

'I think everyone dreams every night, but we only remember a fraction of them, and even then, this small fraction is only fragments of perhaps several dreams.'

'Do people dream in sequence?'

Ilan looked at her, a quizzical frown on his face. 'I don't understand.'

Jennifer took a sip of wine. 'I mean, do people dream in such a way that the narrative of one dream follows another? Like, if you're watching a television series, the events of each episode follow in sequence and each episode takes the story forward. And, if that is the case, will there eventually be a dream that concludes the narrative? You know like the last episode of a series?'

'I have absolutely no idea. Why are you asking me this, Jennifer?'

'Because I've been dreaming for ages now. The same dream. Well, almost the same. Remember, I told you years ago, just after you and I met? I'd been dreaming about a couple in England. In Yorkshire. Their names were Lucy and Charlie?'

Ilan nodded. 'Yeah. I remember you telling me about them, and if I remember correctly, you said on another occasion you dreamed you were giving birth.'

'I did. Since then, she's had another daughter. She's also quit her teaching job and is now a free-lance photographer. A very successful one, I might add. And then I told you that they – the dreams – seemed to be in their correct sequence. But you said that it was probably only one dream and I was only remembering fragments of it, which is why I thought I was dreaming every night.'

'Go on,' he said.

'I'm still dreaming Ilan, and no matter what you say, they are in sequence. At least they are now. They were a bit jumbled up until I figured out the narrative. I want to understand why this is happening to me and I want to know what it means. Do you understand?'

He spread his arms out and casually shrugged his shoulders. 'What? Do I look like a fortune teller to you?'

Jennifer burst out laughing, almost choking on her wine in the process. 'Yeah, I can so easily picture you wearing a brightly coloured headscarf, large hooped earrings, and peering into a crystal ball!'

'That's not quite the image I want you to have of me.'

'Okay, I'll picture you naked apart from the headscarf and the earrings. How does that work?'

Ilan shook his head.

'Well, I'm sorry, it's stuck in my mind now,' Jennifer said as she grinned and tapped the side of her forehead. Then her face grew sombre once more. She looked out towards the night sky and she thought she could hear the waves lapping on the beach in the distance. 'But seriously Ilan, from what I've read on the subject, and I know that maybe I shouldn't be asking you this, but have you ever heard of remote viewing?'

He looked at her for a moment, then got up from the chair and walked over to the edge of the terrace. Jennifer watched him as he stared down at the silhouettes of the fig trees on the ground below.

'I've heard of it,' he finally told her, still looking down at the darkened landscape. 'It's a myth. Nothing more than the stuff of science fiction, or tin foil hat-wearing conspiracy theorists.'

'Oh yeah, there are definitely a lot of conspiracy theories out there,' Jennifer said. 'But I did some research on the subject and it wasn't a myth back in the seventies. The CIA did use it, as did the FSB, or KGB as they were known back then and, according to the articles I've read, there were some positive results, so it might still be –'

'Do you believe everything you read on the internet?'

'Of course not. But I wondered if it were remotely, pardon the pun, possible for someone to be able to dream about being in another place with other people and be able to see that place, and those people, and what was happening there. So, I read up on it and –'

'It's not real, Jennifer,' Ilan said as he turned around to look at her.

'I know, but isn't there a possibility it could be?'

'No. I'm familiar with the articles you've read. Most of them are crackpot theories. Yes, there was a program in the United States back in the seventies which did consider the possibility of utilising remote viewing, and for a short time, they did experiment with it. A lot of money was spent on it, twenty million US dollars I believe. A good amount of money back then. But it came to nothing. No useful intelligence was ever obtained and it was scrapped back in the mid-nineties. It was all part of the Cold War paranoia that was rampant at that time.'

'Did Mossad ever work on it?'

'I believe they considered it, around the time the Americans were doing the same, but nothing ever came of it.'

'So, they, I mean Mossad, don't use it today, do they? Under any circumstances? At least that you know of?'

Worried that she may have hit a nerve, Jennifer got up off the chair and stood beside him, close enough to touch but not quite touching.

'Of course not,' Ilan said. He raised his voice slightly in exasperation. 'Why on earth are you asking me these questions?'

'Because I thought maybe, oh God, I know this sounds so stupid. I've been having these weird dreams for so long now that it can't be normal. The details are so amazing and realistic, it's almost as though I'm not only witnessing events, I'm *living* them. I must have read something once about remote viewing and it seemed slightly familiar – like what I'm experiencing now. And that bugged me enough to google it and when I read up on it – I thought you might know something about it. Seriously Ilan, it was only a passing thought. I was wondering why I've been dreaming so much, and then, I don't know why, but I thought maybe you were –'

'Using you to spy on someone by remote viewing? How could you even think that? It's insane!'

Jennifer covered her eyes with her hands and shook her head. 'I'm so sorry Ilan. It really does sound so 'tin foil hat brigade' doesn't it? Maybe you should lock me up now and throw away the key!'

Ilan set his glass down on wall. He took hold of her hands in his and gently pulled them away from her face. In the candlelight, she could not make out the expression on his face.

'I would never, ever use you for those purposes or for any purpose related to my work. You must believe me, Jennifer. Please tell me you believe me.'

'Yes, I believe you. I... well, it is a bit of a coincidence, isn't it?'

'What's a coincidence?'

'That I began having these strange dreams around the same time I met you.'

He pulled back from her. 'Do you honestly believe that?'

'No. Of course not. It just seems so strange.'

Ilan took another step back from her, shaking his head sadly as he turned away. She reached for his arm, grasping it firmly.

'I'm sorry,' she told him.

He glared at her. His eyes were dark and menacing. 'I cannot believe you would accuse me of using you in such a manner?'

Jennifer shook her head as she reached for his hand and pulled him back towards her. 'I'm not accusing you of anything. Honestly. I'm trying to figure out why this is happening to me every night when I go to sleep. It isn't *natural*, and it frightens me! It began around the time I first met you and I couldn't help but put two and two together and –'

'And came up with a million,' he said.

Jennifer laughed and punched Ilan's arm lightly. 'Haven't I've told you a billion times not to exaggerate?'

'Oh, very funny,' he said.

It was difficult to distinguish his sarcasm from his annoyance at her.

'Well, I thought so. But do you understand what I am saying Ilan? I'm trying to figure this out. I thought I could do it alone. But this crazy idea of remote viewing was the only thing that made a button of sense when you consider my situation and how disturbing it is. I am dreaming another life, Ilan. *Every* night when I go to sleep, I dream about someone else. A woman. A year or two older than me. She's completely different from me, yet I know almost everything about her.' Jennifer slowly shook her head back and forth. Partially in denial. Partially in reluctant acceptance.

Ilan stared at his wife.

'And the most disturbing part of all,' she said. 'I think she is dreaming *my* life while I'm dreaming *hers*!'

'Are you fucking serious?'

A seed of fear crept into Ilan's soul. Could it be possible? As far as he was aware, Mossad had abandoned the project many years ago, around the same time that the CIA had decided it was a waste of money and resources. Was it possible that some other agency – Britain's MI6 or the French DGSE – had continued the research on remote viewing? Both had been included in the original project, but as best as he could remember they had all abandoned it around the same time. Or so the histories of the various intelligence agencies told the story. But history was inevitably written by the winner.

'I'm deadly serious,' Jennifer said. 'The funny thing is, other than the concern that there might be something wrong with me, I *enjoy* it. It's somewhere different I can go to in my head. It's interesting. I like her – this woman called Lucy. I like her life. Her husband is nice. He's a funny, likeable and hard-working builder. He's attractive, but not as sexy as you.'

'Go on.'

'Well, that's about it. I wouldn't want to live her life, but I do enjoy experiencing it. It is a bit like a TV series, and I'm –'

'It seems a bit more like virtual reality,' he remarked.

'Yeah, it does. I don't think it's dangerous. I got curious about it and that's why I did the online research for similar dream phenomena. Remote viewing was the most plausible. I also did a bit of research on astral projection or astral travel, because I remember reading a book on it – a horror story actually – when I was young – '

'I believe I know the one you are referring to. I've read it and I can assure you it's complete fiction.'

'Well, the one I'm thinking of didn't make a whole lot of sense in relation to me, so I went back to the remote viewing scenario. Now I'm beginning to wonder if maybe this woman is doing the same – using remote viewing – to spy on you. Remotely, that is, through me. Is that likely?'

'No,' Ilan told her. 'In fact, it is a ridiculous suggestion. It makes no sense at all. Even if such a thing were possible, what would be the point? Do they need to know how good I am in bed? How well I can cook? My life here with you, my relationship with you, has nothing whatsoever to do with my work. There is nothing they can learn about my work from you.'

'I know that,' she said as she paced back and forth. 'I'm sorry. I don't know why this is happening to me. It's interesting, but it also worries me.'

Jennifer stopped pacing and looked at him, a grin spreading across her face. 'How good you are in bed? How well you can cook? I love how you worry about the important things.'

'Well yes, of course,' Ilan said as a grin also spread across his face. 'My techniques and skill, in both the kitchen and in the bedroom, are very important and unique to me. Naturally, I would hate them to fall into the hands of some foreign intelligence service!'

'Full of yourself much?' Jennifer laughed.

'But seriously, Jennifer, why are you thinking this?'

'You think I'm crazy, don't you?'

'I don't think that. I do, however, think you require an explanation for these dreams you're having. They frighten you and you are trying to understand why this is happening to you. Do you honestly believe any of what you have suggested? This remote viewing?'

'No, of course not. I just thought… I don't know what I thought. I mean, there's another possibility which frightens me so much I can't bear to think about it. So, instead of facing that frightening reality, I latched on to the implausible scenario instead.'

He turned to look at her. In the darkness, the glow from the candles was not bright enough to read her expression but he could hear the note of concern in her voice.

'What is this… *other* possibility?

'That I…' Jennifer hesitated. 'That I might have a brain tumour.'

Chapter 32 - Jennifer's Dream

'A brain tumour! Oh my God!'

'Did you say something?' Charlie asked as he stuck his head around the door, a toothbrush in his hand and a smear of toothpaste on his lips.

'Er, no. I was thinking out loud. Planning what I'm supposed to be doing today.'

'What are you supposed to be doing today?' he asked in between rinsing his teeth.

'Not a whole lot. I have some orders to post, which I'll do after I take the girls to school. Then invoices to send out and that's about it. I'll maybe meet Claire for lunch. Depends on the weather and if she's free. What about you?'

'I'm going to be busy all day. I've several estimates to look at and some orders to sort out for that new build we're starting next week. And I'm putting in a tender for a council contract. Keep your fingers crossed for me on that one.'

'I will,' she told him.

He pulled on a sweater and jeans, gave her a quick kiss on the cheek and disappeared down the stairs.

Lucy busied herself getting the girls ready for school, all the while thinking about Jennifer's theory. She had no idea what Jennifer meant by remote viewing. It was a term Lucy had never heard of and she couldn't even imagine what it meant. She intended to google it when she had a free moment. But, for now, she was more concerned by the notion there might be a more organic source for this situation. It was possible that there was a medical reason for the dreams, and a serious one at that, and that frightened her more than anything.

A crash and a squeal interrupted her thoughts. She turned around to see Amy with an apologetic expression on her face and her breakfast bowl upside down on the floor. Milk and soggy chocolate cereal spread in an off-white bloom across the kitchen tiles. Ross, the new puppy, ran in fear from the sound of the crash. But he found his courage again and leapt forward in delight at this unexpected windfall.

'I'm sorry Mummy,' Amy said, an expression of wide-eyed innocence on her face. 'It fell off the table all by itself.'

Well, of course it did.

Amy rarely accepted responsibility for anything, even when caught red-handed. If there was no one else around to blame then, according to Amy, it just happened. Charlie had nick-named her The Poltergeist. The name suited her.

It's gonna be one of those days. Lucy sighed as she cleaned up the spilt milk, trying her best to keep the pup away from it in the process. She poured fresh cereal into another bowl, added milk and this time kept a close eye on Amy until she was finished. She checked her watch.

'Ready and in the car in five minutes, girls,' Lucy warned them of the time.

As she drove along the narrow road towards the village, listening to the girls chattering contentedly in the back seat, Lucy glanced at the ominous clouds gathering in the distance. The forecast this morning had been for snow later in the day, and it was looking highly likely there would be a fall by this evening.

It wasn't uncommon for snow this late in the spring and Lucy hoped there would be a decent covering this evening and overnight.

Tomorrow was Saturday and it would be great fun to spend the day playing with Charlie and the girls outside in the snow. They could go sledding, build a snowman and have a good snowball fight. Then she would make hot chocolate, with added marshmallows for the girls and brandy for the adults.

If there's enough snow, I can go nuts with the camera!

An idea for Christmas gifts of winter-inspired festive canvasses, mugs, coasters and place settings, along with matching Christmas cards, had popped into Lucy's head back in October and she had been waiting for all winter for the opportunity to get some good snow scene photos.

She loved snow, but for now, she would be happy if it would hold off until this evening, so the girls and Charlie could get back home safe and sound.

With lots of kisses and hugs and a stern warning to behave themselves, Lucy dropped the girls off at primary school. The sleepy little village had a school, three pubs and a pokey little corner shop which struggled to sell anything with a 'best before' date that was in the future. But no post office. And it was a post office Lucy needed.

A fifteen-minute drive took her to a nearby large town that did. After only one loop of the town, she managed to find a parking space and nabbed it before anyone else did. She made her way, struggling with her large sack of envelopes, into the post office where she joined the long queue. She glanced impatiently at her watch every few minutes as she inched slowly towards the counter.

Next stop was Tescos which, thankfully, wasn't busy. The panic buying hadn't begun yet. Lucy only needed coffee and eggs but she figured she might as well get her weekly groceries while she was there.

I've caught bad weather stock-up syndrome. Lucy laughed to herself as she put a pound coin in the slot to release the trolley. Once inside, she flew around the aisles, grabbing items from her mental shopping list that she hoped was identical to the written one she had left on the kitchen table.

Back home in record time, Lucy did her best to ignore Ross as she carried the groceries into the house. All the puppy training books and YouTube videos said do this to prevent him peeing with excitement when someone walked through the front door.

The trouble was, Ross had not read the books or watched the videos, and he wagged his tail and peed right in front of her.

But he was a good dog and he helped Lucy tear the paper towels into shreds while she wiped up the urine and barked frantically when she sprayed the floor with a disinfectant that was supposed to discourage puppies from peeing in certain areas. So far, it wasn't living up to its hard-hitting advertising campaign.

She played with him for a while, incorporating some basic training in with the play. After a while, and a surprising degree of progress, Ross either got bored or tired and strolled off to his bed – a well-chewed cardboard box lying on its side in the utility room. He curled up for a short nap on his blankie. To recharge the batteries, as Charlie put it. Once Ross was settled, she made a cup of tea and began the boring task of filing her invoices and orders, all the while keeping an eye on the gathering clouds in the distance.

Once she had finished filing her paid and posted invoices, Lucy spent another hour emailing a batch to clients who had made online purchases but were still waiting to pay her. As she stretched to ease her aching shoulders – she hated being hunched over a keyboard – she could hear the wind howling outside. It had picked up considerably in the last thirty or so minutes and the possibility of a blizzard later was becoming more and more likely.

Might be a good idea to cook dinner now, then I can heat it up later.

In the kitchen, Lucy set about preparing the meat and vegetables for a beef and tomato casserole that they could enjoy by candlelight if necessary. She listened to the weather reports on the radio, while she chopped the onions and carrots and the radio announcer told her it was going to be a big storm. Lucy added the herbs and the red wine and glanced out the window. From the look of the sky outside, the weather guy was spot on.

Lucy enjoyed extreme weather. She loved nothing more than to be cuddled up safe and warm, in front of the fire, while the elements fought their battle outside. But right now, she crossed her fingers that the storm would hold off until her family could be home with her, safe and sound.

She lit the fire and it burned burning brightly with cheery warmth. The central heating was on and the two torches they kept in the kitchen drawer had full batteries. Lucy checked them twice. She also had candles and a box of matches. Both her laptop and mobile phone were fully charged.

Leaving the casserole to cook slowly in the oven, Lucy opened the back door and stepped outside with Ross hot on her heels. She braced against the cold wind as it slammed into her, scattered some bird feed on the small bird table by the window and filled the feeders up with nuts, keeping an eye on Ross as she did so.

Lucy shivered as she waited, encouraging him to hurry up. The puppy ran around in circles, sniffing the grass and was almost blown over by the wind. Finally, he crouched down, he was still too young to cock his leg, and peed for what seemed like ages. Then he was off at a run again, racing around the garden at full pace. In his mind, Lucy suspected, Ross was racing on some imaginary Grand Prix track. He down-shifted and braked through the pear tree chicane, accelerated hard down the long straight behind the apple tree and then gave it all he had around the sweeping last corner before, to the delight of thousands of cheering fans, he took the chequered flag.

He stopped and did the rest of his business in celebration of his fantastic victory. Lucy praised him to the ends of the earth as she ushered him back indoors, thankful to be back inside, away from the wind, and wrapped in the warm comfort of the house.

Even though it was afternoon, it was almost dark. Dark enough for Lucy to worry about the power going off. In case it did, she lit several candles and placed them around the house. Two in the kitchen. Two in glass jars in the hallway and one in the living room. Then she ran upstairs and lit one in the bedroom and another in the en-suite. They would burn safely all evening and prevent her from stumbling around the house in utter darkness.

One more mental check to make sure she was fully prepared for what the weather forecasters said was going to be the biggest snowfall for many years. Lucy would be madder than hell if they were wrong.

The fires were lit and the central heating was on, both pumping out warmth and cheery comfort. The puppy would be okay for a few hours. The cat, Gene Pitney (AKA, The Genie) – named because of his high-pitched howling in the middle of the night – was curled up asleep on a chair. His litter tray was strategically placed where *he* could avail of it, but where Ross who, much to everyone's disgust, considered it a snack box, couldn't get his nose into it.

Dinner just had to be warmed up on the gas hob once everyone got home and, most importantly, there were two bottles of wine chilled in the fridge.

I'm all sorted. Bring it on!

Then her phone rang. It was Charlie.

'I'm so sorry, sweetheart,' he said. 'It's proper snowing here. About five inches down already and they've closed the roads. I'll not be getting home tonight.'

'What about the girls?' A seed of concern began to grow in her heart, imagining her daughters huddled in the school gym, burning their textbooks to stay warm, and smashing the snack vending machine to feed themselves before starting on the smallest kids.

'They're here with me,' he said. Amy and Chloe yelled 'hello' in the background to confirm his statement.

'Kenny and his missus said we can stay with them overnight so I'm at their house now. The girls are fine and think it's a great adventure. But are you going to be okay on your own? I could give it a shot, maybe ask the police to let me through.'

'No. You stay with the girls. I don't want you risking your neck on dangerous roads. I'm not happy about it, but I'll be okay.'

'I'm sorry, love. There's nowt I can do about it.'

'I know.'

'Keep the heating on while you have electricity, and make sure you have plenty of wood for the fire for when it does go off.'

Oh, shit! I forgot the extra wood for the stove.

'Uh, yeah. I have plenty,' she lied.

I'll get it when I get off the phone.

'Lucy, I can hardly make you out. What did you say?'

'Don't worry. I'll be fine,' she yelled. As if yelling would make the reception any better.

'What?'

'I said, I'm okay.'

'Gotcha. Love you. Stay warm.'

She was about to reply when the signal disappeared and the line went dead.

'Looks like it's just you and me tonight boy,' she said. Ross wagged his tail. 'Well… you, me and the kitty cat. But first I need to go out and get us some firewood.'

By nine-thirty, there was almost a foot of snow lying on the ground. It was still falling heavily and showed no sign of abating. The electricity had failed just as Lucy had finished her bowl of warmed-up stew, poured another glass of wine, and was about to settle down to watch a movie on TV.

She decided to call it a night and tried to get Ross to go outside for a quick pee before bed. He took one look at the whirling flakes and the layer of icy whiteness that covered his usual toilet and ran back inside, safe from the cold and the howling wind.

'Okay,' Lucy told him. 'I don't usually condone letting you pee in the house but this is an exceptional circumstance, so it's okay to use these puppy training pads. But just for tonight. And please, don't eat them.'

Ross looked up at her with an expression that said, 'I have absolutely no idea what you are saying so I'll sit here wagging my tail, with a look of adoration on my face, while I'll pretend to understand. Does that work for you?'

'Good boy,' she told him as she filled his bowl with fresh water, tidied the blanket in his bed, made sure he had all his toys close by and gave him his bedtime dog biscuit.

But Lucy knew that if she went to bed, she would be too cold, and too worried about any storm damage to be able to sleep. Since the electricity was likely to remain off until tomorrow, she realised it would be warmer downstairs by the fire. She dragged the duvet off the bed, carried it downstairs and threw it on the sofa. More wood on the fire and she settled down with her glass of wine, mesmerised by the candles as they flickered, and the shadows they created around her. Outside, the wind howled and the snow continued to fall. Lucy was warm and comfortable and bored out of her mind.

She passed the next couple of hours on the sofa, tucked under the duvet watching a DVD on her laptop. After the movie finished and the battery was too low to watch another, Lucy picked up a paperback but found her eyes getting sore as she struggled to read the print by candlelight.

Her thoughts strayed to her dreams and, as she drank her wine, she decided to have a little chat with Jennifer.

'Jennifer. Hey, Jennifer! Can you hear me?'

Lucy spoke aloud to the dimly lit room and gulped a mouthful of wine for courage. This was her second large glass and she felt a bit daft and somewhat nervous about what she was doing. Gene, who had joined her earlier, lifted his head and meowed in response to her voice but went back to sleep when she didn't react to him.

She pulled herself upright on the sofa.

'You said we need to discuss this, whatever this is. This psychic connection, for want of a better term. Well okay Jennifer, let's discuss it. Let's talk about it.'

She paused and gathered her thoughts. 'When you told Ilan you were worried you might have a brain tumour, I'll confess that frightened me. But your MRI

scan was clear, and I really enjoyed your first trip to
Israel, by the way. Oh, and that Berlin experience – nice
needlework. But, let's not digress. It's obvious something
else is causing our little connection and, regardless of
what it is and what it means, you want it to end. It alarms
you and you're worried that I might be… spying on your
spy. Well, I'm not. Honestly.'

Lucy giggled. 'Although I must confess, I do
sometimes spy on him when he's wearing his swimming
trunks. Nice body. *Very* nice body. But that's the only
reason I spy on him. I'd be mad not to, wouldn't I?'

She took another drink of wine, enjoying the
welcoming buzz. Outside she could hear the wind and she
wondered if the snow was still falling. It was tempting to
nip outside and have a look, but she was too warm and
comfortable to be bothered and, as she sipped her wine,
she thought about what else she wanted to say to Jennifer.

'You wanna know something, Jennifer? I don't
really like you all that much. I mean, you're okay, but I
doubt we'd be friends if we met. You know, if we were
neighbours and knew one another. In real life, so to
speak. Seriously, you can be a bit full of yourself
sometimes. Up your own arse, as Charlie would say.'

Whoa. Don't overdo it.

Lucy paused before she said something she might
regret later. She had a feeling Jennifer could be
dangerous even if she did turn out to be nothing more
than a character in her dreams. Lucy frowned. That hint
of disquiet, of menace, that she felt sporadically when she
thought about Jennifer didn't make a whole lot of sense.
It was merely a feeling and something she wouldn't be
able to explain if she were asked.

She poured another glass of wine and continued.

'I'm sorry. I don't really mean that. You're probably
a nice person, really. I do think you're a great interior

designer and I know how much you love Ilan. Anyway, maybe we should try and sort this out. Unfortunately, I have no idea how on earth we do that, and I'm not totally convinced I want to. You see, although I might look like a bored housewife and mother, I'm not. I have a wonderful family, a lovely home, an interesting career and a husband I love with all my heart and soul. But sometimes I'm alone a lot. Charlie often works away from home – when you think about it, that's one thing we *do* have in common – Ilan is frequently away for longer periods than Charlie. Hey! Do you think that's why we share each other's dreams? Are we both that lonely?'

She considered the words she had spoken.

Am I that lonely?

A shiver ran through her, despite the warmth from the fire, as she struggled to convince herself that this was neither the case nor the reason.

Okay, I'll admit, when the girls are at school and Charlie is working away from home, there are some days when I don't have anyone to talk to, but I like it that way now and then. Not always, but it's good to have time to myself. Some quality me time.

'I do enjoy dreaming about you, Jennifer,' Lucy continued. 'You're – you and Ilan – are like my favourite characters in my favourite TV series. I look forward most nights to tuning in for another episode. And you know what? I don't want to stop tuning in. I'm not going to. If you want to try and stop, fine. Do that. But I intend to continue. And with that, I'm going to sleep. Sweet dreams Jennifer!'

Lucy drained the last of her wine from the glass and set it down on the coffee table. She put more coal and logs in the stove and settled down on the sofa for the night, pulling the duvet snugly around her, cocooning herself in its warmth. She fell asleep immediately.

Chapter 33 - Lucy's Dream

Well, we'll have to see about that.

Jennifer awakened to noises from the kitchen that told her Ilan was making coffee. Then he switched on the television to listen to the morning news and she couldn't hear anything other than the voice of the news announcer – reporting on an economic trade deal or something. She tuned it out as she climbed out of bed.

Jennifer was angry. Lucy's drunken soliloquy had made her so angry she wanted to scream and lash out at something or someone. Preferably Lucy.

Dressing quickly in faded jeans and her favourite purple T-shirt, she made her way into the kitchen and opened a can of cat food which she took out to the terrace. She ignored Ilan. That spy super sense of his was sure to pick up on her mood and right now she didn't want to experience his remarkable interrogation techniques. He would elicit answers from her that she would not be comfortable revealing to him.

She fed the two cats who were waiting patiently below the potted palm tree and took a seat on one of the sun loungers. It was going to be warm today. Warmer than usual for this early in the season and they had planned to spend the day at the beach – some swimming and maybe some fishing later.

She sat there, arms crossed and still angry, and mulled over Lucy's message from her dream. *All that shit about me being up my own arse. Who does Lucy think she is anyway? Here I am, enjoying a sun-kissed island I call home. I have a husband as loving and caring as Charlie the builder. A successful career I didn't just luck into and lots of good friends. I'm happy and I'm never lonely.*

Not like Lucy, sitting there all alone in her big house, bordering on alcohol dependency, and whining on and on about how she loved to experience someone else's life in her dreams because her own life was so sad and boring.

Well, screw you, Lucy. Look at the difference between us. My husband is making a tasty breakfast which we'll share out here on this beautiful terrace. Then we'll go swimming and I'll sunbathe for a while. What are you going to do today, Lucy? Freeze your tits off because you have no electricity and no heating and there's a foot of snow outside your door? And where is your husband? Your family? With you? Nah, I don't think so.

This ends tonight! I won't have you in my head any longer. I'm bored with your life. Your kids and your new puppy, and your photos, and your husband. It ends tonight and I'm going to do whatever it takes to make sure of that.

'Pancakes?' Ilan was holding a plate of them drenched in maple syrup and two smaller side plates with cutlery balanced on them. He set everything down on the table and split the pile of pancakes between them onto the smaller plates.

'You look very serious, neshama. What are you thinking about?'

'I'm hoping the sea isn't too cold for a swim.'

Jennifer kept a happy smile on her face as she tucked into her breakfast and made up her mind to sort this out once and for all. She had an idea how she would do it, although she would have to wait until she went to bed to put her plan into action.

Just get through the day and sort it all out tonight.

Ilan and Jennifer spent the day swimming and sunbathing as they had planned. Lunch was mostly wine and snacks and by afternoon, Jennifer was happy to fall asleep on the sun lounger for an hour or so. By evening she was content and happy and, more importantly, wide awake. But she wasn't taking any chances and made herself another coffee.

'Do you realise that will be your third cup of coffee this evening? You won't sleep tonight,' Ilan remarked as he watched her add a tiny splash of milk to the large mug of steaming hot liquid.

That's what I'm aiming for. That's why I did hardly anything other than snooze all day so I wouldn't be tired.

'I'm fine,' Jennifer replied. 'I have a craving for coffee tonight. And I could murder a bar of chocolate. I'm sorry, I have a couple of design ideas running around in my head and I know I'm not going to be able to sleep until I flesh them out in more detail.'

It wasn't exactly a lie. She did have several ideas for a whole new range, and she probably would work on them this evening and well into the night to keep her from giving in and falling asleep.

'Well, if you end up tossing and turning because you've overdosed on caffeine do not disturb me.' There was a warning tone in his voice which he softened with a smile.

Jennifer smiled wryly. She had no plans to disturb him but she was determined to stay awake all night in the hope she could break this insane connection with Lucy.

By eleven o'clock Jennifer was engrossed in a movie. Ilan gave it ten minutes then declared it the worst movie he'd ever seen and went off to bed, the paperback he had been reading earlier tucked under his arm. Jennifer crossed her fingers that he would read only a few pages before settling down to sleep.

She slipped into the kitchen, poured another cup of strong black coffee and settled down again in front of the television, her notes and a sketch pad of designs on the coffee table in front of her. There was another movie that looked interesting so she downloaded it and decided to do some work before watching it. After that? Well, she would think of something, anything, to keep her from sleeping. Maybe a walk. Nothing too brisk. A gentle stroll in the fresh night air to stimulate her and keep her from any tempting thoughts of climbing into bed and curling up beside Ilan.

By now, normally – though normally wasn't a word she would use to describe her situation – she would be in a deep sleep and living in Lucy's world.

Personally, Jennifer had nothing against Lucy. In some respects, she even liked her. But this couldn't go on. It was becoming too intrusive – the way she would remember things that were not part of her life as she went about her day. It had to stop, and if staying up all night and sacrificing her sleep meant she could make it stop, then she was more than happy to stay awake for however long it would take.

She glanced at the clock. It was a quarter to three. *I'm almost there.*

In a few hours it would be daylight and Ilan would be stirring. She knew she would have to slip into bed before he wakened and she could pretend she had been there all night, fast asleep beside him.

This plan wasn't as simple as it sounded. Ilan had almost cat-like instincts and would awaken, instantly alert, at the slightest noise or movement. Over the years, Jennifer had learned how not to disturb him, but it wasn't easy. Her movements had to be slow, silent and deliberate.

Alternatively, she could put on a fresh pot of coffee and pretend to be up before him. This might be the better option and one that she might well consider come the morning.

Jennifer yawned and stretched as weariness began to catch up with her and that annoying beeping noise was still in her head. Normally, she could ignore it and get on with her day but now, in the quietness of the night, it was incessant and disturbing. If anything, it seemed louder than before.

She frowned and rubbed her arm and wondered why it felt tender as if she had been pricked by a needle or, more likely, bitten by an insect. But there was no itchy lump, bruise or puncture wound of any kind. There was no explanation for it other than she must have bumped it, or something had scratched it, so slightly that it would hurt but not show. She also had a niggling sore throat and hoped she wasn't coming down with a cold or the flu.

It was still dark outside with no hint of the dawn breaking yet and Jennifer knew she was going to be a wreck all day. But there was nothing she could do about it.

On the plus side, ideas for her new designs had come thick and fast and she was pleased with what she had achieved. If nothing else, that alone was worth the exhaustion.

Her eyelids grew heavier and heavier and the minutes crawled by so slowly now. This was the longest night of her life. She remembered when she was in her twenties and could go clubbing and partying all night long, stopping at a café somewhere for breakfast before going home to crash for a couple of hours. How did she manage it?

I can't be that old now that I'm not capable of staying up for one night. I'll wait until it's almost seven then I'll take a shower. Ilan will think I'm just up. God, I'm knackered. I wonder what Lucy will think of this?

Chapter 34 - Jennifer's Dream

Nothing. Not a single image. Not even a fragment.

No voices. No sounds of traffic through the open window. No cats meowing for food, or a radio playing in the background. No day-to-day events. No sailing or swimming, or sex, or dinner out on the patio. Or the terrace as Jennifer called it.

Nothing.

Lucy felt a creeping sense of disquiet wash over her as she realised that this was the first morning in a long, long time she had no recollection of dreaming. She was so used to reflecting on Jennifer's day while she planned her own that she felt bereft – as though she had lost a friend.

Has something happened? What changed since that night way back in March? Back then? It seems like it was only a couple of nights ago – that night when it snowed so heavily and I was all alone in the house and ended up a little drunk – okay, a lot drunk – and I spoke aloud to Jennifer?

Lucy had said some things she regretted the next morning. But she hadn't thought about it since. Until now.

Have I pissed Jennifer off somehow?

She had no way of knowing… and that disturbed her even more.

Despite being in the company of her family and her friends, the sensation of being alone remained with Lucy all day. She felt detached from everyone around her. *With* them, yet *apart* from them. It seemed like she was watching them through an old window pane, rendered almost opaque with years of dust and grime.

Even their voices were distant – she could hear them but they sounded so far away. Amy and Chloe along with Claire's kids – Lily, Karen and Mark – had temporarily abandoned the paddling pool and were running around squealing with laughter as Charlie sprayed them with the garden hose. Ross barked in delight as he joined in the game. He was snapping and biting at the jet of water as it hit him, soaking him, and he shook the water off, making all of them laugh even harder.

Gavin was in a lazy mood and, armed with a giant yellow super soaker that contained about a gallon of water, he had positioned himself behind the largest of Lucy's hydrangeas, where he was playing the role of sniper and shooting a powerful jet of water at anyone who got within his firing range.

It was a typical scene of two families, all of them good friends, playing on the lawn on a warm summer's day and Lucy was right there in the garden with them.

Or am I?

She frowned as the question slipped, unwanted, into her mind. Something was off. Like there was a delay in time, or a watch with a sticking hand, and she was out of step with the world around her. It wasn't a good feeling. It seemed to be getting stronger as if she was moving farther and farther away from them.

'Are you alright?'

'I'm sorry, what did you say?' Lucy blinked and turned to her friend who now stood beside her. She could have sworn Claire had been relaxing on one of the sun loungers.

There was that sense of time distortion again.

'You're standing there as white as a sheet like you've seen a ghost or something. What's wrong?' Claire asked.

'Nothing. Nothing at all,' Lucy replied.

'Are you sure about that? You looked totally out of it for a while there.'

I'm out of phase. Isn't that what they call it in sci-fi movies? Am I in a sci-fi movie?

'No, I'm fine. I have a bit of a headache. A migraine and it's making me feel a little queasy.'

'Are you hungover?' Claire asked.

'I haven't had a drink all week. This is my first glass of wine since last Saturday.'

Lucy looked at the glass she held in her hand. She took a sip and grimaced. The ice had melted and diluted the taste of the wine.

'This is disgusting. I need a fresh one,' she said and headed towards the door, hoping Claire wouldn't follow her inside.

But Claire was right behind her. She leaned against the kitchen counter and watched Lucy tip the contents of her wine glass into the sink, open the fridge door and pour herself another glass. Lucy then topped up Claire's glass, added a couple of ice cubes to her own and turned to face her best friend.

'What?'

'I don't know what you mean, Lucy.'

'Claire, you are following me around like a lost puppy, asking me if there's anything wrong, and even when I tell you there isn't, you still persist.'

'There's something not right with you, Lucy. Something amiss that I can't put my finger on. Fuck's sake! We're best friends and we've known each other since we were wee bairns at school together.' Claire had picked up a lot of Gavin's Scottish words and was claiming them as her own. 'I know you better than anyone and I'm telling you something's off with you.'

'You're wrong, Claire.'

'You know you can tell me anything, Lucy.'

Lucy smiled and looked at her friend. 'Honestly, there's nothing to tell. I have a headache and an annoying beeping noise in my ear and I'm tired – this week has been so busy. I thought I could recharge my batteries this weekend but they're still a bit flat.'

Claire gave her a look that told her she wasn't even a little bit convinced, but Lucy shrugged her shoulders and waited to see if her friend was going to let it drop or continue with her interrogation.

Lucy fidgeted with some crumbs on the counter as she waited. Claire seemed unsure of what to do or say. But Lucy refused to give her the opening.

'Wanna go and watch the rest of the gunfight outside?' Claire asked as she finally gave up.

'I have a much better idea,' Lucy replied and went to the cupboard in the utility room. She returned with two super-soakers like the one Gavin was armed with.

'Let's join in,' she said with a grin.

They filled the giant water pistols from the kitchen tap, finished their wine and like a pair of Wild West gunslingers – that rare kind of Wild West gunslingers who wore bikini tops, denim shorts and flip-flops – they went back out into the garden to do battle.

Chapter 35 - Tel Aviv

Seven days since the accidents.

Ilan couldn't move. He was paralysed by fear as he sat quietly in the doctor's office. His shoulders were hunched forward and he kept his hands flattened on the seat underneath his legs to stop them trembling while he waited.

He wanted to look at his watch, but what was the point? Time didn't matter anymore. He could sit there for an hour or a day or even a week and it wouldn't matter. Nothing would matter until Jennifer was with him again.

An eternity passed – or it could have been five minutes – then the door behind him opened and the doctor rushed in. He was carrying a plastic cup of coffee in one hand and he had a thick file under his arm – that threatened to slip out and spill onto the floor. He appeared flustered.

'I must apologise for my tardiness. I was dealing with another patient and it took a little longer than I anticipated. Please forgive me.'

The doctor didn't wait for a response but merely set the file on top of the cabinet behind the desk and sat down. He placed the coffee to one side where it couldn't be knocked over accidentally, and where he could conveniently forget about it. Of course, calling it coffee was stretching the definition somewhat. It might look like coffee and even smell like coffee, but like all vending machine coffee, it didn't come close to the real thing. He only bought it out of habit and if he forgot himself and took a sip, he was very quickly reminded that he was trying to give up vending machine coffee.

He took off his glasses and rummaged around in one of the desk drawers until he produced a cloth. He then proceeded to give the glasses a good cleaning – breathing on them, rubbing them, and then holding them up to the light several times to check his progress.

'How is she?' Ilan said. He was tired of waiting. He needed answers. It had been seven long, terrible days. This waiting and not knowing was killing him.

'One moment, please,' the doctor replied. He put on his glasses and peered at his computer screen. He jiggled the mouse back and forth, and up and down, before he clicked it a couple of times. 'Let's see what the latest updates have to say.'

Ilan leaned forward in his chair as he awaited the doctor's words. He needed to hear them but he also dreaded what the man in front of him might tell him.

'Jennifer appears to be making progress. It's early days yet and she is still being weaned off the sedation, but we believe she is slowly awakening. She is responsive to sound and pain stimuli. Not to a great degree yet, but she is proceeding in the right direction. Judging by her increased gag reflex – it is still relatively insignificant, but it is there – she appears to be beginning to fight the intubation. That is a definite sign of increased wakefulness and, as such, it is good news. By tomorrow afternoon she will be off the sedation drugs entirely and we are hopeful we will see signs of her regaining consciousness. Her latest CT scan shows more… normal brain activity, which is exactly the result we have been hoping for. Have you any questions?'

'This sounds positive, but will she wake up fully?'

'That we do not know. All we can do is hope, but the signs are good.'

'Are you certain?'

'As certain as I can be with the evidence in front of me.'

'When will you know?'

'That I cannot answer. Look, you must understand we can still only wait. It's up to her now.'

'She was... I mean... she is a strong woman.'

The doctor nodded. 'That is in her favour.'

Ilan shook hands with the doctor, thanked him and left the office to go back and sit by her bedside where he belonged. As he held her hand in his, he tried to hold on to the tiny seed of hope that was beginning to grow in his soul.

Chapter 36 - Jennifer & Lucy's Dream

Jennifer glanced at her watch, switched off the bathroom light and made her way into the bedroom. It was almost one-thirty in the morning, which meant it was two hours earlier in the UK, and since Lucy tended to be in bed by eleven at the latest on a weeknight, she was most likely asleep by now.

I hope she hasn't changed her routine.

Jennifer slipped under the covers beside her husband. Ilan twisted around in his sleep, curved himself against her back and his arms pulled her close to him. She felt herself drifting away the moment her head hit the pillow and she sighed contentedly as she felt his body against hers. Her eyelids grew heavy and she fell into a deep, deep sleep.

Lucy casually pulled the chair out from the table and, with a smile, invited Jennifer to take a seat beside her.

Jennifer moved the chair a little bit further to the left, making a show of putting a more comfortable distance between her and this woman who was, technically speaking, a stranger. She reluctantly sat down, keeping her face neutral as she glanced at the woman in front of her.

'Would you like something to eat or drink?' Lucy asked.

At her words, a waiter materialised from out of nowhere and handed each of them a leather-bound folder containing the kind of lunch menu one would find in a five-star restaurant. Before she had even studied all the items on the menu, Jennifer arched her brows at the opulence of the fine leather that was so out of character with the small sidewalk café where they were sitting.

Jennifer glanced around her. The street was familiar yet she could not place it. It looked a little bit like Paris but it could as easily be an older part of an American city – New York or Los Angeles perhaps. The sky was bright blue, almost too bright, and interspersed with fluffy white clouds that floated gently across its expanse. The scent of jasmine surrounded her, yet light pink petals of cherry blossom skipped along the pavement, carried along by the gentle breeze. She could have been in Tokyo, although it didn't seem overly Asian. It merely hinted at it. Vancouver sprung to mind because, in some respects, Vancouver had an Asian quality to it. She had been there twice and this place reminded her slightly of the city.

But something was off. There was something strange about this place and she couldn't quite put her finger on it. Everything was a little too perfect. The sky was too blue. The clouds were too fluffy and white. The scents of the flowers were too strong. They should have been diluted by the normal every day smells of a large city – exhaust fumes, food, people. But they weren't. It seemed too perfect to be real.

'We should order,' Lucy's voice interrupted her thoughts.

'Should we?' Jennifer asked, arching an eyebrow at the pleasantly casual tone of Lucy's voice.

The waiter hovered nearby, pencil and notepad at the ready.

'Yes, of course,' Lucy replied, smiling brightly. 'What better way to discuss this… situation of ours than over a nice lunch and maybe a glass or two of wine in these beautiful surroundings?'

'Where are we precisely?' Jennifer asked.

'Ah, I thought you might ask that. I don't know, to be honest. I don't even know how I got here. One minute I was standing in my kitchen, talking to my husband. I had a headache because I fell and bumped my head yesterday. I'd been hiking, taking photos and on the way home I tripped, sprained my ankle and hit my head on a rock. I'd also drank about a bottle and a half of wine last night. It was a lovely evening and the girls were staying with friends, so Charlie and I sat out on the patio until it got dark. Just relaxing. Talking and drinking and enjoying the lovely weather and the sunset.'

Lucy smiled at the memory of the night before. It had been one of those rare, nearly perfect evenings.

'Then this morning,' she continued. 'I had a hell of a headache. And suddenly it got sharp like a knife going through my skull. It was blinding. Agony. It stopped me in my tracks and I couldn't move, and I remember standing in the kitchen. I was about to ask Charlie something – dunno what – and I remember falling and I could hear Charlie yelling, and sirens, and I thought something was wrong with one of the girls. And the next minute I was sitting here, waiting for you to join me.'

'Seriously?' Jennifer raised an eyebrow.

'Yeah, seriously.'

'This is crazy,' Jennifer said.

'How did you get here?' Lucy asked.

'Well, I walked here. I came from over there. I, uh…' Jennifer frowned and glanced in the direction she thought she had come from. It seemed wrong. She had no recollection of walking along the pavement, of avoiding the nearby puddle or walking past the newspaper stand or the shoe shop. Like the waiter, she had suddenly appeared here in front of the table she was now sitting at.

'I don't remember how I got here,' she admitted.

'What's the last thing you do remember?' Lucy asked.

She frowned in concentration. 'Late last night. We were in the car. Ilan was driving. He was driving really fast because we were being chased.'

She stopped as the memories came flooding back.

'Take your time,' Lucy said.

'We… grabbed a few things – clothes, and passports, and stuff. And his gun. It was serious. That's why he had the gun with him. You see, he's a…' Jennifer hesitated.

'I already know he's a Mossad officer, Jennifer,' Lucy rolled her eyes. 'Go on.'

'We were running because someone wanted to kill Ilan. They were going to shoot him and probably me, too. And we were trying to get to a safe house and these men were following us. Ilan was angry, but he was frightened too. Like I was. Frightened, I mean. Then he spotted a narrow side road into the forest and he turned sharply and we thought we'd lost them. But we couldn't be sure so he still had his foot down. Then we drove around a corner, and there was a truck – one of those big brutes they use for hauling logs. It was right there in the middle of the road, and… I was screaming as we hit the truck almost head-on, and we were spinning around, and I could hear glass breaking all around me. It seemed like we were spinning forever. I was wearing my seatbelt but I think I hit my head on something. Then the car stopped moving and… Ilan was sleeping beside me. I could see his head on the pillow. I thought I had dreamt it, but I'm thinking now that the pillow was the airbag. I was so tired and all I wanted to do was close my eyes and fall into a deep, deep sleep.'

Jennifer shivered despite the warm air. 'And now I'm here. How is that possible?'

Lucy shrugged. 'I have no idea. Anyway, I'd love a bite to eat so let's order and we can talk about it over lunch.'

As if by magic, the waiter appeared at her side once again. Lucy ordered a Caesar salad and a large glass of white wine. He jotted it down and turned his attention to Jennifer.

'I'll have the same.'

The waiter took the menus from them and disappeared. Jennifer and Lucy sat there and stared at one another, unsure what to say or do.

'Where do you think we are?' Jennifer asked to break the silence.

'I don't know, Jennifer. You tell me.'

'It looks familiar, but I can't place it. It reminds me of Vancouver a bit, but it's not quite Vancouver, if you get what I mean.'

'You're kidding. Right? How can all of this be reminiscent of Vancouver?' Lucy waved her arm dramatically in the direction of the street.

'I beg your pardon. What on earth are you talking about?' Jennifer asked. 'It's… well, it could be any city. Anywhere. But, to me, it's a bit like Vancouver. The cherry tree, this café, these streets.'

'Streets? Is that what you see? Okay, this is becoming seriously weird? I don't see streets. Or cherry trees for that matter. As far as I'm concerned, you and I are sitting at a wooden picnic table outside a visitor centre in the middle of a forest park. I know this place, but I can't put my finger on where I know it from.'

'So, you're in the middle of a forest park and I'm in the middle of some large city. But it's somewhere you think you know, is that correct?'

'Yeah, that about sums it up,' Lucy replied with a frown. 'Like I said, it's very familiar to me, just as whatever you see around you is familiar to you, but at the same time it isn't. We could be anywhere in the world. Or not.'

'What do you mean?' Jennifer asked.

Lucy shifted in her seat and frowned as she considered her answer. 'Truthfully Jennifer, I'm not sure. But I have a terrible suspicion that neither of us are in the world right now.'

Jennifer nodded thoughtfully. She felt something similar. It was as if they were here and not here at the same time.

'Are we in a dream?' Jennifer asked.

'I think so.'

'Why?'

Just then the waiter arrived with their plates. Lucy and Jennifer glanced at one another and raised their eyebrows when they noticed he had added ice to Lucy's wine, the way she liked it. She hadn't asked him to do this and it only added to their suspicions.

Yet both women began to eat. Hesitantly they tried a small amount, chewing cautiously but not sure why. To their surprise the Caesar salads were delicious.

Lucy set her knife and fork down on the empty plate and licked her lips in pleasure. She considered that the best salad she had ever tasted. Jennifer must have thought so too for her plate was also empty.

Lucy took another mouthful of the wine. It was also delicious, and she dabbed at her lips with her napkin. She needed some more of this heavenly nectar.

The waiter must have read her mind because he appeared at the table immediately, carrying another two large glasses of the wine. One of the glasses contained ice.

This is more than a little weird.

As soon as the waiter left, Lucy lifted her glass and took a sip, savouring the taste. She looked at the woman across the table from her. It was strange seeing her in the flesh, at arm's length from her, when up until now she had only ever seen her in dreams. She suspected Jennifer was thinking along similar lines.

'Do you want to know what I think? What I *suspect*?' Lucy asked.

'Go on,' Jennifer replied.

'Well, obviously something happened to us. I mean, your car accident and my fall resulted in this weird connection between us, and –'

'Yes?'

'I'm not sure, but I don't think it can be stopped.'

'I'm not following you.'

'I don't really understand it myself, but it seems we've experienced each other's lives through our dreams beginning from two significant, and very distinctive, points in our lives. In your case, it was when you met Ilan. In my case, it was when Charlie and I decided to buy our house.'

'Like one of those cases of your-life-flashing-before-your-eyes-when-you-are-about-to-die sort of thing?'

'In a way, yes. But in our situation, it was your life that flashed in front of my eyes and my life you saw in your eyes. Do you get what I'm trying to say?'

'Yeah. What happened to us occurred at roughly the same time, give or take a few hours and, because of that, we made some sort of psychic connection that seems to be manifesting itself in… an exchange of dreams is probably the best way of describing it. Yeah, I think I get it. So, if that is the case, what do we do about it?'

'I'm not sure. I think, and this is what worries me, only one of us can stop it and only one of us can come out of it.'

'One lives, one dies?' Jennifer asked. 'Why?'

'Yes. Maybe,' Lucy nodded. 'I can't explain it. It's a feeling I have. And I can't explain why I feel this way. Maybe I know that I'm dying. Maybe my injury was more severe than yours and I won't recover. Or you're dying. Or something. Like I said, it's just a feeling I have.'

'Do you know which one of us lives and which one dies?'

'That, my dear Jennifer, is the million-pound question.'

Chapter 37

Eight days since the accidents.

Ilan sat by his wife's bedside. He didn't know it but, in another hospital in England, a man called Charlie was by his own wife's bed. Both men had been sitting in their respective places since the accidents occurred. The chairs they sat on were not comfortable, but neither man noticed. Or cared.

Like Charlie's, Ilan's world had shrunk since the accident. Once his world was full of life, and love, and happiness, and the anticipation of a long future spent with Jennifer beside him. Now, it consisted of only the space around her. It consisted of a bubble of time and space that encompassed her and expanded enough to allow him to occupy that bubble with her.

Inside the bubble she was safe. She was alive and, like in a mother's womb, it nourished and protected her. Ilan was connected to her by the umbilical cord of her hand in his.

This bubble was made of such fragile stuff. If it were to burst...

He refused to allow that thought any purchase, and focused on her hand in his. Her skin was cool against the warmth of his and it was only the steady beep of the monitors that reassured him she was still alive. The scent of the jasmine plant he had brought her, a reminder of her life with him, was a nudge that he hoped she would recognise as a plea for her to come back to that life.

The world outside the bubble no longer existed for Ilan. He had rejected it, wanting only to remain in her world.

He didn't hear the doctor step into the room, and he jumped in surprise when a hand gently touched his shoulder. He stood up quickly.

'I'm sorry,' the doctor said in a hushed voice. 'I didn't mean to startle you and I apologise. Please sit down again.'

He obeyed the doctor's request, all the while watching his face in a futile attempt to read it. But the doctor was well-practiced in keeping his features non-committal.

The doctor picked up the chart from the foot of the bed and glanced through the pages of notes. Deep in thought, he nodded to himself a couple of times as he scanned the pages.

'Jennifer is doing very well,' he finally said.

'She will wake up soon?' Ilan permitted his hopes to soar for a moment, then reeled them back in again. It was too early to hope.

'Well, she is breathing on her own since we removed the intubation tube early this morning. It appeared to be causing her distress and that is a good indication of consciousness returning, so we removed it to see if she could breathe without it. She did. She met all our expectations, including her increased response to pain stimuli and sound.'

'What happens now?'

'She will wake up when she is ready. I suggest you talk to her, hold her hand as you have been doing. Squeeze it gently. Above all, speak to her. Tell her things about your life together. Tell her about the weather or what you had for breakfast. Anything that will make a connection. Most of all, she needs to hear your voice. It will help bring her back.'

'That is all?'

'That is all for now. Like I said we must wait for her to waken. It could be today. It could be tomorrow. It could be any time in the future. We will have to be patient.'

'When she wakes up, will she... will she be okay? I mean will she have brain damage?'

'We will see.'

The doctor patted his shoulder gently. Ilan didn't know if it was in celebration or in sympathy.

Chapter 38 - Jennifer & Lucy's Dream

'Can you hear that?' Jennifer asked. She ignored the tone of Lucy's voice. Usually, any conversation that included the patronising words 'my dear Jennifer' would have gotten her gander up but she refused to bite. This time.

'Hear what?' Lucy asked.

'That beeping noise. I've been hearing it for a while and it seems louder now. Do you know what it is?'

'You still hear it?' Lucy's eyes widened in surprise. 'I don't anymore. I heard it for ages but it seems to have stopped now. I think it's a form of tinnitus but I'm not sure. Why?'

'No reason,' Jennifer said as she shrugged and stared at the woman sitting opposite her. She looked slightly different from the woman in the dreams. Her skin tone wasn't as dark as Jennifer remembered and her eyes were slightly more rounded. Her hair was longer and she was a few pounds lighter. Having known her from so many dreams, Jennifer could tell from her expression that she was worried about their situation.

She hides it well, but not well enough. I wonder what she thinks about me?

'Why did both of us hear it?' Lucy asked, remembering her surprise when she had awakened from a dream in which Jennifer had also been complaining about a noise in her ear.

'It's possible it has something to do with our accidents. At first, I thought it was tinnitus, although it's a bit outside the definition of tinnitus. The more I think about it, and the fact that you heard it too, makes me wonder if it might be hospital equipment and it's part of the world – the real world – bleeding into our dreams.'

'So, what you are saying is that somewhere in the real world both of us are in a hospital because of the accidents we had?' Lucy said.

Jennifer nodded. 'In two hospitals, most likely. You'll be in a hospital somewhere in Yorkshire, and I suppose I'm in one in Cyprus. Or maybe Israel. That's where we were going.'

Lucy traced the pattern on her plate with her fork as she considered what Jennifer had said.

'So, what do we do about it?' she asked.

'Well, I'm not sure, but I think if one of us stops dreaming then the other one will die. But we have to stop, or at least one of us has to stop,' Jennifer replied.

'Yeah, that's what I figured,' Lucy said. She sat back and folded her arms defensively in front of her. 'So, which one of us gets to live and which one dies?'

'I don't know. I think we have to decide.'

'Fuck that for a choice!'

'I agree with you that it isn't fair, but I think that's the way it works.'

'No seriously, fuck that for a choice. I'm certainly not going to give up my life for you. In fact, I'm getting out of here right now,' Lucy said as she pushed her chair back and stood up.

'Where are you going?' Jennifer asked.

'I have a family waiting for me, so I'm going home. Bye Jennifer,' she said as she turned and walked away along the pavement, her steps determined and sure.

Jennifer watched Lucy walk away, past the newsstand and the shoe shop. She either hadn't seen the puddle when she stepped in it or her pride was forcing her to pretend her feet weren't wet at all. Then, instead of crossing the road, she turned left at the corner at the end of the block, and she was out of sight.

Jennifer leaned back in her chair and gazed around her. At the tall buildings and the pretty cherry trees, and all the while inhaling the scents that surrounded her. For a large city centre, it was such a peaceful place.

She closed her eyes and relaxed in the warm, spring sunshine, and she waited.

Her eyes opened at the sound of a chair scraping on the pavement as Lucy angrily pulled it out from the table and sat down, a scowl on her face as she folded her arms in front of her.

Well, that didn't take long.

'I thought you were going home,' Jennifer said, trying her best not to laugh.

'I thought I was,' Lucy told her. 'I walked back along the path towards the river, turned left by the oak trees and found myself back in this picnic area and you sitting here sunning yourself.'

The waiter materialised beside them again with two leather-bound menus, his pencil and notepad at the ready. Both women looked at each other in astonishment.

Lucy found herself tempted again by the Caesar salad but she resisted and ordered a large glass of white wine instead. Jennifer asked for the same. They watched the waiter scribble their order on his pad. He seemed alarmed by the fact that they hadn't ordered any lunch.

'I don't understand how I ended up back here,' Lucy said. 'I definitely didn't take a wrong turn.'

Before Jennifer could reply, the waiter reappeared with their wine. It tasted as refreshing and as delicious as it was the first time around. Lucy's, once again, had ice in it.

'Do you always drink your chardonnay with ice in it?' Jennifer asked.

'Not always. It depends on the weather. A scorching, hot day like this, yes.'

A scorching hot day? This isn't a hot day. It's a pleasantly warm day. But then I live on an island in the Mediterranean and you live in Yorkshire so I guess it's all relative.

'In the wintertime, on a cold day, I wouldn't think of it. In fact, I usually drink red wine in the winter. Red wine or rum and coke. And once in a blue moon I'll take whiskey because Charlie likes it, but I'm not fussy. Maybe a hot toddy now and then. In the summer it's nearly always white wine with ice or a gin and tonic.'

'Makes sense. I drink red occasionally but I prefer white, and if I fancy spirits, I usually drink vodka or whiskey. Ilan likes whiskey too, so I often drink it with him.'

'What do you imagine all this means?' Jennifer asked. She wondered how close Lucy's answer would be to her own notion.

'You mean me coming back here?'

Jennifer nodded. 'Yeah.'

'Well, it could be that we're stuck in some sort of loop.'

'That's what I was thinking,' Jennifer said, taking another sip of the wine. It really was delicious. Maybe she should ask the waiter to bring out a bottle.

Her eyes widened as he did just that. A full bottle wrapped in a crisp, white linen napkin and resting in an ice-filled bucket on a stand which he placed beside the table. He nodded briefly in acknowledgement of Jennifer's unspoken order but his face was angry and he refused to make eye contact with either of them. He did, however, look pointedly at the two menus he had placed on a nearby table as if to say, 'you should have ordered the Caesar salads.'

'This is seriously getting weirder and weirder by the minute,' Lucy remarked as she lifted the bottle out of the bucket, shook the moisture off the bottom, and topped up her glass. 'But who cares, so long as there's wine, eh?'

'I don't think sitting here and getting plastered is the answer,' Jennifer warned her.

'I know, but right now it's working for me. If you think of something let me know.'

'I have an idea, but I need to try something first,' Jennifer told her as she drained her glass, set it down on the table and stood up. 'I'm going home. See ya.'

Lucy sipped at her wine as she watched Jennifer walking away, down the path through the pine trees towards the river. At the grove of oak trees, she turned left, out of Lucy's sight.

Lucy poured another glass of wine, added a couple of ice cubes, and sipped it slowly while she waited.

She didn't have to wait for long before Jennifer came walking back towards her. Her expression remained neutral. Lucy pulled out the chair and she took her seat again. The waiter made to step forward, but one glare from Lucy put him back in his place.

'Well, that settles that,' Jennifer said as she poured herself another glass of wine.

'What now?' Lucy asked.

'I think we have to work out who gets to go home and who gets to leave. Each of us puts forward their argument and whoever's is the most valid – wins, I guess.'

'Who picks the winner?'

'I dunno,' Jennifer replied with a shrug of her shoulders. 'Maybe the waiter does.'

'I don't want to die, Jennifer.' Lucy decided it was time to say what was on her mind.

'Neither do I,' Jennifer responded.

'I'm not going to die. I think you should give up because I will fight you on this, and you really don't want to know me when I'm in a fighting mood, because I intend to go back home to the people I love.'

Jennifer looked at her. 'What makes you think your life is more important and more deserving of saving than mine?'

Lucy swirled the ice around in her glass. 'I don't, honestly. But I have a husband who loves me, and two little girls who I love beyond reason and who need their mum to be in their lives as they grow up.'

'I have a husband too. He's my whole life and I'm his. The fact that you have children and I don't doesn't make my life any less valuable.'

'I know that, but –'

'I'm sorry, Lucy but I *will* fight you on this. You know that, don't you?'

'As long as it's a fair fight, I don't care. I won't give up my family, Jennifer. I'll fight to stay with them with all my might.'

Jennifer looked at her and raised her glass. 'Then, may the best woman win.'

Lucy raised hers and they clinked them together. 'Now, we just have to figure out how to get out of here.'

Chapter 39 - Lucy's Dream

As she threw back the duvet and climbed out of bed, Jennifer glanced out the window to a beautiful sunny day. She smiled as she watched the trees swaying in the gentle breeze – a breeze that took the away the harshness of the sun's heat and filled the air with the gentle scents of the morning.

This morning she felt so much more energised and alive than she had in a long time. She showered and dressed quickly, eager to embrace the morning and all that the day promised her.

Ilan was already up and outside. She found him feeding the cats and she stood there for a moment listening to him murmuring gently and lovingly to each of them. As he spoke, he stroked the backs and scratched the ears of the tame ones who rubbed against his legs and wound in and out between his ankles as he dished out the food. He kept a cautious distance from the feral ones. They were thankful for the food he offered, but still wary of human contact, even if it only ever offered kindness.

He glanced up as she stepped outside to join him and he greeted her with a smile.

'There is something different about you this morning, but I can't figure out what it is,' he told her, a quizzical expression in his eyes.

'Nothing different. I feel fantastic this morning,' she replied with a shrug of her shoulders. 'Full of beans, as they say.'

'You look great.' Ilan caught his wife in his arms and pulled her close to him. His eyes drank in her features and he kissed her gently on the lips.

'I'm making coffee, toasted bagels and fresh fruit for breakfast,' Jennifer told him, reluctantly breaking away from a kiss that promised so much more. 'Want some?'

'Maybe later,' he replied with a gleam in his eyes and he gently kissed her neck, under her ear. His warm breath tickled and the familiar desire awakened inside her.

Jennifer tilted her head back and looked up at him, a gleam in her own eyes now. 'I think coffee tastes so much better when it has brewed for a while, don't you?'

She caught his hand in hers, pulled him towards the door, and led him back inside the house.

Jennifer closed her eyes and tilted her head upwards, as she allowed the water to cascade over her. The simple pleasure of the water on her body stilled her for a few moments and she smiled contentedly as she recalled the reason for her second shower of the morning.

As she dried herself and put her clothes back on again, the aroma of coffee from the kitchen made her stomach grumble.

Well, good sex will do that.

She towel-dried her hair, scrunched it into place and thought about her dream from the night before.

Meeting Lucy at the café, or the picnic table as Lucy called it, had been interesting, yet disturbing. They both thought they were going to be stuck at that table forever, drinking wine and eating Caesar salads under the watchful eye of their mysterious, and somewhat disapproving, waiter. Taking turns to attempt to leave, only to find themselves back at the table, until Jennifer came up with the idea that they should try leaving together.

It had worked. They left the table, two empty wine glasses sitting on it, and walked for a short distance until they came to a busy four-way junction with a pedestrian crossing, although Lucy claimed it was a fork in the gravel path through her forest. Jennifer felt compelled to go in one direction and Lucy in the other. They stood together for a few moments, each one of them feeling as though they should say something, but unsure of the correct words. Goodbye? It's been a blast? Bon Voyage?

Should they hug? Shake hands?

Nothing seemed appropriate and so they said nothing and did nothing. They stood there facing one another and then Jennifer felt what could only be described as a disturbance in the air between them – a sort of shimmering, almost invisible force that seemed to have created a barrier between them.

She didn't know what it signified and she wondered if Lucy was aware of it also.

Lucy gave no hint that she was aware of anything between them. She shrugged her shoulders. Jennifer nodded her head in reply and then both of them turned and walked away in opposite directions. Lucy had turned left down the gravel path that led into the forest and Jennifer had turned right towards the busy city centre.

Jennifer had wakened shortly after that, relieved to be away from the dream about the café. For all its pleasant location and ambience, there was an underlying, and very disturbing, creepiness to it that she couldn't quite explain. She remembered, as she walked away from it, with each step she took, the sense of unease had slowly lifted. She paused and turned to steal a glance back at Lucy. Lucy had also stopped and turned around. Jennifer noticed the concerned frown on her face and it was obvious Lucy wasn't experiencing that same sense of relief. If anything, Lucy had been growing more and more uncomfortable the further they got from the café and Jennifer could see the hesitation and doubt clearly on her face. She got the impression that Lucy had changed her mind, but it was too late. Then it seemed that Lucy had finally realised there was nothing she could do, for her shoulders slumped in defeat and she turned back towards the forest again.

The pedestrian crossing light turned green in her favour and Jennifer continued on her journey.

A good sleep, and the nature of last night's dream, had left her feeling refreshed and excited and looking forward to her day. She felt so alive and happy. Making love to Ilan had been the most delicious icing on the cake.

Ilan planted a kiss on her cheek and poured coffee for her as she walked into the kitchen. She was still wearing her satisfied smirk and she noted he was wearing one of his own. It had been a passionate, enthusiastic session that left both of them laughing and gasping in temporary exhaustion and also in surprise at how amazingly good it had been.

Jennifer sipped her coffee and prepared breakfast as Ilan stepped into the living room to answer his phone. It was his private one and she knew from his side of the conversation he was speaking to his daughter, Nurit. Jennifer popped her head through the door, caught his eye, and mouthed 'tell her shalom from me' then went back to slicing the kiwi fruit.

At the café, while they were racing towards the bottom of that second bottle of wine, Lucy told Jennifer she wanted a discussion on the matter before any decision was reached. Jennifer agreed at the time. She meant every word she said when she had told Lucy that she would talk it over with her again in another dream before they decided.

But now, and for some reason she couldn't explain, her promise seemed to have been, not so much broken, as cancelled. Jennifer knew in her heart there would be no more discussion and that the decision had been made.

But she had not made it. She didn't know how or why, but somehow it had been taken out of her hands.

But why, and in whose favour?

That was something she did not know.

Am I feeling this good because I've won and there'll be no more dreams? Or is it because I've lost and this is my last day.

Chapter 40

Nine days since the accidents.

Someone or something was choking her. Hands were around her neck, squeezing tightly. Blocking her airways. She clawed at the hands with her fingertips.

'I'll kill you,' a voice said.

It was familiar. It was a woman's voice but she couldn't be sure who it was, or why this woman wanted to kill her.

'I had to die so you don't get to live,' the woman said. 'You promised we would find a way.'

She couldn't speak. Couldn't explain.

With all the strength she had left, she pulled at the woman's hands, forcing the fingers apart. Slowly, gradually she felt the death grip loosening. She took a deep breath, sucking in the life-giving air as she pried the fingers away from her throat. And then suddenly she was free.

Her throat was dry and painful and felt constricted. It was almost impossible to swallow and each breath was a desperate struggle as she gasped and tried to suck in great mouthfuls of life-giving air.

She opened her eyes and tried to sit up. It hurt to swallow and it hurt to breathe. It hurt everywhere. Inert muscles screamed in white-hot protest as adrenaline coursed through her system. Her heart hammered in her chest and she thought it would burst out through her ribs.

The familiar beeping noise was still there, but it was no longer in her head. She could hear it beside her, beeping faster and louder as the warning alarms sounded to signify her increased heart rate and awakened state.

She opened her eyes and turned her face towards the noise in an attempt to get her bearings.

She was lying on a bed. In a room that was hidden in semi-darkness. All she could see through the gloom, were faint, small lights and a screen with numbers on it – some of them flashing in sync with the warning alarms.

She opened her mouth to call for help, but only a raspy sigh came out. Her mouth was as dry as sandpaper and her parched throat was aching.

Where am I?
What happened?
Am I dead?

Fear settled over her like a linen shroud.

Her eyes frantically searched the room, as a wave of dizziness washed over her and nausea threatened to bubble up to the surface. She was spinning out of control and she needed an anchor. A fixed point that she could grasp tightly and hold on to.

The faint light cast a pale glow and, as her eyes became accustomed to it, she began to see objects. A window first and the faint light that filtered in from it allowed her to see a door and walls, a table and a chair. There was a figure in the chair. It rose up and began walking towards her.

Her mind screamed out a warning. *It's her!*

It was the woman who had tried to kill her and she was coming towards her now to finish the job. She crouched back against the bed, felt the pillow against her shoulder blades. She was trapped. She had nowhere to go. No way to escape.

She tried to scream again, to cry out for help, but the words would not come. She tried to get away but she could not move. Her limbs were like lead as her body betrayed her.

More figures emerged from the shadows. They scurried about, switching off the alarms, and pushing away the spectre that had been in the chair. It stood in the background, watching and waiting. She allowed her fear to recede a little, somehow knowing that these people would protect her from it.

One of the new figures reached up towards a switch on the wall and suddenly there was a bright, blinding light. She blinked her eyes against the brightness.

Voices called out to her, but she could not understand them. She did not know what they wanted from her. She shook her head from side to side as one approached her holding a syringe. She wanted to scream as the figure forced something into her veins.

Her heart rate and her breathing began to slow. She closed her eyes and took deep, slow breaths and fought down the nausea that threatened to overcome her.

Still, the voices spoke to her. Words that made no sense. They were trying to tell her something and she forced herself to concentrate on what they were saying.

'You were in an accident,' they said. 'You were hurt, but you are going to be fine.'

'You've been asleep for a while,' they told her. 'You are awake now and you're going to heal and you will be okay.'

They repeated the words over and over again. A soothing mantra.

She wasn't sure if she believed them, she didn't know who they were and she didn't trust them. Not yet. But she felt almost calmer. Almost reassured.

She tried to speak, but her voice was still a raspy croak.

'Don't try to talk yet,' they said. 'Sip this first.'

A glass of water with a drinking straw in it was placed at her lips.

'Sip slowly,' one of them told her. 'A little at a time.'

She tentatively took a small sip, the coldness of the water shocking her, yet it was soothing against her dry tongue and it eased her throat when she swallowed. Still wary, she permitted herself a second sip, then another and another. Then it was taken away. She made a mewling sound and her mouth opened and closed like a hungry new-born baby searching for the nipple.

Her eyes widened in terror as the figure from the chair came towards her. She shrank back as it approached her. Then it came into focus.

It was not the woman who wanted to kill her. It was a man.

He was tall and he was smiling. But there were tears in his eyes. His tears spilled over and he laughed and cried. He took her hand in his, lifted it to his lips and kissed her fingers. He held her palm against his cheek and she felt the warmth of his tears as they splashed onto her hand.

She did not know who this man was and, more worryingly, she did not know who she was. Her memories began from the moment she awakened. As if she had been born a few moments ago in this darkened room, surrounded by these figures she now recognised as nurses. Although she didn't know how she knew that. The man was still there but he had been ushered back to the corner of the room, a stern warning given for him to stay there. She would have preferred him closer. Her terror of him had abated and, if anything, she felt inexplicably comforted by his presence. She fixed her eyes on him, while the nurses busied themselves around her.

He was the steady anchor in a sea of activity. The fixed point she had been searching for.

The nurses finished their appointed tasks and one by one they stepped out of the room. The man approached her again. This time she felt no fear and she welcomed him as he came closer. She still did not know who he was, but her instinct told her she could trust him.

Why do I know that? Who is he?

He took her hand in his. She tried to sit up.

'Slowly,' he cautioned her.

'No,' she said and her voice sounded strange to her ears. She reached for the water on the table beside her but his hand got there first and he steadied the straw as he held it to her lips.

She took a long drink and leaned back against the pillow.

'I need to see you properly,' she said. 'I feel I know you from somewhere, but I'm not sure from where, or how. Should I know you?'

'Yes. You know me well,' he replied. He smiled but she could see the concern in his eyes.

'How?'

'You're my wife,' he told her.

She blinked in shock. 'No. That's not possible. It can't be. I would remember something like that. Why can't I remember anything?'

'Because we were in an accident. You hit your head and required surgery. It happened nine days ago and you've been in a coma since then. The doctor told me it might take some time for your memory to return and it's nothing to worry about. It's normal. I'll let him explain it properly when he speaks to you.'

'What is my name?'

When he told her, it seemed familiar but she wasn't sure. It could be that, or it could anything. She didn't know.

There was so much she wanted to ask him. So many questions.

What happened? What is your name? How do I know you? Are we really married? Where do we live? Have we any children?

A thousand questions raced through her mind. So many, she didn't know which one to ask first.

She thought maybe she had two children – two little girls – but she wasn't sure, and she wondered where they were. What kind of accident had she been involved in? Where was she now?

She couldn't remember anything. Not a single thing. She could sense it on the tip of her tongue like a dream that disappeared the moment you waken. That thought made her frown and brought her fear bubbling to the surface again.

Why does the thought of a disappearing dream disturb me so much?

'Tell me who I really am,' she begged him.

Then the door opened and another man she didn't recognise walked in.

She sensed the air of authority about him even before he introduced himself as her surgeon.

'I am the one who had to cut off your lovely hair,' he told her. 'For that, I apologise profusely, but I had to do so in order to operate to repair the damage to your brain.'

Her hand flew to her head, feeling her scalp through the stubble where it had been shaved and had now grown back ever so slightly. Through the scratchy stubble, her fingers touched the scab and the stitches, proof that what he said was true. He had operated on her brain.

'Why?'

'We had to perform a craniotomy to alleviate the pressure on your brain when you struck your head.'

He began explaining the diagnosis – the trauma that had caused the pressure and its consequence and the details of the procedure. Most of it was beyond her knowledge and she found her thoughts moving forward as she tuned out his voice. She needed to know who she was and why she was there. She looked at the man who called himself her husband in an unspoken plea to help her remember. He could only shake his head.

She turned her attention back to the doctor, her eyes boring into him, demanding that he tell her the truth. 'Is this why I can't remember anything?'

'To a degree, yes,' the doctor said. 'It is partially caused by the anaesthetic but mostly as a defence mechanism by your consciousness to protect itself from the psychological aspects of the trauma you suffered. It's all a vital part of how the brain heals itself. Your memory should begin to come back in a day or so. You'll find it gradual at first then it will come back at such a great speed you might find yourself a bit overwhelmed. Please don't worry, we are all here to help you.'

He smiled reassuringly.

'Thank you,' she replied.

'Now, I will leave you in the care of your husband for a while. He's a good man and I know he loves you very much. But not too long though, as you need a good sleep and –'

'Haven't I had enough sleep?'

'No. You were sedated. A completely different animal. You need some natural sleep now.'

'I'm not sure if I want to go back to sleep.'

The doctor frowned and looked at her. 'Why not?'

'I don't want to have any more dreams.'

The doctor and the man who said he was her husband exchanged looks.

'You have had dreams?' A look of surprise flitted across the doctor's features. 'What sort of dreams? What do you remember about them?'

'Not much,' she replied evasively, preferring to keep as much as possible to herself for now. 'But I do remember I experienced them. I just can't recall the details of them. Apart from the last one. In my last dream, this woman was trying to strangle me – trying to kill me.'

'I see. It's possible this was merely a part of the process of waking up. We removed the intubation tube two days ago because you were beginning to struggle against it. That may have accounted for the choking sensation. It's not unheard of for coma patients to experience some form of dream state while they are unconscious and to remember it, and we do believe you were in REM sleep for considerable periods throughout the past nine days. You should not concern yourself. And believe me, a good, natural sleep will make you feel so much better.'

'Okay,' she nodded, still not convinced.

'I will look in on you later.'

She watched him as he tapped the tablet he was carrying and added some remarks to her notes. Then he motioned one of the nurses over and issued a few murmured instructions to her. The nurse nodded in compliance and, with a smile and a nod of reassurance to his patient, he left with the nurse in tow.

In a way, she felt relieved the doctor was gone, although she had many questions that she wanted to ask him. But they could wait. She had to be certain of something first.

'Where can I find a mirror?' she demanded of the tall man who was still standing beside her bed. The one who said he was her husband.

'There's one in the bathroom,' he told her. 'But I'm not sure if that is a good idea.'

She pulled back the sheet, swung her legs out of the bed and attempted to stand up. Her legs seemed to disappear from under her.

The man who claimed to be her husband caught her in his arms before she collapsed to the floor.

'Well, that didn't work out so well,' she said with a feeble attempt at humour.

He held her close to him. The sensation of his arms around her sent, not only a feeling of comfort and familiarity but, a spark of desire that coursed through her body. It delighted and frightened her in equal measure. He seemed to be a stranger, yet she could not deny the powerful physical attraction she felt for him. She did not find it difficult to imagine making love to him.

'Maybe you should wait until tomorrow when you will be stronger?' His arms were still around her, holding her, keeping her safe. It was good but it was not enough.

'No. I'm beginning to remember things. But I'm not sure if they are the correct memories. Not sure if they're my memories.'

He looked at her with a quizzical expression on his face.

'I think I know you,' she said. 'And I think I know who I am, but I need to see my face. I need to see what I look like. Then I'll know which one... I'm sorry, that sounds so crazy, and maybe it is. Maybe I am crazy. But I need to do this. It's hard to explain, but I'll try, as soon as I know. Will you help me?'

'You know I will.'

'Actually, I don't. But for now, I'll believe you.'

She leaned against him, thankful for his proximity, as she attempted to walk the few steps to the bathroom. But she was so weak she could barely put one foot in front of the other, and she allowed him to pick her up and carry her into the bathroom.

The lights came on automatically. He gently lowered her until her feet touched the ground, but he kept his arms around her as she cautiously stepped forward to stand in front of the mirror.

The face before her was that of a woman she was not sure she recognised. The eyes were sunken and surrounded by black circles. An ugly, yellowing bruise covered the left temple, spreading above and around the eye socket and disappeared up into her hairline towards the scabs that formed the operation site.

Ouch. Is this because of the surgery or a result of what necessitated it?

She did not know.

A few minor cuts and scratches were dispersed over her chin, nose and cheekbones. The cheekbones themselves were prominent and the sallow skin stretched over them gave her a haunted, half-starved look. The hair had been shaven close to the scalp, and the regrowth wasn't sufficient yet to give any indication of colour or shape.

Curly or straight? I don't know. I don't even know what kind of hair I have. I don't even know the fucking colour!

She could see the partially formed scar from the surgery and she raised a hand to touch it. Her fingertips traced its path and she was tempted to pick at the scabs and the remains of the stitches. It was the ugliest thing she had ever seen.

Her eyes connected with his in the mirror. She could see all the emotions in them – fear and concern and, above all, love. Emotions he usually kept guarded from the world but not from her. With her, he wore his heart on his sleeve.

And suddenly, it was this that she remembered.

She watched him as his tears threatened to spill over again and she felt tears of her own beginning to form, hot and stinging.

'No,' he whispered, his mouth close to her ear as he stood behind her to steady her. 'No tears. You are alive and safe and your hair will grow back. You'll heal and be strong and healthy again. There's no need for you to cry. I can do that for both of us.'

'I know that I loved you,' she said. 'That I do love you. I can feel it in my heart and in my soul and I remember most of it now. Almost all of it. But I can't make all the connections in my head yet. But I will in time. I promise.'

She tore her gaze away from his and went back to studying the face in the mirror.

Her eyes locked with the reflected eyes. With the mouth that matched her mouth. The nose that was her nose. She nodded and an expression of sympathy and sorrow crossed her brow. It was her reflection and yet it was not.

For a moment the face changed. It became someone else. It became the woman whose life she had shared so intimately for so long.

How could it have been only nine days? It seems like so many years?

The face of the woman stared back at her. She could read the emotions written there. Sorrow and grief and hatred.

She didn't blame her one bit, even though she had no say in the matter.

'You promised,' the face in the mirror told her. 'You promised we would decide together.'

'I am so very, very sorry,' she whispered to the face in the mirror.

Then it faded and when she looked in the mirror again all she could see was her own reflection. But the guilt written on her features was almost overwhelming. She knew in her heart that this guilt for the woman who died when she lived would always be with her.

Her hand reached for his, squeezing it. She held on tightly to the one thing that anchored her to this world. The one certainty she understood and the one thing that had made her journey back possible. This man. This strong, loving man who was the love of her life.

She gently touched the plaster cast on his left arm, turned her face to his and smiled, her love for him shining through the pain and the horror of the last nine days that was etched on her face.

'I'm Jennifer,' she told him, nodding to herself as the remainder of her memories came flooding back to her. 'And I know who you are. I remember you now. You're Ilan.'

Chapter 41 - Tel Aviv

Five months later.

Gasping for breath and with a stitch in her side that threatened to double her over, Jennifer realised she still had a long way to go before she was back to full fitness. She stood on the pavement for a moment before facing the task of climbing the short flight of stairs up to their apartment. Before – in that other lifetime – she could have run three or four times the distance she had managed this morning without a second thought.

She was angry and frustrated at the slow pace of her recovery, even though she was told, day and daily, that she was on schedule… that she was getting there. The fitness regime, the physiotherapy and the counselling all combined to bring her back to the woman she had once been.

It was just taking so bloody long!

Jennifer stopped herself from automatically reaching up to tie her hair in a ponytail the way Lucy would have done. It was cut short again, back to her usual style, and the colour was once more the white-blonde shade she had been for so many years. She had grown it almost to shoulder-length, but it reminded her too much of Lucy each time she caught a glimpse of herself in the mirror. She had to cut it – to become Jennifer again. But the habit of tying it, like the residual images of Lucy that still haunted her, had not quite died yet.

She opened the front door and headed straight to the fridge in the kitchenette for a small bottle of water. She gulped down nearly half of the water, grateful for its coolness, and went to look for her husband.

Ilan was out on the small veranda of the apartment they were renting, sitting in one of the two plastic chairs that took up most of the space. He had his feet up on the railing and was balancing the chair back on two of its legs, rocking gently as he spoke on the phone.

The apartment was nice – comfortable and modern – but neither of them considered it a permanent place to live. It was convenient to the hospital for her physio sessions, fully furnished and the rent was reasonable. Sufficient for their needs at this present time, it was a place to live until they could find somewhere to call home.

Jennifer would have loved to return to Cyprus. But that was out of the question. They could never return there.

She had found it difficult at first. But with Ilan to comfort her and help her rebuild her life here – her life with *him* – she had come to accept that Israel was her new home.

Ilan was no longer operational. This was due to the threat to his life, not because of the broken arm and other minor injuries he sustained when they collided with the truck. Now, he was reluctantly desk-bound. Jennifer sensed his frustration and she sympathised aloud with him, but quietly she was relieved. He was home every evening and she no longer worried about where he was in the world and what he was doing.

It had taken a while but gradually they made Israel their home and she was adapting well to the culture and the country.

Jennifer loved Tel Aviv. It was a beautiful and vibrant city, full of life, and she enjoyed being a part of it. But she wanted a home somewhere quieter, away from the noise and the fast-paced activity. Somewhere nearby would be ideal and if they could find a house similar to her home in Cyprus it would be a dream come true.

They were looking for just that place. In time, they would find it. She was content to wait.

Ilan was speaking softly in Hebrew when Jennifer stepped out onto the small veranda. She noticed that the kitten they had recently adopted was curled up on his lap. Good homes had been found for the ones they had left behind and this new one was a delight even though she was, occasionally, a painful reminder of all they had lost.

She sat down beside him, aware that she was still sweaty from her run. She would shower later but right now there was something she wanted to discuss with him. She inhaled the scent of the jasmine plant he had bought her. In the hot, still air it lingered and surrounded her like a lover's gentle caress, as she waited for him to finish his phone call.

He eventually said shalom to whomever he was talking to, set his phone down on the small table and smiled at her as he reached for her hand, always needing the connection of her touch.

'Will you still love me when I'm old and grey?' he asked.

'You're old and grey now and I still love you,' Jennifer replied with a cheeky grin, admiring his hair and the grey at his temples and in his short beard. There was more now, but it suited him. She had some grey herself but that was a secret known only to her and her hairdresser, and she was quite determined that it would *remain* a secret.

'You know what I mean.'

'Of course, I will. Why?'

'Because right now I feel very old and grey. I've just been informed I'm to become a grandfather. Nurit is pregnant and Reuben has proposed and they're getting married a month from tomorrow.'

'Like father, like daughter,' she grinned.

'Not quite,' he scowled. 'I had already planned on marrying her mother when Nurit was conceived. And I thought Nurit was only dating Reuben because she was on the rebound from Yonni.'

'Hey, sometimes a rebound romance turns into the real thing,' she told him. 'Reuben is cool and I like him. He has a wise head on his young shoulders and I know Nurit is very much in love with him. She's twenty-nine now, almost thirty – hardly a lovestruck teenager. She knows what she wants and it's Reuben she wants to spend the rest of her life with. Besides, I wasn't crazy about Yonni. And I know you weren't either, even though you wouldn't admit it.'

'You'll come to the wedding with me? You're invited, but both Nurit and I will understand if you feel it would be too much for you.'

'No, I'll be fine. I'd love to, but there's something I would like you to do for me first.'

'What?'

Jennifer took a deep breath and she didn't plead, nor did she demand it of him, but she made it clear she wanted to go back to the UK for a couple of days – a long weekend at the most. She also made it clear she would go alone if she had to, but she would prefer him to come with her.

'I know it carries an element of risk for you, but please, if it is possible, come with me. I think I need you there with me.'

'I don't think you're up to travelling,' he said. 'And why? Do you want to visit your parents?'

'No. Although we could do that as well. I'm fine to travel. The doctors told me last week. I have to go because there's something I need to do. I can't explain it but it's connected with the time I spent in the coma and what I experienced then. Ilan, it's something I need to face before I can let go completely what happened to me. I know you don't understand, but I need you to believe me when I tell you I must do it. I need you to trust me. When we get there and I can confirm it, I promise I will tell you the whole story.'

Two weeks later they flew El Al from Israel to London. When they finally got through baggage reclaim and the long queue at customs, they made their way to the rental desk and hired a car for their long journey northwards to Yorkshire. Jennifer programmed the postcode of the hotel they had booked into the sat nav and they set off, stopping a couple of times along the way for a bite to eat.

Ilan still had no idea where they were going, or why.

Chapter 42 – Yorkshire

Jennifer took Ilan's hand in hers. She held onto it for dear life while they stood together in front of the entrance gate to the small country churchyard on the outskirts of a village that was so familiar to her, despite only having ever seen it through Google earth on her laptop.

She took a deep breath and stepped through the gate.

Still holding her hand in his, Ilan walked beside her as they followed the gravel pathways between the rows of graves. Jennifer glanced at each headstone, studying every inscription, reading the names and the dates, as she searched for the grave she was looking for.

Finally, she found it.

The sharpness of the lettering cut into the clean granite headstone remained untouched by the weather and bore witness to the fact that this grave was months rather than years old.

As Jennifer looked at it, a shiver ran up her spine that had nothing to do with the coldness of the March weather and the drizzling rain.

It was all true. It had all happened.

It was not a dream. It was not a dream. It was not a dream. The words echoed in her memory like ghostly whispers.

She ran her palm over her rain-soaked hair, touching the scar gently, as she stood in front of the grave. Ilan stood beside her and she squeezed his hand again, needing his strength to comfort and reassure her she was alive and well and this was not her grave – that she was not a ghost, even though one resided in her mind.

It was not a dream.

Do you think I don't know that now?

The simple, yet elegant, epitaph carved into the stone read.

Lucy Nicola Wilson, beloved wife of Charles
And devoted mother of Amy & Chloe.
FOREVER WITH US IN OUR HEARTS.

The date of birth was irrelevant, but the date of this woman's death was the same day she had awakened from the coma. Ilan frowned in confusion.

'Who was she? Did you know her?'

'This is going to sound like the craziest thing you have ever heard, but I think she was me,' Jennifer answered in a quiet voice.

'I don't understand,' he said as he looked at her. It was still beyond him as to why she had driven this distance. Some unknown knowledge or instinct had directed her along the roads to this small graveyard nestled in a village at the edge of the Yorkshire Dales.

Jennifer met his gaze and took a deep breath as a sob escaped her lips.

'That's not exactly true. I mean, she isn't me but she might as well be. Or at least a part of me. It's hard to explain. At first, I thought she was a figment of my imagination, part of whatever I was going through when I was unconscious in the hospital. But ever since I woke up, the memory of her – and her life – is still in my head, as if I lived it. The frightening part Ilan is that I think she had to die for me to live.'

Ilan frowned. 'What are you talking about?'

'All the dreams I had, after the surgery when I was unconscious, were about this woman and her life. Do you remember when I first told you about them, you thought I was crazy, then you worried that I had a brain tumour or something but you still enjoyed the details.'

'What are you talking about? What dreams?' His dark feature etched with concern, Ilan put his hands on her shoulders and turned her around to face him.

'I told you about them. About how I lived her life every night when I went to sleep. I knew her, Ilan. She was a wonderful photographer and, with her husband, she turned an old stone farmhouse into a beautiful home for her and her family. I knew what her favourite food was and I knew that red wine gave her a migraine but she could cheerfully down a whole bottle of chardonnay and hardly suffer a hangover the next day. I remember her grief when her first dog died and how guilty she felt when she got another puppy only a few months later. I know how much she loved Charlie. He was her soul mate. I... she loved her two daughters more than life itself. I remember me, I mean her, giving birth to them. Amy's birth took almost eighteen hours. Chloe, the youngest, came quickly, but Amy's delivery was so painful and exhausting that I... I mean *she*, wanted to die! I felt it, Ilan, I lived it. She was me. She was me, Ilan!'

The words poured out of Jennifer's mouth and along with them came the tears. Ilan held her tightly. She buried her face in his coat and his arms were around her, holding her up, as he had done when she had awakened in the hospital. Now, he kept her from falling to the ground beside the grave of this other woman.

'This is insane, Jennifer,' he said. 'It is not possible.'

'It's true. Every night when I went to sleep with you beside me, I would dream I was waking up in her life and living it. And I told you that I thought she was doing the same – dreaming my life each night when she went to sleep. You were worried and frightened by it. You took me to different doctors and psychiatrists, and I started to think you were right, that there was something wrong with me.'

'What are you talking about, Jennifer? I did *not* take you to any doctors or psychiatrists. This is the first I know of any of this.'

'You do know. You were so angry when I asked if you if the Mossad were behind it? I googled remote viewing and how the different intelligence agencies had studied it over the years. And I thought you, or they, were using me to spy on someone through remote viewing. You became angry with me. You yelled at me and threatened to leave me for even thinking such a thing.'

He stepped back from her, shaking his head. 'No, Jennifer. I know nothing of what you are suggesting.'

'I realise that now. What I thought were conversations you and I were having was another aspect of the dreams. It was probably the same for Lucy when she thought she was telling her friend, Claire, about her dreams. But I did dream all of it, Ilan. Then, when I woke up in the hospital, it was the car crash and my head injury all along. Even the part about me telling you about my dreams. It was all in my mind. Or so I thought.'

'What do you mean?'

Jennifer took a deep breath and wiped away a tear. 'While I was unconscious, I was in some sort of dream state. Even you know that. The doctors told me I was in continuous rapid eye movement sleep and, while I was in it, I was dreaming this woman's world and she was dreaming mine. But when I regained consciousness, in the hospital, I could still sense her. I could remember, not just images, but thoughts and feelings.'

Jennifer looked at her husband, urging him to believe her. 'I can still sense traces of her. They're not so clear now, but they are still there.'

She glanced slowly towards the gravestone again – **beloved wife of Charles and devoted mother of Amy and Chloe**.

The words slashed and gouged her heart and her soul. The grief and guilt Jennifer felt was raw and agonising and almost made her knees buckle, but Ilan's arms were around her and it was his love for her that kept her from falling.

'The worst part – the part that makes me feel so guilty – is that she had to die so that I could be here with you. I love you so much that I let her die so I could be with you. You see, Lucy and I met and we talked about it and then we –'

'What do you mean – met and talked about it? Where? How?'

'I don't know exactly. It was in the dreams. There was this place. To me it was a city sidewalk café but to Lucy it was a picnic bench in a forest park. We ate salads and drank wine. Boy, did we drink wine! And we talked. Turns out she had suffered a head injury from a fall at roughly the same time you and I crashed... maybe a few hours earlier or later, I'm not sure. But we realised that our consciousnesses had become linked, or exchanged, or something, and we experienced each other's dreams while we were both unconscious. We both wanted it to stop and we realised only one of us could wake up and that the other would die. Don't ask me how we knew. We just knew. So, we promised each other we would meet again and talk it over and decide together who would live and who would die but I went ahead and came back without telling her. I didn't do it deliberately, it just seemed to happen. When she realised what I was doing she tried to kill me. She was choking me and I fought her. Physically fought her. I thought I was going to die but, in the end, I won. I must have, because I woke up after that.

I think I killed her. She hated me because I wanted to live. But I don't blame her. She had a husband and two beautiful little girls and she only wanted to be with them. But I killed her. I had to.'

Jennifer fished a paper tissue out of her bag and blew her nose. 'I can still sense her here with me. I think she will always be with me – a residual echo of who and what she was. Maybe that's why I felt compelled to let my hair grow long for a while. You know, she had the most luxurious hair, almost down to her waist, and I felt I had to grow it in memory of her but, in the end, it was too disturbing, so I cut it again.'

She leaned against him, resting her head on his chest, feeling the strong, steady beat of his heart against her cheek.

'I am so sorry she's dead – that she had to die for me to live,' she told him. 'Because this was what I wanted. This is what I could never give up, even if it meant her death. You are what I want, but just at this moment Ilan, because of the part of Lucy that remains in me, I can feel how much it hurts to leave behind her husband and her daughters and the life that she lived with them. And I feel so guilty. I can't help this guilt because in choosing to be with you, I made her die.'

Shocked and concerned by her revelations, Ilan held her tightly to him as they stood there in the cemetery in the grey Yorkshire drizzle, a million miles away from their old life in Cyprus and their new life in Israel. He had no intention of ever letting her go.

He held her for what seemed a lifetime but gradually her tears subsided and, still in his arms, she looked up at him. A thousand questions raced through his mind but right now there was only one that was important to him.

Before he could ask it, Jennifer drew in a deep breath and let it out slowly in a long sigh. It seemed that she had come to a decision.

She looked into his eyes and smiled and his heart did its usual flip when she gave him that smile

'I'm okay now. At least I will be in time. As long as I'm with you,' she said. 'Let's go home now.'

Epilogue

Saul Mueller had been the deputy director of the Mossad for many years and had known Ilan Ben-Levi for almost the same amount of time. Since before he had recruited him out of the army.

The file his assistant had placed on his desk that morning was a briefing from Ilan and this was his second reading of it. Ilan, as always, was concise and to the point. As Saul had taught him to be.

'We need facts, Ilan. Always the facts. Flowery language and romantic prose belong to the poets and the storytellers among us. Are you a poet or a storyteller, Ilan?'

Ilan Ben-Levi had shaken his head and told him that no, he was neither a poet nor a storyteller.

'But you are a romantic?'

Ilan had shrugged his shoulders and nodded in reply.

'Romance is good,' the deputy director had told him. 'We all need some romance in our lives. Yes?'

'Yes,' Ilan had replied.

That had been many years ago and Ilan, though young, had learned well.

He noted the request in the last paragraph. Ilan was respectfully asking that this report not be entered into the system. It was, he insisted, nothing more than his own speculation regarding the subject of a conversation between himself and his wife.

Everything she had told him concerning the dreams she experienced while in a medically induced coma appeared to be true. This had been confirmed when they had travelled to the UK and visited the grave of a woman whom his wife insisted had been connected to her in her dreams. A Google search of the English woman backed up everything his wife had told him concerning this woman, her life and subsequent death at the exact instant his wife had awakened from her coma.

His wife further stated that while in a dream state she had discussed the possibility of her being involved in a 'remote viewing' scenario or experiment with him. In her dream, he had strenuously denied the existence of such a program as he would have done if she had genuinely asked him.

In conclusion, Ilan stated that, while he would not permit under any circumstances, his wife to be involved in such a program, should it ever have occasion to be activated, he felt she could perhaps, on occasion, give useful input and advice if required.

The report concluded with Ilan stating that he would prefer that this information regarding his wife be classified for his, the deputy director's, eyes only.

A yellow 'post-it' note attached to the report had personally, on the strength of their long-standing friendship, reiterated this request.

Saul closed the report and placed it carefully on top of his desk.

He was old enough that he should be retired by now, and old enough that he should not be surprised or amazed by anything anymore. But this? This was beyond surprising or amazing.

This was the sort of thing that kept him from retirement. Kept him from the terrifying prospect of spending the rest of his life gardening. He couldn't write his memoirs, obviously, and he hated crosswords and daytime television with a vengeance.

That left gardening: Pruning roses, planting climbing flowering clematis, or growing begonias from seed.

Could begonias be grown from seed? He didn't know and he didn't care to find out.

Or the other option – round-the-world cruises with his wife. This was her dream for their retirement. It had been for a couple of years now. She was always leaving not so subtle hints in the form of brochures lying on the kitchen worktop, or on the coffee table beside the television remote control.

Saul loved his wife dearly, but the thought of spending weeks, or more, on a large ocean-going vessel with only other retired old fogies for company, made him want to die right now.

Right here.

But *this*? This was enticing. This was exciting. It awakened all the old memories and it took him back to a time and place when spies were spies. Proper spies. Not the high-tech loving bureaucrats of today. The good old days.

He hoped someday he would have the opportunity to meet this remarkable Englishwoman called Jennifer. Ilan Ben-Levi's wife.

He ran his hands over the file, relishing the old-fashioned notion of a paper file in a folder that bore the legend – 'DD And Above Eyes Only'.

Shortly, he would file it in the appropriate place, but for now he merely sat there, his hands resting on the cover of the file, and he stared thoughtfully out of his office window, across the rooftops of the city and he wished he could do it all again.

Amanda Sheridan
March 2020

If you enjoyed this book, I would love you to leave me a review on Amazon.
https://www.amazon.co.uk/gp/product/B086H3HQ4M

or on Goodreads –

https://www.goodreads.com/book/show/53570380-rapid-

eye-movement

You can also find me on Facebook –

https://www.facebook.com/Amanda-Sheridan-Author-

104074121231229

and my Instagram account –

https://www.instagram.com/amandasheridanauthor

Drop by and say hello.

Now published and available here -
https://www.amazon.co.uk/gp/product/B08MB3Z785

The Dreaming.

Jennifer and Ilan have settled into their new life in Israel. But Jennifer is still haunted by the memories of her accident in Cyprus and the experiences that occurred as a result of her injuries.

Then Ilan is called away from his office job to take on one more mission.

A very dangerous mission.

And it is up to Jennifer to utilise her experiences to try and save him.

In ways she could never have imagined.

Acknowledgments

I would like to thank the following people. Without them, I would never have written this novel.

My beloved husband Hugh, who gave me time and space to write, brought me tea or wine when I needed it, and tried his best not to distract me by playing the radio or shouting at the football match on TV.

David Kessler for finding all my lost commas and so much more. Todah!

Simone Kessler for her assistance with the Hebrew translations. Todah!

Lesley, Ralph, and my wonderful Aussie cousin, Alannah, for taking the time to read the manuscript and giving me praise and constructive criticism in equal measure.

Cover by Amy Hunter Designs, from an original photograph by Giulia Marotta.

Formatted by Vicky Peplow, VAP Books.

And last, but by no means least, my late mother, May Sheridan, who always said I should write a book because I told such fanciful stories, usually to get out of trouble! I wish you could have read it, Mum.

Printed in Great Britain
by Amazon

67920691R00196